DEATH'S TOUCH

MASE EVANS

DEATH'S TOUCH

ISBN 979-8-9874613-0-3

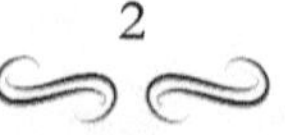

Dedication

To Brain, for always being as helpful as he could – even
when he wasn't.

Chapter One

I ride my bike along the old sidewalk and into the part of the neighborhood that's been abandoned for longer than I've been alive. Someone owned all of it at one point, and when they moved, they couldn't seem to get it sold for the million dollars they'd been asking for. Big surprise there.

Eighteen years later, they finally managed to land a sale with a company that wants to come in and tear it all down so they can build a bunch of fancy townhomes. I'm not exactly happy with this arrangement for multiple reasons, but it's not like my opinion regarding their little "project" matters at all.

I've spent years of my life biking up and down the old sidewalks and exploring the properties that I'm now technically allowed to since the old "no trespassing" sign fell down 5 years ago. It's a rule that goes without being said, sure, but no one lives here and it's not like there are any hidden cameras around, so what does it really matter?

I spend my free time – when I'm not enduring the torture that is school and homework, that is – here. I bike through the overgrown properties, testing out tricks, falling into ditches, reading books, watching birds, and all-around actually enjoying myself. I don't know what I'm going to do when they destroy this place.

This place has been my entire childhood. It's a place where I can have fun, let down my guard, and not hate every waking moment of every day.

And I don't have to worry about accidentally hurting anyone here.

A few blades of grass are nothing when compared to killing another living creature, human or not. I could hurt this place, but even if I did, I couldn't possibly do as much damage in one day as that construction company is going to do. I have an awful gift, yes, but I know how to keep myself from hurting anything.

I run my gloved hand along the side of one of the old houses with its rotting walls and rusted nails. Something about this place is magical to me. It has a story, but one that no one knows. It's like it's holding secrets back from everyone who lives around here, and no one actually cares enough to uncover them.

I guess it kind of reminds me of me.

My phone goes off in my pocket and I jump. I pull

my hand away from the old house. I'm easy to startle, to say the least.

I swipe to the right before putting the phone up to my ear. "Yeah?"

It's my mom on the other end; no doubt asking if I'm at least on my way home by now. I know she doesn't like it when I'm out this late, but I don't have much else to do around the house, and this is probably the safest place for me to be, no matter what time of day it is.

"Honey, it's getting dark," she says, and I mentally put another tally-mark on the list of times I've guessed her words before they're out of her mouth. I'm at sixteen this week and it's only Tuesday. "And dinner will be ready soon. Are you on the way home?"

Seventeen.

"Yeah," I answer, holding my phone between my cheek and shoulder as I climb onto my bike and start on the ride home. "I'll be home in about ten."

"Alright," my mom says, sounding weirdly relieved; like she'd thought I wouldn't be coming home at all for some reason. "Be careful on the way back, okay?"

Eighteen.

I sigh. "I will," I promise, and pull the phone away from my ear before hanging up.

I've been out here all day, so I guess it makes sense that she's calling to check up on me, but she knows I'll be back by the time dinner is supposed to be on the table. I was only ever out after dark once, and it was because I'd been exploring the inside of one of the broken-down houses and my phone had died beforehand. By the time I realized how late it was, I was already half an hour late to dinner.

I hadn't gotten close to being that late in a long time and I didn't ever plan to be again. Neither my mom nor my dad seemed to believe that, though.

The breeze blows past me as I ride. It pulls at my hair, doing its best to take the long, black strands with it.

The wind feels good against my bare face and neck, like seeing a long-lost friend for the first time in years. The wind itself is my long-lost friend, though, and it's the only friend I've ever had or needed.

Slowly, I remove my hands from the handlebars of my bike as I slide my jacket off of my shoulders. The tank top I'm wearing beneath it leaves my chest and shoulders bare. I carefully tie my jacket around my waist and grasp the handlebars again.

I stand up while I ride, welcoming the warm air against my skin as it envelopes me in its embrace.

I close my eyes and breathe in a deep breath, letting the air fill my lungs before slowly letting it out again. A feeling of calmness settles itself over me and drowns out my feelings of frustration. Riding has always calmed me in this way. I don't know what about it does, but I love the feeling.

When I open my eyes again, I find myself at the cross street where I'll have to make a left to get back to my house. I jerk my handlebars quickly, making sure to avoid ending up on the street when I do. My mother has always told me to ride on the sidewalk because it's safer than riding on the street, even if I'm technically not supposed to.

"Damn it," I breathe, and a rush of adrenaline surges through my body.

I hadn't been paying enough attention when turning onto the cross street. At least, not enough to see that a guy is walking on the sidewalk a few feet away from where I am.

My mind races, noticing the car in the street, the guy in front of me, the ditch on my other side.

Before I have a chance to decide what the smartest course of action would be, I turn my bike again, throwing myself straight into the ditch.

Only, it doesn't go as smoothly as I hoped it would.

My front tire hits a rock in the ground, and I'm thrown off of my bike.

My mind goes blank and the next thing I know, I'm lying in the middle of the ditch, my jacket snagged in my bike's chain, my bike on top of me, and my limbs thrown in various directions that I can't even pretend are comfortable.

I do my best to sit up as a groan escapes past my lips.

Blood drips down my right arm from a large gash in my tricep; no doubt from a rock that decided injuring me was a good form of entertainment. If I'd just kept my jacket on, I wouldn't have gotten the cut.

I grip the wound with my left hand.

"Oh my gosh. Are you alright?" a frantic voice asks.

I turn to see the guy who I'd almost managed to hit after making the turn. Would it be completely rude for me to blame this all on him?

The guy shoves his phone in his pocket before climbing down next to me in the ditch and untangling my jacket from my bike's chain. Once he's finished that, he pulls the thing off of me. He's wearing the hood of his jacket over his head and, from here, I can't see his face.

I ignore responding to his question as I look at my bike. It doesn't look damaged, which is a damn good thing, or I'd be holding him personally responsible.

"Your arm," the guy standing in front of me says, turning back to face me. He reaches over like he wants to check and make sure it's alright, but I flinch and move away.

The guy freezes, then pulls his hands away and stands up straight.

Great. I don't need another person finding me suspicious.

"It's fine," I say, glancing back down at my arm. I remove my hand, hoping the blood won't start flowing again so he won't insist on helping me. "Or, at least, it will be." I look up at him. I can see his face now. I hadn't originally thought so, but he doesn't appear to be much older than I am.

The worry in his dark brown eyes subsides a bit, and I let out a breath. Good, he isn't going to pester me about it anymore. Hopefully that means I'm in the clear.

"I'm so sorry," he tells me. "I wasn't watching where I was going. My friend from out of state texted me so I was talking to him instead of paying attention, even though that's really stupid and-"

I cut him off before he can make me any later getting home. "It's fine," I tell him, shrugging like doing so didn't just cause a wave of agony to spread through my left collar bone and shoulder.

Well, I guess I broke that.

I move to get up. My mom's going to kill me if I'm even a couple minutes late.

"Here," the guy says, rushing forward to help me up.

"No!" I shout, which to him is really uncalled for and probably rude, but to me makes perfect sense. He freezes again before taking a step back. "I-I've got it," I tell him, unable to meet his confused gaze. This is so awkward and uncomfortable. I really wish I could just get up and leave like nothing happened. It would've been so nice if he hadn't noticed my existence.

"O-okay." The confusion is apparent in his voice, and I feel bad because he shouldn't need to be so confused. He was trying to be nice and help a hurt girl up, but he can't do that. *No one* can do that.

Painfully, I stagger to my feet, though I try to play it off as though it's nothing.

I glance over at the guy standing beside me. He looks worried, to say the least.

"Are you new in the neighborhood?" I ask him, before he can get a chance to try to help me or apologize again. I snatch my jacket from where he put it on top of my bike and put it on, every muscle in my body begging me not to, but I ignore the pain to the best of my ability. I manage to avoid using my left arm as much as possible in the process, though.

The guy gives me a weird look, and I realize that I just put my jacket back on over a blood-soaked arm. Oops.

"Yeah," he says, shaking his head like he's trying to get the thought of how strange I am out of his mind. "My dad and I just moved here from Virginia." I mentally note that he didn't say "parents," though I don't know why I bother. "I was just going to check out the old, abandoned part of the neighborhood because-"

"I've gotta go," I cut him off again, realizing that I've given myself a great way to waste even more time by opening my mouth at all instead of just dealing with the seemingly endless awkwardness of this situation. "Sorry, I just realized the time and my mom is expecting me back and I can't be home late again or she'll kill me." I don't know why I'm rambling. I don't usually ramble at all, but my best guess is that I have the guy in front of me to blame for it. "Sorry," I say again.

"Yeah, well it's not important, anyway," he says,

giving an awkward laugh. "I'm sorry again. For not paying attention."

"I wasn't either," I tell him, which is totally not something I'd say, so I don't understand what the heck just came out of my mouth. I shake my head and pick my bike up off the ground, completely relying on my right arm, despite the blood I can feel seeping through my jacket. "Well, bye."

"Bye." He waves awkwardly as he climbs out of the ditch and starts back on his way down the sidewalk in the opposite direction as me.

I get a whole whopping two steps before I'm interrupted again.

"I'm Chase, by the way," he calls back to me, and I can feel myself physically cringe when he does, but I do my best to hide it.

I turn so that I'm walking away from him still, but backward at the same time so that I'm facing him. "I'm Thana," I answer.

Chase frowns. "That's a-"

"A weird name?" I interrupt, sighing. "Yeah, very. Kinda stuck with it, though. *Bye*." This time I wave, hoping he'll get the message that getting his butt out of my life would be the preferred thing at the moment.

"Bye again," he calls, and I turn my back on him, sighing a breath of something that I can only guess is relief that I don't have to talk to him anymore. I'm bad enough at interacting with my parents and siblings. People I don't know is just about twenty thousand times worse. It hadn't been all that bad until he seemed to want to strike up a conversation with me which is A) not wanted and B) something I don't have the time for.

It's not that I hate people. It's that I literally can't get involved in anyone else's life if I want them to not end up hurt. If someone has a death wish, then sure, I'll be their friend, but I don't think anyone actually wants that.

It only takes me another couple of minutes to get back home. It feels like it's a lot longer than it actually is because of my broken collar bone and bloody arm, but the last thing I want is to have to tell my parents about what happened. I just don't exactly see a way out of it.

They expect me to be more careful than I was being while riding, and I don't want to make them worry that I'm being unsafe because I don't want them to not allow me go to the abandoned part of the neighborhood anymore. As it is, I already don't have as much time with the place as I'd like.

I don't know when they're going to start building there, but I doubt it's going to be all that far in the future.

Once they start, I'm going to lose the only safe place I've ever had. I can't go sit in a coffee shop like normal people can because I can't risk being that close to other people. But the idea of constantly being shut up in my room to avoid interaction with other human beings is not something I ever want to think about. It sounds like my own personal version of hell more than anything else.

I park my bike alongside the house before I go around the back and push open the door. My family has never been the best about keeping the doors locked. They only ever stay locked at night or when everyone has left the house. Other than that, it's about as easy for someone to rob us as, well, it is for me to just walk in.

Every movement I make hurts, but it's not like I can just not make any movements and expect it to go away. Pain meds are what I need. And a sling. Luckily, I have both up in my room. If only I didn't have to tell my parents about my broken bone and could just walk around with an arm in a sling and have no one notice.

At the sound of the door softly closing, Fayre, my little sister, sticks her head around the corner and takes notice to the fact that I'm home.

"Thana's back!" she announces.

I flinch at her sudden shout, which hurts my banged-up body even more. "Scream it a little louder, why don't you?" I hiss, sarcasm and irritation dripping from my tone. "I don't think they heard you in Iceland."

I know I don't need to be such a jerk about her shout, but I'm in some serious pain and that didn't exactly help, so I think I have some reason to be upset. And I know she doesn't know that I'm in pain, but she's bound to figure it out as soon as she or anyone else takes a good look at me. I'm pretty sure my broken collar bone is visible even through my jacket. It's remarkable that no blood has managed to seep through the sleeve yet from the gash in my right arm, but I doubt my luck will last.

Fayre gives me an irritated look as she steps into the foyer. "Grumpy mu-?" She stops in the middle of her accusation and freezes dead in her tracks. "Ana, what'd you do?" she snaps at me as she seems to come out of her trance, and takes a step over to me. She places her left hand on my upper arm and her right hand on my shoulder that isn't hurt.

I grimace beneath her touch, even though she's gentle enough that it doesn't cause the pain to be any worse than it already was.

My sister sighs. "Broken?"

I glare at her. "What do you think?" I snap.

Fayre returns my unpleasant expression. "Don't give me that," she tells me, sounding much more like she's my mother than my younger sister by nearly three years. "What'd you do?"

Just as she asks it, my older brother, Daemon, rushes into the room and stands alongside my sister. "What the hell, Than?" he snaps at me when he notices my shoulder; like I intentionally broke my bone just to get on his nerves.

My mom trails behind Daemon, her hands covered in flour from whatever it is she's making us for dinner. She looks worried, even though she hasn't noticed my collar bone yet because the only place she's looked is straight at my face. "Thana, I thought I told you to be home by – oh my," she says, catching herself before she can finish scolding me for being late.

"Yeah, yeah," I say, moving away from Fayre and taking multiple steps back. They never seem to take the time to notice me until I don't want them to. That's when I get all the attention in the world. "I've got a sling in my room. Can we please not bother with the x-ray again?" I beg, which sounds pathetic, even to my ears.

My mother crosses her arms at me, which tells me what I already know: there's no way I'm getting out of this.

I groan and my siblings snicker at me. Well, Fayre does. Daemon looks frustrated; like me not wanting to go to the emergency room again is a personal offense to him.

Daemon has always been extremely overprotective. He's a year older than me but, much like Fayre does in certain situations, he treats me like he's one of my parents and not like he's just my older brother.

I know part of the reason all of them are so protective of me is because of my "curse" or whatever it is, but it feels beyond blown out of proportion sometimes. I'm sixteen. I'm pretty sure I know by now that I have to be extremely careful. Why do they think I go to the abandoned part of the neighborhood every day?

My mother dusts her hands off on her skirt before she starts bossing me and my siblings around.

"Daemon and Fayre, dinner is done except for the cookies." Well, that explains her flour-covered hands. "Thana, get a book or something to keep yourself entertained and get your broken butt in the car." There's no room for argument with the way her eyes meet mine: daring me to disobey.

I sigh, but haul my "broken butt" up to my room to find some form of entertainment.

Chapter Two

The x-ray I get at the emergency room reveals the same thing I suspected it would. All I need to do is wear a sling until it's healed and keep my shoulders straight as much as possible so that my bones don't heal in a way that they aren't supposed to.

It feels like a giant waste of time, but at least the fact that I got it done pleases my mom.

"Wasn't the secretary boy cute?" my mom teases, nudging me with her shoulder.

I can feel the disgust that shows on my face. "Ew. Mom, he's gotta be in his twenties. That's gross," I moan.

"Oh, not for me," she says, waving a hand at me dismissively.

"Oh, you mean for me?" I challenge. I know this game well. She wants to know what my type is for some reason. Well, lucky for me, I don't plan to give that information away. Besides, whoever said I have to have a type? And it's not like it would matter. I couldn't ever date anyone unless I wanted them dead, anyway.

"You're no fun," my mom pouts playfully, but I'm less amused than I think she wants me to be.

I don't find this game half as fun as she seems to think I do. It doesn't matter if I like anyone, be they a guy or a girl or anything in between. I *can't* like anyone. It doesn't matter that I've found multiple guys attractive before because that could never be anything more than just a crush.

"Yup, just boring old me here." I roll my eyes. "Go tease Daemon," I tell her. "Or Fayre. I'm sure either of them would find it more enjoyable."

"That's not my place," my mom says, unlocking the car door before she climbs in. Once I'm in the seat beside her, she continues. "Your father is responsible for making Daemon uncomfortable, and Fayre still hasn't shown any interest and I'm fairly sure she's still too young, anyway."

I seriously doubt that, considering that when my sister talks about a few boys, her eyes become all sparkly and she gets giddy with excitement every now and then. She's good at hiding it around everyone who isn't me, but I get the feeling she wants me to ask her about it, which is why she shows it to me. I haven't yet gotten around to asking, though.

"You hungry?" mom asks as I fasten my seatbelt,

doing my best to keep from getting my glove snagged on the mechanism that keeps it in place.

I shrug, but my stomach growls a second later, giving away the truth.

My mom side-eyes me with a knowing smile before she puts the car in reverse and pulls out of the parking lot.

I watch out the window as the buildings go by. I've never been overly fond of the city with its high buildings and crowds of people bustling around, but I've never known anything else. We've lived in the city my whole life. My parents have always lived here, too. It seems as if I'm part of a family of city folks, not that it bothers me all that much. I just can't seem to help but wonder what it would be like to live farther out.

The thought of living in the country was a pleasant one for me. It seemed peaceful and relaxing; not like how it is here. Here I have to be careful everywhere I go. I can't even go out to get the mail and not worry that I might bump into someone walking down the street.

"So, you never exactly told me what happened," my mother says, bringing me away from my thoughts of what a perfect life might be.

"Oh." It's the only thing I can think to say. I don't want her or anyone else to trust me even less than they already do. I need some amount of freedom, if nothing else. "I just fell off my bike again." I shrug. It's not a complete lie, but I am leaving out quite a bit of the story.

"Ah."

My mom looks pleased with the answer, which is enough to make some of the tension leave my body. I sink deeper into the seat, but not deep enough that I'm unable to keep my shoulders and back straight.

"Is that all?" she asks a moment later, which means she noticed something was off about my expression or my tone of voice, and she knows I'm keeping something from her.

"What else would there be?" I ask, my body stiffening again, but hopefully not enough for her to notice this time. She's so good at these games, though. It's so annoying when I can't get away with things.

My mom shrugs and turns back to watching the road. She turns on her turn signal and gets into the left lane, checking over her shoulder to make sure her blind spot is open. "I was hoping you would tell me."

I want to groan. She's too good at this.

"Nothing more to tell," I say. "A bird just distracted me is all, and I turned wrong and crashed in a ditch." That'd be almost completely true, too, if the bird didn't go by the name Chase and speak in perfect English.

"Alright." She obviously doesn't believe me, but she doesn't press the subject. I'm thankful that she doesn't. I really don't want to be unable to go out on my own anymore. So maybe I almost killed someone today, but that doesn't mean it happens all the time, and usually I'm more careful. If it happens again, I'll have to tell her or my father, but, at least for now, I'm okay.

In all honesty, the person I'm worried about the most is Daemon. Sure, my parents would definitely consider taking away my privileges to go out riding on my own, but Daemon would be beside himself at hearing what happened. I doubted he would leave my parents alone about it until my privileges were completely gone. He'd be so worried I'd probably end up required to have a chaperone on the way to school. Not that he doesn't make that his responsibility already.

A few minutes later, we pull into a parking lot and my mom parks the car.

"Mom," I hiss as I jog to catch up with her. She's halfway across the parking lot by the time I'm out of the car. "Mom, you know I can't eat in there." I jerk my head toward the yellow and tan building.

"They're in wrappers. Don't worry," my mom says dismissively as if I'm being overly paranoid about the situation. Maybe I am, but if anyone besides my mom sees my hamburger turn grey, there are going to be some serious problems.

I just stare at her as we walk. Even if I am just being paranoid, this seems far too relaxed to be normal.

My mom holds the door for me when we head inside and I thank her as I walk through. I may be a sarcastic pain in the ass with an attitude problem, but I still have manners.

We go over to one of the giant tablet-looking screens and put in our order before we head over to a booth in the corner. It's big enough to seat at least 5, but it's the safest place for us – or me, if I'm going to point fingers – to sit, even if it is rather rude to any large groups coming in.

Out of the corner of my eye, I notice two men walk in. They're both wearing suits, which I find strange considering we're in a fast-food restaurant, of all places. One is wearing a black suit and the other a grey one. They punch in their order just like my mom and I did. They're laughing and the one in the black suit slaps the other on the shoulder.

"I'm going to run to the restroom and wash my hands," my mom informs me as she stands up.

"Cool," is my only response.

She smiles at me as she walks past and plants a kiss on the top of my head. Thank goodness I'm wearing the hood of my jacket up today.

I see the two men in suits who walked in a moment ago take the table beside the booth my mom and I have claimed. Their voices aren't whispered, but they're quiet enough that eavesdropping is entertaining. Mostly because I'm a curious person and, even though I'm not usually much for gossip, I doubt they've got any information about who's dating who and what scandalous events happened between which high schoolers over the summer.

"Yes," the one in the black suit says, laughing. "It'll take some getting used to, but we won't be going anywhere before they're done, and maybe not even after, so we might as well get as comfortable as we can."

Grey suit nods his head. "I appreciate you doing this for me," he tells the other man.

"It's nothing," black suit responds breezily as he leans back in his seat. "The company needed someone to come, and after everything happened, I think it'll be a good change. Besides, you're the one who paid to put me here." He chuckles lightly.

I tilt my head a bit, trying to hear better. I can't decide if this is a business meeting or not. And, even though it's none of my business, I can't help but wonder more and more what the two men are talking about.

"Yes, well, you're my brother regardless of the company," grey suit says. "And as far as the company is concerned, I own it and, therefore, I have the ability to choose who I put where. I think you will do just fine overseeing this project."

Huh, so it is a business meeting of sorts, but the two men have family bonds, and those seem to matter more to grey suit than whatever is going on regarding his company.

Black suit nods, but not in a smug way like he expects his brother to think highly of him. "The demolition crew will be there fairly soon. We're looking at another month or so for the designs to be completely finished and I don't want them destroying the place before that's done. I'd much rather disrupt the neighborhood for as little time as possible."

Wait. Demolition crew? Neighborhood disruption? Were they talking about…

"I agree," grey suit says to his brother. "Chesterfield has been abandoned for years. I'm sure the neighbors have gotten used to the quiet area."

The blood in my body goes cold.

They were talking about the abandoned part of the neighborhood. Chesterfield was the street the old houses sat on. The whole place was going to be destroyed in a matter of a couple months…

I can feel my heart sink in my chest at the realization. Sure, I knew they'd tear it down at some point, but to know about when it's going to happen… that's a different thing all together.

I decide then that I hate these two men regardless of the fact that they're trying to be nice to the other people who live in the neighborhood. They were going to take away my childhood and my safe place. How could I not?

Their conversation fell into talk about when they'd both last talked to their mother, and then their families, and, by the time they got that far, mom was coming back over to our table with a tray full of food.

I don't forget about the men beside our table, but my stomach growls when my mom sets the tray down in front of me, and that's enough to pull most of my attention away from the burning pain of anger and sadness in me.

I reach for the burger my mom got me, but I freeze just shy of taking a bite. I have to be careful. I can't risk anyone seeing.

Carefully, I pull the wrapping around the burger as much as I can, trying to hide anything that my lips will touch. Once I've gotten it as covered as I can manage, I take a huge bite of it, letting the taste of MSG overflow my senses and kill as many of my brain cells as it wants to. It tastes so good, how could I not let it? I haven't had a hamburger from a restaurant in forever.

"Mmm," I sigh as I chew the food. It's like an explosion of flavor in my mouth; far more exciting than anything I've eaten lately.

My mom chuckles across from me as she pops a couple fries in her mouth.

I notice black suit look up at me, and that's when I realize my mistake. I'm holding the burger low against the table.

I jerk my hands up when I notice and look away from the man. I can see him shake his head out of the corner of my eye. He no doubt noticed the fact that my burger was not the color it should be, but seems to think he's just crazy or something as he gets back to his meal with his brother.

Great job, Thana.

After getting back from the restaurant, I did my best to take a shower without causing my collar bone much pain. Unfortunately, that proved much more difficult than I wanted it to be. I'd managed to get through it, though.

Now, I have a towel wrapped around my body with my practically useless left arm holding it in place as I keep it plastered to my torso beneath my breasts. With my free hand, I run a brush through my tangled mess of hair.

My mom used to help me brush it each time I got out of the shower, but now I do it myself. It's become a habit of mine, even if it's basically useless when I'm going to be heading to bed right after.

I sigh as I stare at my reflection in the bathroom mirror. I look nothing like my mother and sister. Or even my father and brother for that matter. My mother and Fayre, who inherited her looks, both have gorgeous blond hair that spills down their backs in a wavy waterfall of beautifulness. They have blue eyes and lightly tanned skin, like they see just enough sun to make them beautiful, but no more than that. They're both average height with curvy hips and breasts that aren't too small or big but just perfect. Everything about my mother and younger sister seems perfect.

My father and brother are both handsome with wavy brown hair and green eyes. They're both muscular, but not ridiculously so, and tall. They're tan and both have easy smiles that light up their faces.

I look nothing like them. Where they all look beautiful, I'm much different. I can't even say I just look plain. I stick out like a sore thumb in my own way.

I have ridiculously straight black hair that falls midway down my back, reaching to my shoulder blades, but that's it. My eyes are grey, but not the kind of grey that's an off blue or green. They have no color to them at all. They're as dull as everything else about me. My skin isn't tan like any of my other family members, not even the slightest bit. I'm sickly pale, and, if it's even possible, there's a bit of a grey tinge to it. Along with sickly pale, I'm almost sickly thin, and short. I'm not curvy like my mother and sister, and by no means have much in the department of cleavage.

I have one strange thing about me that would stick out if anyone knew it was truly how I looked, though. Instead of pale pink lips like normal people have, my lips are black as night; the same color as my hair. Everyone has always thought it's just lipstick I'm wearing, but I've never touched a tube of lipstick in my life. Or any makeup for that matter, though it would help my appearance a lot.

As boring and dull as I am, I've somehow never been very self-conscious about how I look. I'm odd-looking I suppose, but I've never cared to impress anyone with my appearance. I've never cared to impress anyone with anything about myself, come to think of it.

I get picked on at school a lot about how I look and how I act, but everyone seems to assume I'm just that gothic kid in the back who wants nothing to do with anyone and who only wears black. Yes, I only wear black, but it helps to keep the true color of my lips hidden if everyone thinks I'm just trying to be a rebellious teen. That, and it's not like I have much of a choice. I wear black and grey because it's my only option.

I set down the brush and stare into my own eyes in the mirror.

School starts back up in a week, and I'm not so sure I'm ready for that. School starting up means dodging other teenagers in cramped hallways and making sure I notice the people who stand along the edges, silently judging everyone else. And Mark. School starting also means avoiding Mark.

This is Fayre's first year in high school, though, and that has me much more worried about the school year starting up than listening to snobby girls poke fun at the weird girl in the corner who's covered nearly from head to toe in black and grey clothing. Fayre is so sweet and gentle, and I don't want the stupid high schoolers I've been stuck with for years to ruin her. I love my sister so much and I couldn't bear for them to do that to her.

And, the worst part of all, is that I don't have the option to do anything to help even if I wanted to. If I were to stand up for anyone, which everyone would see as picking a fight, I couldn't back it up. Well, I could, but at the risk of their bare skin touching mine and killing them. As much as I would want to kill anyone who tried to hurt my sister, that isn't something I can actually do.

Besides, that's basically Daemon's entire reason for being, anyway. He'll take care of Fayre, whether or not

I'm able to be there to help, too.

I leave the bathroom and go to my room. The bathroom I was in is attached to my bedroom. It was one of the accommodations we had to have for me because if I used any other bathroom in the house, especially one that guests might use, they'd be keenly aware of the room being completely black and grey. Taking the risk and hoping that anyone who went into the bathroom would just think that's how we had decided to decorate it wasn't something my parents were willing to do.

I get changed into a pair of comfortable pajamas before I climb into bed, hoping that sleep will come easier tonight than it did yesterday.

Chapter Three

My alarm goes off at the ungodly hour of 8:00 in the morning two days later. We still haven't done our shopping for notebooks and pencils yet. Not that we really need anything more than we already have for our next year of school, but my mom is a complete office supply junky. Now that everything's gone on super sale, she's extremely excited to get to the stores to do some shopping. See, my mom isn't like stereotypic women who go shopping for jewelry and clothing and handbags and whatever else. Instead, she goes for dumb little things, like sticky notes and erasers that fit into her mechanical pencils.

I slam my hand on the alarm clock's snooze button absentmindedly and, as soon as the blaring sound stops, I'm asleep again.

Unfortunately for me, it goes off again 5 minutes later.

I wake with a start and I glare at the noisy thing. Would it really be that bad if I threw it out the window and told my mom I hadn't heard it go off at all when she comes to my room and wakes me up herself?

Groggily, I shut the thing off and climb my sleepy butt out of bed. Yawning, I lift my arm above my head, stretching the sleepiness from my body. It doesn't help as much as I want it to, and I consider flopping back down on my bed. It takes me a moment to convince myself that getting out of bed myself and going to eat breakfast is a good thing.

I grab my gloves off of my nightstand and slip them onto my hands before I head over to my closet. My clothes consist of basically all the same stuff – plain T-shirts, jeans, and shorts – so I literally only have to decide whether or not I want to be sweating my butt off while we're outside or if I want to be freezing cold while we're inside. Neither option is one that sounds pleasant, but I decide that wearing jeans and dealing with the ridiculous heat outside is better than wishing I had a jacket inside of a store.

I head over to the bathroom to change. I'd rather avoid making my floor black along with everything else, if I can.

I peel my socks off of my feet before I strip down to my underwear and replace my pajamas with the clothes I grabbed a moment ago.

A knock comes on my door as I'm pulling on my shirt. "What?!" I shout, my voice muffled by the fabric.

"Breakfast is ready," Daemon replies, and I hear his steps retreat down the hallway. Thank god he doesn't want to keep pestering me like usual.

I let out a breath of relief I didn't know I was holding in and pull my shirt down over my stomach so that the hem is around my hips.

Before leaving my room to get food, I snag my wallet off of my desk and stuff it into my back pocket.

When I get to the dining room, I plop down at the dining room table with my brother and sister. Despite the fact that the food is done, my mom is standing in the kitchen, eating a piece of toast while she goes over a pile of papers for some purpose that I'm unsure of. Fayre is texting instead of eating, which I seriously doubt she won't regret later in the day, and Daemon is, well, I don't really know what he's doing. He's just sitting there.

A fact about our family is that we hardly ever actually eat at the table, but we do sit at it a decent amount. Just not usually for eating purposes. The reason I haven't gotten food yet is because food right after waking up makes me nauseous, so I'll be waiting a bit.

It takes less than a minute for me to become bored.

If I had any contacts in my phone, I'd be doing the same thing Fayre is doing right now. Unfortunately, though, the girl with the ability to kill people and who either gets made fun of almost constantly or gets completely ignored at school doesn't have any friends.

When the silence starts to become unbearable, I decide that I should probably do my best to engage in some conversation with my siblings to keep any and all discomfort that is starting to sink in from getting any worse.

"Looking forward to your senior year?" I ask my brother, raising an eyebrow at him. My brother is the stereotypic popular good kid. He gets good grades, he doesn't pick any fights but will stand up for people when he sees they need help, and he's got a circle of nice friends.

Daemon looks over at me, seeming surprised that I'm talking to him and not just ignoring his existence like usual. "Um, I mean, I guess?" he responds, sounding more like he's asking for my approval of his answer or something rather than straight-up giving it to me like I would've preferred.

"Interesting." I smirk at him. "Gonna finally ask Lauren out, or are you gonna wait until the two of you have graduated college?"

Daemon rolls his eyes at me.

"I don't know," he tells me, but doesn't give me any more of an answer than that.

He's never been the most fun to tease, so I suppose I have no reason to be disappointed. I do wish I could get some more entertainment out of this than just a simple answer, though. I mean, come on. At least a tinge of red in his cheeks would be enough, but there's nothing.

"Huh," I say beneath my breath, not loud enough for him or anyone else to hear.

Once I thought about it, that was the first time me mentioning Lauren hadn't made him blush at all. Was he over his little crush finally? Or was he just so comfortable with the thought of liking her that it didn't make him feel awkward anymore?

I pull my phone out of my pocket and open up the messaging app. Once inside, I tap Fayre's contact and text her "good morning" because I know that will get a quicker response than me actually talking to her in the real world.

Instead of answering me with her voice like a normal person, she texts me back without even glancing in my general direction. She doesn't even seem to notice, or care, that Daemon and I are here.

Good morning! I read on my phone. There's a little smiley face emoji beaming at me through the glass.

I can't remember the last time I texted anyone and used an emoji, but I'm also talking to my sister, so I guess it fits her a lot better than it does me.

Mind acknowledging us irl? I text her back, trying not to let my mild irritation become apparent in the words.

Fayre's phone goes off when my text goes through and I catch a hint of pink rise in her cheeks. She either thought I was one of her other friends again, or she knew it was me but didn't register the fact that I'm sitting right in front of her.

She opens her mouth to say something, but just as

she does, mom walks out of the kitchen and over to the table. "Have you all eaten? Because I'm ready to get this show on the road," she says, her voice bright and happy.

Mom's eyes pass over each of us as she waits for a response. Her eyes fall on my arm in the sling when she looks at me, which I can only guess means that she's still wondering what exactly I did that caused it to break.

"I did," Fayre tells her, the blush fading from her cheeks.

Daemon just nods his head.

I can't tell if that means he ate too, or if he's just confirming that Fayre did, in fact, eat.

Instead of responding, I just stand up and grab a piece of toast off the plate on the counter. I put it between my teeth as I pull my phone from my pocket and plug my earbuds into the audio jack.

They're all looking at me when I come back out, waiting for me to say something, I guess.

I pull my toast out from between my teeth. "We leaving or not?" I ask, like I'm already in the car and have been waiting for them for the past hour.

My sister and I weave through the many aisles of school supplies. Mom needed to go grab other things in the store and Daemon, who had already finished picking out what he needed by then, offered to go with her. I was responsible for staying back with Fayre, though I didn't quite understand why I felt like I should be babysitting her when she's fourteen.

Though I know it's strange and that I'm going to get a lot of weird looks for it, I plop myself down on the floor and lean my back against a shelf full of spiral notebooks. I already have everything I need, and I don't feel like standing around while I wait for my sister to finish.

Fayre raises an eyebrow at me before she goes back to flipping through a stack of folders.

Even though she's going to be going into high school in a matter of a couple days, she's still obsessed with everything covered in pink glitter. She's already managed to find a sparkly pink pencil case, a fancy pen with sparkly pink ink and a giant pink pompom on the end of it, and now she just needs a folder that will match.

I purse my lips as I look her up and down.

Everything about the way she's dressed screams sixth grader, but there's no mistaking how gorgeous she is. Fayre is young at heart, but I doubt that will last as long as anyone wants it to. She's going to be the talk of the school when we get there Monday. Every guy is going to want to take her out, which is going to make the hot, popular girls jealous. I just hope Fayre is smart enough to avoid letting them get their hooks in her.

"Do these match?" Fayre asks, spinning around to

face me with her pompom pen in one hand and a folder so sparkly it's practically blinding me in the other.

I shrug. "I mean, they're both making me wanna wretch," I tell her, by way of answer.

Fayre rolls her eyes at me, completely unamused by my answer. She turns back around and continues on her quest to find the perfect glittery pink folder.

I can't help but hope it'll end soon so that I don't have to stay here much longer.

Sighing impatiently, I pull my phone from my pocket and start a round of solitaire.

Solitaire has been my distraction from the world for years. When I was ten, I saw a boy playing it with an actual deck of cards in the cafeteria one day. He was sitting on the floor and looked bored out of his mind as he poked at his food with a disgusted look on his face. He'd ended up starting the game and hadn't looked up until he was done.

After that day, I learned how to play and started carrying around my own deck of cards. When I got my phone, the first thing I did was download the game so I could play it whenever I wanted to. Somehow, though, even after all of these years of playing the game, I'm still terrible at it.

"Hey," a familiar voice says from somewhere not far off.

My head snaps up and my eyes land on a guy I've had to deal with every year for as long as I can remember.

He's not talking to me, though. He's talking to my sister, which is enough to piss me off to a whole new level.

Mark crosses his arms and leans cockily against the shelves less than a foot away from my sister. "You're the girl who came over to help my sister with a science project, right?" he asks, a smile on his face that can make any girl's knees buckle beneath her, my sister being one of them.

My sister giggles before she looks away from him and down at her shoes, her face bright red.

Before I even have time to register the thought, I'm on my feet and marching my way over to them as I stuff my phone back into my pocket. I don't stop until I've matched his position, but am standing so that my face is a few inches from his and my body is separating him from my sister.

"She's three years younger than you, *Mark*," I snap, my disgust apparent in how I say his name. "Get out of here and don't you dare ever think about coming anywhere near my sister again." I glare daggers at his stupidly perfect face with his blond hair and gorgeous eyes.

Mark puts his hands up and takes a step back. I can tell he doesn't feel bad at all for what he was no doubt thinking, though.

Mark has made it his job to make my life a living hell ever since I first met him nearly three years ago when he took an unwanted interest in the goth girl just like most other people tend to. Only he seemed to be much more set on trying to figure me out than anyone else ever seemed to be. When he couldn't find anything weird about me aside from how I dress, he seemed to decide that just being a bully in the meantime was good enough.

"Your sisters hot," he says in response, shrugging. "Can you blame me for being interested?"

My rage hits a boiling point and I reach forward and slap him across the face, leaving a bright red handprint on his cheek.

I can't help but wish I'd thought to take my glove off before doing so.

"Thana!" Fayre says behind me, not sounding angry so much as surprised and confused.

She grabs my shoulder with a hand, but there's literally nothing she could do that would stop me from saying or doing whatever I feel necessary to get this jerk to back off.

I stare directly into his hazel eyes, my index finger a centimeter away from poking him in the nose. "Don't come near her again," I growl, my voice barely above a whisper. "And trust me when I tell you this: I can do *much* worse than a bruised cheek."

Something that looks vaguely like curiosity flashes over his features, but it only lasts a second before its covered up by his usual smirk.

"Thana!" Fayre says again, but her voice is weak this time.

"Easy, honey. No need to worry your pretty self about it." He gives me the same smile that makes every girl but me fall instantly for him as he reaches to stroke my cheek with the back of his hand.

I smack him away, my eyes not leaving his. "Flirting will get you nowhere with me," I hiss, wishing I'd let him touch me just so I could watch his body turn to grey dust before he died. "And you and I both know I'm not pretty."

Fayre's grip on my shoulder tightens, which is enough to snap me out of my angry trance.

"Well, as nice as this has been," Mark says, his amusement all over his face. "I really need to be heading out." He looks over my shoulder. "See you at school, Fayre." He winks at her before he spins around and walks off.

If Fayre hadn't been holding a fistful of my jacket in her hand, I would've pounced on him and had him dead before he even would've realized I was there.

"LET GO!" I shout back at her, adrenaline, rage, and hate burning white-hot in every inch of my body.

Fayre's expression changes to fear as she lets go and takes a step back.

My feet slip beneath me on the tile and I fall to the floor.

My cheek connects with the floor before I'm able to catch myself.

White-hot pain rages through every inch of my body, and I bite my tongue hard enough to make it bleed to keep myself from crying out. It doesn't keep the tears from spilling down my cheeks, though.

Damn collar bone.

"Thana!"

Fayre rushes over to me, dropping everything she'd been holding a moment ago to the floor. She kneels beside me, her hand on my shoulder as she moves my jacket away so that she can see my left collar bone.

"It looks fine," she says, her voice breathy.

Her face has gone pale in just the past few seconds and I realize that I probably wasn't the only one who thought I might've injured myself even more than I already am.

"It sure hurts, though," I say through gritted teeth as Fayre does her best to help me to my feet.

I take a moment to stand there while the pain passes and Fayre doesn't rush me.

I know everything I just did was extremely stupid and immature, but Fayre is my sister and I love her more than anything else. To have some creep like Mark Denson looking at her like nothing more than just a toy for his own amusement makes me sick. And gives me more than a mild urge to sink my fist into his face and watch him die a slow, agonizing death.

"C'mon," Fayre says once I've recovered from the pain. "Mom and Daemon are probably waiting for us by now."

I nod my head and grab my stuff off of the floor before I follow her to the front of the building where the registers are. The black mark on the floor from where my cheek connected with the tile is visible out of the corner of my eye when we turn to leave the aisle.

Chapter Four

I wake to someone pounding on my bedroom door. There's no doubt in my mind that it's Daemon, checking to make sure I'm up and getting ready for school.

Groaning, I roll over in bed and bury myself deeper in my covers. The warm air beneath my blanket beckons me to let the world slip away into sleep again, but I know my brother won't let me even spend a moment longer in bed if he can help it.

"Thana!" Daemon's voice calls. "We leave in twenty!"

My eyes snap open and I sit up in bed. Twenty? Why didn't they wake me up sooner?

"Coming," I mumble beneath my breath, my voice raspy from sleep.

I get changed and grab my backpack – which I was

smart enough to pack the night before – before I leave my room and head out to the kitchen.

I'm so late getting out of my room that pretty much all of the food is gone by the time I actually get into the kitchen. I've never been able to eat that much in the morning anyway, though, so I'll be just fine waiting until lunch for a proper meal.

"Okay, let's get this show on the road!" mom announces as I make my way into the dining room.

Three. And it's only Monday morning.

She ushers us out to the car and climbs into the front seat as everyone else plops themselves in the unoccupied ones. Daemon takes the front passenger seat as usual and Fayre takes the seat behind our mom, which leaves me with the one behind our brother.

Mom puts the key in the ignition and turns the car on. Once it's on, I roll down the window and lean my arm against the ledge so I can feel the warm air against the tiny bit of bare skin on my arm where my jacket sleeve is pulled up. It's not much, but it's more than I get to feel unless I'm out at the abandoned part of the neighborhood.

I let out a shaky breath when my mom pulls the car out of the driveway. The first day of school has always made me nervous, but I thought I was past worrying day in and day out that I'll hurt someone. Apparently, things like this don't loosen their hold as quickly as I wish they would.

The drive to school takes about ten minutes, which

isn't terribly bad but is also longer than I wish it was. Most of the kids who go to this school live in the neighborhood over from ours. It's already been developed, so most of the kids are snobby rich kids who can't stand the fact that some of us can't afford to buy name brand clothing.

I've never had to deal with it much, but I've seen plenty of other kids who do. I'm just the kid who no one likes anyway, so why bother tormenting me about my clothing when there's so much other stuff that's off about me?

Mom parks the car, and the three of us grab our stuff and climb out.

"Hey," mom's voice is gentle when she says it, but what catches my attention is her hand on my knee.

Any touch at all is something I usually avoid and those around me do the same. I'm deadly, so why would anyone take the risk? Even my parents, who love all of us to death no matter what, have never taken the risk of coming into my room at night to give me a hug before I climb into bed. Fayre holding me back from Mark yesterday was one of the rare times someone has dared to touch me, and it wasn't in a loving way, like how my mom is touching me now.

I meet her gaze. "Hmm?" I ask, not able to form actual words through the surprise that's taken over every inch of my body.

"You're gonna do just fine today," she tells me, a kind smile on her face. There's no doubt in her voice at all. Nothing that makes me think that maybe she's forcing these words out. Nothing that makes me think that she's only trying to be a good mother in telling me this. She truly believes it. She thinks I'm going to go in there and be like every other kid instead of the weirdo in the back of the room who has no friends and who keeps their head down in the halls to avoid making eye contact with anyone.

I smile back at her, but it's forced. "Yeah," I say, but it doesn't take a genius to know I don't believe any of it.

My mom sighs.

I can't seem to help but feel bad as I climb out of the car and make my way inside. Sure, she believes that I'll do fine and maybe even come off as slightly normal, but that doesn't mean I actually will.

And I prove that to myself already as I walk from the car to the school doors with my head bowed like I'm afraid of the world; as though my only comfort is to watch my feet and the ground right in front of them.

I let my bangs fall over the left side of my face as I hike up my backpack in a way that makes my whole jacket moves up with it, and my hood fall further over my face.

There's no reason to hide, and I know that, but it makes me feel like everyone else is safer from me if I'm hidden. I know hiding isn't going to make me any less dangerous, and that if someone stumbled into me and their arm brushed against my cheek, it would still kill them, but it gives me peace of mind to know that most of my skin is covered when I'm hiding like this.

"Thana?"

I can't help it when I flinch.

Damn it...

What's he doing? Why's he talking to me? I almost hit him with my bike, but that doesn't give him the right to talk to me. Especially because I'm, well, *me*. No one talks to me unless they've got something rude to say. Is that why he cares that I exist?

"What do you want?" I snap, probably harsher than I should've, but do I really have any reason to not expect something bad out of this? I know he doesn't know about all of my past encounters at school – or maybe he does because he's about to add another to my long list – but it's really hard to convince myself that being polite might be the right thing to do in a situation like this.

"Geez, what'd you do to your arm?" Chase asks, his eyes on my sling. His eyes widen a second later. "That's not because of me, is it?"

"No, it was the troll who lives in the culvert under my driveway who decided to attack me on my way home for entertainment purposes." I roll my eyes. "What do you think?"

I really shouldn't be as rude as I am, especially since he just confirmed that he isn't here to destroy my life, but I can't seem to help it. I don't like him, even if I can't place why I don't and he hasn't given me any reason not to like him. I trust my impulses though, and right now they're telling me to not like him and to get him out of my life as quickly as possible.

I'd prefer to just stand here and glare at him rather than even talking to him, but I think that's kind of overdoing it a bit. I can make it clear enough that I don't want him around with some rudeness in my voice and it might actually be a bit more fun than just looking at him like he's a disgusting bug that I'd like to introduce to the bottom of my shoe.

"I'm so sorry," he says sheepishly, looking away from me and down at the floor.

I let out a breath. I can't help but feel guilty for how I'm treating him. I don't want anything to do with the guy, but all he's been is nice to me. Even I can't justify my own rudeness with only the fact that I feel like I should hate him.

"It's fine," I tell him. "And it's not your fault either. I was the one on the bike."

I wish I could say I'd meant for those words to come out of my mouth and that they hadn't seemed to appear out of nowhere, but that'd be a lie if I did. I'd meant to leave it at "it's fine" and walk off, but, for some reason, my words didn't stop there. They seemed to form on my tongue out of thin air.

Surprise flashes in his eyes for a second, but as quickly as it showed up, it vanishes, leaving behind the same expression he wore a moment ago; something hard to read beneath the sheepish yet caring look.

"Well, I guess that makes it both of our faults, then." He doesn't look like he fully believes that, though. "But I got away without a scratch and that's far from how you ended up," he adds. "Just let me know if you wanna break my arm in return or anything."

He winks at me teasingly, and a smile almost makes its way onto my face before I manage to catch it and bury it deep inside.

I'll manage smiles that aren't directed at my family sometimes, but it's rare that I let them make it to the surface.

And, most of the time, those only get shown to people I somewhat enjoy being around, like my younger cousins or my grandparents, or when whoever earned it can't actually see that it's on my face. Laughs are out of the question.

"It's my collar bone," I inform him, my face blank and my voice holding no emotion whatsoever. If he saw the start of the smile, that's all he'll ever see of it. He's not worth my face twisting into such an awkward and uncomfortable position.

"Ah," he responds, something that looks vaguely of disappointment flashing in his eyes before he hides it, just like I did with the smile.

The bell rings then, and I can't help but feel completely relieved when the piercing sound reaches my ears. The sooner I can get away from this guy in front of me and this awkward conversation, the better.

"Gotta go!" I announce, and before he can respond, I do an abrupt about-face and march off in the general direction of my homeroom.

I keep my eyes on the floor the whole way there and do my best to become invisible again.

I wish it worked better.

Someone knocks into my shoulder as I'm walking, sending me sprawling to the ground. I land on my right side, which makes it less painful for my broken collar bone, but the jolt still sends a flare of pain through me.

I have to bite my tongue to keep from crying out.

I grip my left shoulder, my eyes not moving high enough to see anything other than the shoes of the jerk who knocked me over.

"Oops," Mark's stupid voice says as he crouches down to look me straight in the eyes.

Well, if he's not going to let me sit in pain in peace, I might as well look up.

It's not like I wasn't expecting this after what I did at the store last week, but I still can't say I regret telling him to stay away from my sister. I doubt he could do anything to me as punishment that would make me think maybe I shouldn't have.

When I meet his gaze, I take notice to the fact that there are two guys with him, one on either side of him.

"Not so tough down there, are you?" he sneers, a twisted, cruel smile playing across his face.

I smirk at him. "If I'm not a threat, why do you have backup?" I look past him at his two minions. "Hey, guys. Nice of you to help this guy with the big, scary, broken girl." I stick out my bottom lip mockingly at him.

That only pisses him off more.

Mark grabs the hood of my jacket and slams me back against the lockers.

My head spins from the pain and my vision goes black for a second before his disgustingly perfect face comes back into view. I'd really love to mess him up.

"Thanks for the migraine," I say, my voice strained from the throbbing pain in my shoulder and now my brain.

"Hey, back off," I hear Chase say from somewhere ahead of me.

Damn it.

A hand grabs Mark's shoulder and he drops his hold on my jacket.

I slip back down to the floor as he spins around to face Chase.

Mark gets right up in Chase's face. "What'd you say?" he asks. Everyone knows full well that he knows exactly what the other boy said, but I suppose giving Chase a chance to change his mind somehow seems more threatening.

"I said, back off," Chase repeats through gritted teeth.

Just leave it alone, you moron.

"She's already hurt, just leave her alone."

I want to scream at him to back off, to let me fight my own battles and not get involved in something that's none of his business, but I'm not dumb enough to think that I won't end up twenty times more hurt if I keep it up with Mark. If he can get Mark to leave me alone, I'll be better off than I would be if I was left to deal with it on my own. I don't seem to know how to not make situations worse for myself, after all.

That fact doesn't make me any less irritated, though. Regardless of if it will help me in the end or not, it's none of his damn business.

"You know what?" Mark says, and I really wish I could see his face so I knew where this was going. "You're right." He pats Chase on the shoulder before he turns back to me. He walks back over to me and crouches down so his eyes are level with mine again. "I'll just wait for you to heal, and then break you again" He leans in closer and his voice is a deadly whisper when he continues. "Because *no one* tells me what I can and can't do."

He slams my head back against the lockers again, another jolt of pain surging through my body when he does.

Once the pain subsides a bit and my head is clear again, the weight of his threat fully sinks in.

Fayre.

That's what he's talking about.

If I won't let him get anywhere near Fayre, he'll find a way. And if she doesn't want him anywhere near her, he'll still find a way.

I'm not sure if I'm overthinking it or if I understand completely, but the gravity of that is like a crushing weight on my entire being, making it hard for me to see, to think, or to even breathe.

By the time I snap out of whatever trance I was in, my breathing is heavy and there's a thin line of sweat on my upper lip. I move to wipe my face with the back of my hand, but my hands are numb.

There's no way he would dare do something to Fayre… is there?

"Are you alright?"

Chase kneels beside me and puts his hand gently on my right shoulder, which doesn't hurt but makes me flinch anyway because it's unexpected and physical contact scares me.

"No," I whisper, my voice barely audible, even to my own ears.

I'm late to class, my sister could possibly be in serious trouble, and it's all his fault. If he'd just left it alone, I'd be broken and bloody but my sister would no doubt be fine. All Mark wanted was to hurt me. What if, now, he decides that hurting my sister while he waits for the perfect moment to break me would be more fun?

"I…" I jump up to my feet, ignoring the pain coursing through every inch of me. My face is hot with anger and my hand is clenched into a fist that I bang against the lockers so hard it sends a stabbing sensation through my arm.

"Woah, calm down. It's alright," Chase says, standing up and putting his hands one on each of my shoulders.

"It's not alright!" I can't help it when I shout.

"Look, thanks for sticking up for me, but next time, don't."

I hike my backpack up on my shoulder before I march off to my class, which I'm already late enough to.

Chapter Five

Not once have I ever wanted to be seen standing outside of the school with one of my siblings. I've never wanted to be seen with anyone because it would draw attention, and even the attention I would get for being Daemon's sister would be something I don't want. He's popular and being in that crowd or even associated with it is a hard no for me. Fayre is still new, though, and I need to know she's okay, which is why I make the exception today when I text her and tell her to meet me by the old oak tree.

On any other day, I would've climbed up the branches and plopped my butt down on a large one in the middle instead of standing around like I'm doing right now. But with my brokenness and all, that'd be rather difficult and I'm not so sure that's something I want to deal with.

I watch as Fayre walks out of the school with a group of other freshmen girls who all look completely overjoyed to see each other after the summer break. She gives each of them a tight hug before she makes her way over to where I'm sitting by the tree.

Without saying anything, she plops down beside me and lays her head against my non-broken shoulder.

Fayre has always been more physically loving than anyone else in my family, so it's not completely unusual for her to be like this. I don't get why so many people are touching me all in the same day, though. Usually, I don't have to deal with this much human contact within a twenty-four-hour timespan.

"I met the *cutest* guy today." Fayre sighs as she leans into my shoulder more, a smile playing on her lips and a love-struck glimmer in her eyes. "I feel like Cinderella when she met Prince Charming, but without the evil step-mother and you're not an evil sister, but you get my point."

She sighs again and I can't help but be reminded of some dumb romance movie. This has never been my favorite topic and I'm pretty sure my sister knows that already. But I also tend to suck it up when I'm around her because she's a full-on love story lover, and probably one of the most dramatic ones at that.

"Um... fun?" I say. It sounds more like a question than anything else, but Fayre knows how this works by now. "What's his name?"

"Drake," she answers. The dreaminess in her eyes comes back.

I crinkle my nose at that. "Stereotypic kinda guy you'd think of when you hear that name, or a nerd who just happens to have a name that really doesn't fit?" I ask, because I'm overprotective.

Fayre turns and glares at me. "What does it matter, so long as he's a nice guy?" she challenges.

"Because every Drake I've known hasn't been a nice guy," I answer, which isn't exactly valid, but it's all I've got, so I'm rolling with it.

My sister rolls her eyes at me and turns away, no doubt still thinking I'm an absolute moron.

"Have you seen Mark at all today?" I ask her. I was going to wait until we'd been talking for a while longer to drop that one on her, or until I could somehow tie it into the conversation, but that doesn't seem to be happening and the overwhelming urge to ask finally took over.

Fayre frowns at me. "You mean the guy from the store?" she asks, and I nod in response. "No. I've really only been talking to the other freshmen." She shrugs like it's nothing, but she still looks a bit confused. I can't blame her. "Why?"

"Uh…"

Damn it.

"Just wondering if I needed to beat anyone up," I answer sheepishly, which isn't a lie but also isn't the whole truth.

Fayre rolls her eyes at me but she doesn't yell at me, so I take that as a good thing. I wish I could ignore how hurt I am that she thinks I'm being overly paranoid and stupid, but I don't know how to. And it's not like I've told her why she needs to be worried about him. I can't help but think that maybe I'm being dumb by not doing it. After all, it is her life. But I also don't want her to be scared. Though I don't know if me telling her would actually scare her, considering that she could probably go around school with a large group of friends and be perfectly fine.

"I'm gonna head out," I inform her as I climb to my feet. I grab my backpack off of the ground and sling it over my shoulder. "Don't have much time left with that sanctuary of mine, so yeah."

She offers me a sad smile before telling me to enjoy myself.

Mom will be here to pick us up soon, but I tend to avoid riding back home in the car and usually just walk. I get home at some point either way. Besides, the walk gives me extra time to be alone with my thoughts.

Usually, I don't have much to think about, but today has given me enough stressful events that I could mull over them for the next three months and still not be satisfied. What had Mark meant by what he said? Did he plan on hurting Fayre? Or did he just mean to scare me so that I wouldn't stand up to him again?

But what if he hadn't even been thinking about anything that had to do with Fayre? What if he was just mad that Chase stood up for me? What if he was just telling me that as soon as he got the chance, he would hurt me? What if he just didn't want to worry about having to fight off anyone else so he can focus fully on hurting me and enjoy it more?

I shake my head.

What if I'm overthinking all of it and he was just trying to scare me like he's always done? I wasn't going to fully write that off, because I've dealt with him messing with me for as long as I can remember, and I doubt my sister coming around did anything but give him more things to use against me and scare me with.

What if that's really all he wants? Just to scare me because he's never been able to get to me as much as he wants. Sure, he gets satisfaction from leaving me sprawled out on the floor and defenseless while I scramble to get my stuff picked up, but what if he just wants to make tormenting me more fun? Fayre would be a great way to do that. Especially after how I reacted to him talking to her at the store.

I let out a breath and push the thoughts from my mind.

Going to the abandoned part of the neighborhood is my escape. It's where I don't have to be me or deal with any of the day-to-day complications of my life. I get to take a step back and be whoever I want to be. I get to be the girl who reads books under the shade of old oak trees, the girl who rides her bike through ditches to see how much air time she can get, the girl who does her best to mimic the bird calls she hears. I get to be *that* girl instead of this pathetic mess of one who everyone else sees.

I ignore everything that happened at school – including all the homework I'll have to do tonight when I get home – during the rest of the walk to the abandoned part of the neighborhood. Instead, I focus on more mindless things, like not stepping on the cracks in the sidewalk as I practically race to get there.

I pass by my house on the way there, which is hard to avoid. It's usually part of my routine to stop by and grab my bike before heading off, though.

Today, my usual plans won't suffice. I can ride one-handed, sure, but riding a bike with a broken shoulder is not the most pleasant thing in the world. Especially since it's still as sore as it is. If I'd thought to bring my pain meds, I'd probably still grab my bike because I'd be able to power through it, but I didn't have that kind of foresight this morning.

When I get to the closest one of the multiple abandoned properties, I climb beneath the fence and make my way over to the house. I lean my back against the wall and let out a breath, letting the comforting feeling of the familiar place wrap me in its arms.

I slide down the side of the house until my knees are pressed against my chest. I wrap my arm around my legs and rest my chin on my knees.

I don't feel like getting up and walking around today. Not yet, anyway.

Slowly, I pull my jacket off and set it on the ground beside me. I'm wearing a sleeveless shirt beneath it, and now that it's off, I can feel the wind against my bare skin. A feeling of freedom surges through me at the feeling of the breeze.

If I didn't have to worry about the sling getting wet and ruined, I would almost hope for rain to follow the wind. I've always loved the feel of the water sprinkling down on me, sometimes light, sometimes hard. It gives me the same feeling the wind does, but stronger.

There's a rustle of leaves somewhere to my right and I jump in surprise. My eyes catch the sight of a squirrel making its way up to its home near the top of the tree and, though the sound seemed to come from somewhere on the ground, I can't see anything else, which tells me it was more than likely that it was the squirrel who caused the sound.

"*'Cause I could be everything you need,*" a voice sings, barely above a whisper.

My heart hammers in my chest, adrenaline coursing through every inch of me.

I don't dare move. Or even breathe, for that matter.

No matter what I tell myself about the sign falling down five years ago, I'm still trespassing.

Another rustle of leaves follows a second later, and this time, I'm not dumb enough to think it's a squirrel.

My attention snaps to the corner of the house as someone's leg comes into view. It's followed soon after by the rest of them.

"If you're the one for me-"

Whatever the line that follows that one is, it dies on Chase's lips.

His cheeks turn the tiniest bit red as his eyes lock on mine and go wide.

I'm not sure if I'm relieved that the person standing in front of me is him instead of the new owner of this place, or if he scares me more than anyone else ever could. With how my heart is racing inside me, my best guess is the latter.

Chase's surprise fades a second later, but he still looks embarrassed at the fact that he'd been singing what's no doubt the sappiest love song ever written. "What're you doing here?" he asks. Confusion is written all over his face when he asks. There's something else in his expression, too, but I can't put my finger on what it is. Fear? Worry? It's both and neither of them at the same time.

Unsteadily, I climb to my feet.

I open my mouth to snap at him, to tell him that leaving is what I'm doing, but it dies before I can even feel the start of the words on my tongue.

I don't know where my fight went, but it's all but burned out as I stand there, too ashamed of my inability to answer that I can't even look him in the eyes.

Nothing about this is right. I shouldn't feel like I'm somehow a failure for not being able to make him come off as the idiot in this situation, but I feel like one. I don't ever want anyone to see me in a weakened state, and that's exactly what he's seeing.

I hate it so much it brings back a little of my usual fire.

"Trespassing," I say, bluntly. "What're *you* doing here?" It's not my usual snippy reply, but it's better than not responding at all. It took long enough for me to reply that the space between us felt awkward, but it wasn't enough that I started fidgeting like I always do when I get nervous.

Chase grins a bit, but wipes it off his face faster than I expect him to. He puts his hands in his pockets, the tension in his body relaxing a bit. He shrugs. "Bored is all," he tells me. "My uncle owns this place and my dad is here as his representative, so technically I'm not trespassing like you." He winks at me, a glimmer of amusement in his eyes.

My attention snaps to him. "Y-your uncle…?"

I hate how pathetic it sounds; like I'm some girl scared of the monster under her bed and am begging my parents to let me sleep in their room.

"My uncle owns a building company in Virginia," he explains. "But he's been spreading out for the past couple of years. This is the farthest project he's had, and it's far enough that he doesn't think he'll be able to properly oversee the work."

I hate how he says the word "project," like his uncle isn't taking the only place I've ever felt comfortable and completely destroying it.

I know it's not his fault, but I can't help but glare at him as though it is. I know he has nothing to do with this. This is because of his uncle's company and because of his father being here to "oversee" the destruction they're going to cause, but it feels like I should be blaming him, too. Like I should be just as mad at him for stripping the best thing in my life away from me.

"What did I say?" Chase asks, looking nervous, but also mildly irritated. I can't blame him. I've been rude to him every time I've talked to him. He didn't say anything that would've made any normal girl mad at him.

I shake my head. "Look at this place," I tell him gesturing around us at the greenery and the old, broken houses. "People used to live here," I say, touching the wall of the house. "Kids used to run around and play in that field, and in that forest. There're stories here. Maybe forgotten ones, but they're still stories, and your uncle's company is destroying them. Uprooting them and killing all that's left of them."

I know I'm probably being overly dramatic, especially with the look he's currently giving me, but I can't help it. I've fallen in love with this place more times than I can count, each time for a different reason, and I don't think I've been the only one to do so.

I know I'll still have memories of this place when it's gone, but I have nothing else to go to. I have nowhere else where I feel safe. I can't even say I feel safe with my family, because, at any given moment, I could kill one of them. Nothing about my life feels safe except for this place, and I'm losing it.

"Yeah, there're stories," Chase agrees. "But look at this place. People left this place to start new stories. This place is going to change but that's so that new people can start new stories." He looks like he doesn't want to say the last bit, but he does anyway, after letting out a breath. "And so that my uncle can make more money, too, I suppose," he mumbles beneath his breath, sounding resigned to the idea of it.

I don't accept it like he seems to, but I don't see any point in arguing with him.

It's a thought I'm not familiar with, but my fight is gone today. And after everything earlier, I just feel tired.

"Is everything alright?" Chase asks, concern in every feature of his face.

I look up at him. The compassion in his voice catches me off guard. Do I not seem alright? And why does he even care?

"What does it matter to you?" I ask. There's no bite to my tone, just genuine curiosity.

An expression I can't read crosses over his face before he shrugs a shoulder, like whatever he was thinking didn't matter at all, which I'm pretty sure it did. "I don't know," he tells me, looking a bit confused by his own answer. "You freaked out after that guy said whatever he did to you earlier and now you just seem… off, I guess."

I roll my eyes. "Because you totally know me well enough to know when I'm acting differently than usual."

The hint of a smile hides in the corners of his mouth. "Call it a hunch," he says. "And I would like to get to know you better. You seem cool."

I search his eyes when he says that. There's no way he's serious. No one ever wants to get to know me. That's an unspoken rule that everyone should know after just a glance in my general direction. He must want to torment me like Mark does or something. There's no other explanation.

I don't see anything in his expression that would lead me to believe that, though, which is enough to leave me dumbfounded.

What leaves me more shocked is when I find myself saying that I'd like to get to know him too, which makes absolutely no sense because if anything, I can't stand his existence.

"But you have to not be the cause of me breaking any more bones, got it?" I say, a teasing tone to my voice that I'm not used to.

I feel like the words coming out of my mouth are completely out of my control, like someone is somehow choosing my words for me and making me say them. But I'm thinking every word before I say it, and I know I'm fully responsible for choosing to say what I do. And yet, for some reason, they keep coming out of my mouth, no matter how much I know I'm going to regret them later.

Chase laughs.

It's a nice laugh. Loud, but joyous and it makes his whole face light up.

"I'm being serious," I tell him, though we both know I'm being anything but. "I don't think I can be friends with someone who's making me fall into ditches all the time."

The word feels heavy on my tongue. I've never called someone a friend before. I suppose Daemon and Fayre could be considered my friends, but they're my brother and sister. Sure, I talk to them sometimes and hang out with them every now and then, but it's not like having a real friend. I can't help but feel like they – Daemon especially – only endure my company because they feel bad for me.

"I'll do my best, but I make no promises," he says, giving me a goofy smile.

Chase doesn't know any of my secrets, though. All he knows about me that he could pity is what happened earlier with Mark. And, strangely enough, I don't think that's enough to make him look at me like I'm something that needs to be protected.

I could be wrong, but he's not looking at me like that right now, which is enough to make me think maybe I'm not for once.

Besides, it's not like I could ever tell him anything that would truly make him see me differently. No one except for my family can know about what my touch does to people, so I don't have anything more to worry about than I do with everyone else.

The worst thing I could do would literally be to kill him, and I doubt that, even if I actually do become good friends with him, I'd ever get the chance to accidentally touch him. I'm careful enough about it and the only time I've ever truly screwed up was when I had my jacket off and I rode straight into the ditch to avoid hitting him.

"So, does that make us friends?" I ask, which I'm pretty sure is not something people ask, but I can't help but ask it, anyway.

Chase grins at me. "Ever had a friend before?" he teases, chuckling a bit. "And, I mean, I don't think friendship is something you just decide. I've never decided to be friends with any of my other friends. We just kind of… talked and somewhere in there, the word 'friend' came about."

I purse my lips. "Interesting."

He looks completely amused by me, but I'll take that over him looking at me like I'm a wounded puppy any day.

Chapter Six

I sit back down and lean against the old house. Chase sits beside me, but far enough away that I'm not uncomfortable with him being there.

"So, what's your favorite color?" he asks, as though that's the deepest question he could possibly come up with. "And you can't choose black because black is the absence of color, which automatically makes it a no." He smiles teasingly at me, and I know he just wanted an excuse to take away my only obvious answer.

"I don't have a lot of color in my life," I answer, which is as close to the truth as he ever needs to get. "And that's not fair." I give him a suspicious look. "What if black really is my favorite color?"

A teasing smirk pulls at his lips. "Too bad!" he announces. "You've gotta go with your second favorite."

"You're despicable," I say, clicking my tongue as I shake my head. A hint of a smile hides in the corners of my lips, but that's as much as I let it show.

I don't know why I'm relaxed with him, but I can't say I'm not enjoying it. Is this how it would be if I talked to more people? Would I be comfortable with them too if they actually wanted me to be around? Or is he just as completely strange and confusing as I've always thought?

"That I am," he agrees. "But you've still gotta pick one."

What if he's not even the reason I'm comfortable around him? What if I'm comfortable because I'm here, where I'm always relaxed? Is it possible for this place to have such an impact on me that even when I'm with someone else, I'm still perfectly relaxed?

"Blue," I sigh. "And it's my favorite of them all. Black is near the bottom of the list, actually."

I tug at the hem of my shirt awkwardly, which is when I realize I'm not wearing my jacket anymore. I snag it off the ground and pull it back on as quickly as I can manage, which I'm sure looks strange, but it doesn't matter that much because everything about me is strange.

Chase laughs. "Really? Seriously was not expecting that." He stands up and walks over to the base of a tall oak tree. It's one of my favorites to climb when I don't have any broken bones. "The black thing, I mean."

"Yeah, well, look at me," I say, gesturing down at myself.

That probably doesn't sound right, considering that he thinks I picked out these clothes, but he doesn't say anything about it, so I take it to mean I'm still in the clear.

He snorts a laugh but doesn't look back over at me. Instead, he looks up at a branch over his head and jumps up to grab it before pulling himself up into the tree and sitting up on the branch he had been hanging from a second ago. "So, why blue?" he asks, as though he didn't just climb into a tree like he never finished descending from apes.

I can feel my cheeks heat up at the question. "I like the ocean," I explain, sheepishly. "And rivers, and streams, and whatever else you want to fit into that category. I've never been to the beach, though. Or to a riverbank, or anything. I know the ocean isn't clean here, but when I think of the ocean, I think of the color blue anyway, and I think I'd love to see it either way if I got the chance to."

My cheeks are red hot by the time I stop rambling.

There are plenty of reasons why I can't go to the beach or touch the ocean water where everyone can see me. I have secrets, and they have to stay that way. But he doesn't know that, so I'm sure he thinks I'm just some strange kid who's never been to the beach before because her family either doesn't like it or doesn't have the time to go. It's not like we live far from one.

When I look up at him, I don't know what I'm expecting to see, but whatever I thought there would be in his expression, it's not what I find. There's something kind there, like he can't help but find it slightly amusing, but also somehow sweet. Like he somehow likes that my reason for liking the color blue is so childish.

His expression changes to something teasing a second later though, and I can't quite pinpoint what else. "You're cute when you blush," he says, and I can tell he means it, but he looks like he's waiting for something when he does.

My face heats up more, if that's even possible. It's not because I'm flattered though, or because I'm embarrassed. It's because that pissed me off. "Don't call me cute," I snap.

There's a glint of something mischievous in his eyes. "Would you prefer to be called a trespasser?" he offers, wiggling his eyebrows at me.

I almost can't help but let a smile slip onto my face, but I catch it before it has the chance to. "The 'no trespassing' sign fell down five years ago," I retort. "Technically, I'm not doing anything wrong by being here."

His eyes sparkle at my challenge. "Do you wanna take that back?" he asks.

I raise an eyebrow at him. "Why would I do that?"

Chase shrugs. "Just giving you the option before I totally turn this around on you. You sure you don't wanna take it back?"

Now there's definitely no way I'm doing that. He can say whatever he wants and I'll turn it right back around on him. I've played this game enough with my dad to know how it works, and I've become quite good at it.

"No, I'm not taking it back," I say, defiantly. I do my best to cross my arms to emphasize my stubbornness, but that doesn't work as well as I'd like it to with my broken collar bone. After trying for a second, I give up and let my arm fall back into my lap.

Chase laughs. "Okay, Trespasser," he says, winking at me.

"And how does that make me a trespasser?" I snap. Whatever the joke is, I'm definitely not getting it. How does me not taking it back make me a trespasser?

Chase hangs himself upside down in the tree. His dark hair hangs straight down, as though each strand is doing its best to reach for the ground, and his shirt slides down his stomach before he pulls it back into place and tucks it into the waist of his pants.

He looks so boyish and goofy like that that I almost want to laugh.

"You were the one who told me earlier you were trespassing, remember?" he says. "I asked you what you were doing here and your exact answer was 'trespassing.'"

Damn it.

"I don't remember that," I lie, but we both know that's all it is. "I would never say something so untrue."

"Snaps at people a lot, is very stubborn, and also sarcastic." He nods his head and pretends to pull a notepad and pen from his pocket. "Got it." He uses the invisible pen to write it down on his notepad.

I scoff at him and roll my eyes.

I seriously doubt he just put those things together. He seems to be able to read me fairly well. He knew I wasn't going to like it when he called me cute, and he knew I was going to be too stubborn to go against what I said. I don't understand how he's doing this, but it's mildly disturbing at the same time that it's endearing.

Slowly, I pull myself up to my feet and walk over to the tree before I lean my good shoulder on it. He's tall enough that even though he's pretty high up in the tree, his face is at eye level with me. "So, what about you?" I ask, raising an eyebrow at him. "What's your favorite color?"

"Black," he answers, which was not what I was expecting. I wouldn't have pegged him for favoring such a dark color. Maybe dark blue or green, maybe even purple, but not straight-up black.

"Wait a minute," I say, eyeing him suspiciously. "Black isn't an option. You said so yourself."

He grins at me, which looks extra silly because he's hanging upside down in a tree like he's six, and he may not be the tallest guy, but he's definitely not short enough to be that young.

"Don't you dare laugh," he says, but it's not a threat so much as it's playful.

I try to hide the amusement that's bubbled to the surface again. I wish I knew what about being around him makes me comfortable enough to actually feel like smiling.

"It's bad, isn't it?" I tease. "The girly-est color there is? Oh my god, you like glittery pink, don't you? My sister will be your best friend if I guessed right."

Chase snorts a laugh but shakes his head. "Almost. Ignore the glitter and you got it right. My favorite color is pink."

Despite the fact that he told me not to laugh, he doesn't look embarrassed about the fact. If anything, he looks completely relaxed, like he's told a million people.

"So, when you have the option to grab a blue cupcake or a pink one, you go for the pink one?" I ask.

"Obviously," he says, looking completely amused. "I'm a sucker for the pink ones."

I have to fight the smile again that wants to pull the corners of my lips toward opposite sides of my face. "Don't worry. I won't tell anyone about your girlish weakness for pink cupcakes." It's my turn to wink at him.

"Phew, I thought you'd go tell the whole school." He laughs and does the most boyish thing I've seen him do when he reaches forward and gently punches me in the shoulder.

I wouldn't have a problem with it, but he hits my left shoulder, and even though it isn't hard, it sends a bolt of pain through my body and I practically double over from it.

I suck in a breath of air through gritted teeth, but it doesn't ease the pain at all.

I know it'll subside in a matter of a few minutes, but it hurts like hell in the meantime.

"Oh my gosh." Chase maneuvers down from the tree by sitting up and then simply jumping off the branch like it's nothing. He turns to look back at me and grabs both my arms before looking at my face. "I'm so sorry, Thana. I wasn't thinking. I didn't mean to do that. I'm sorry."

The pain is down to a dull throbbing by the time I register that he's in front of me.

"How did you do that?" I ask, dumbfounded. "I've been climbing trees for years, and that would still kill me."

I've tried to pull things off like that before, but I've never been good at sticking the landing. Or working up enough stomach muscles to properly pull myself back up instead of struggling to the side and using my arms to do the work. It took forever for me to even feel comfortable hanging upside down in a tree and not like I was going to be stuck hanging there because I couldn't figure out how to pull myself back up.

"Do what?" He looks over his shoulder like the answer might be behind him. He doesn't find his answer there, though, because he looks back into my eyes less than a second later.

"How'd you get down from the tree so easily? Are you like, spiderman's brother?" I look at the tree then back at him. "Dude, I've had to have climbed this tree ten thousand times and there's no way I could do that and not die."

Chase frowns and looks back at the branch he'd been on a moment ago. "I… practice, I guess?" he answers. It sounds more like he's asking me if that's what I think it was, though.

I've spent too much time with my brother to pass this opportunity up. "Well, if you're asking my opinion, to me it looked like you were trying to be a show-off because there's a girl standing in front of you, but I could be totally wrong." I shrug innocently. Not my best material, but it's more than Daemon has given me lately.

He snorts a laugh. "God my little sister used to think I was trying to impress a girl every time I opened my mouth. Don't tell me you're going to be doing that now, too." He gives an exasperated groan that would have been completely convincing if I didn't know the circumstances.

I mentally note how he spoke in past-tense when he was talking about his sister, but I don't press him by asking. I should know well enough that there are some things people would rather avoid talking about. I don't know if his sister is a tough subject or not for him, but I don't want to test that.

"I've been stuck teasing the same two people for forever, and my sister isn't as much fun as my brother, which means I really only get to tease one, so I've got an open slot that needs filling," I tell him. "If we're gonna be friends, I don't see why I shouldn't fill that spot with you."

He rolls his eyes at me, but he looks amused.

It's then that I realize he's still gripping my arms. I think he realizes the same thing though, because he takes a sudden step back and let's go of me.

I almost want to laugh at the situation.

"You never laugh, do you?" he asks, tilting his head slightly when he does. "Or smile, for that matter."

"Nope," I answer, and I can't help but sound a bit too pleased with myself when I do.

"Instead of smiling, you do this weird thing with your face." He smiles but then scrunches up his face like he's got an itch on his nose and then the smile is gone.

I don't get the feeling he's trying to make fun of me when he does it, though, which keeps me from getting annoyed with him.

"I don't look that ridiculous," I retort.

Chase laughs. "It's so ridiculous it's almost better than a real smile."

I roll my eyes. "Get used to it," I tell him. "I don't remember the last time someone saw me smile and I don't intend to start up again now."

"Is that a challenge?" he asks, raising an eyebrow at me.

I know he wants it to be, but that's not what I was going for. I should've suspected that would be how he'd take it, though. He seems to enjoy a challenge even more than I do.

I shrug. "Sure, why not? But I'm not betting on it because, even though there's no way I could ever lose, I don't have money to set aside for that."

"Seeing you actually smile will be fulfilling enough," he says, and climbs back up into the tree like it's nothing. "I like it when people smile."

I almost want to laugh at that. I can't believe he thinks he'll actually get a smile out of me. He hasn't known me for long at all, but he seems to be able to read me well enough, and I would think he'd be able to tell that I would never let down my guard enough to lose a challenge like that.

The challenges with my dad have only succeeded in making me better at this. I may have slipped earlier, but I hadn't expected the challenge to arise from it. I know this one is here. That'll make it impossible for me to forget about it.

"Is there a time limit or does this challenge never end until I actually smile?" I ask, hoping a little more than I should that it's the latter. I want to prove him wrong, even if that's not really possible if the challenge never ends. I want to see him try to make me smile, only to have it fail.

"Give me two months and you'll crack," he says, smirking at me playfully. "My friend back in Virginia thought he could go six and I broke him just before he reached the two-month mark. I don't think it's possible to be more stubborn than him, so that's the time limit."

Damn it. I guess I can live with it, though. At least he didn't say a week. That wouldn't be satisfying at all. At least this will come with a mild feeling of victory.

"Whatever you say." I scrunch up my nose at him mockingly, mimicking what he said my amused face looks like just a few moments ago.

Chase laughs and almost manages to fall out of the tree before he catches himself.

When I scrunch up my face this time, it's actually to keep myself from smiling. He's so dorky in such a boyish way that's strange to me at the same time that it's somehow endearing. I can't tell if he's immature for his age, or if he just hasn't managed to lose his ability to be comfortable with being silly in front of other people.

"Hey! I know I gave you the option to break me back, but just one bone, not my whole body!" he jokes.

I roll my eyes at him in response.

My phone goes off in my pocket and I can't help it when I jump.

I glance behind myself where the street that leads back home is. I can see the sun setting behind it, which means the person calling is my mom. I should've been paying more attention before now, but I've honestly been enjoying myself quite a bit, which has apparently made me oblivious to what I'm supposed to be keeping track of.

I pull my phone from my pocket. I swipe right on the screen and put it up to my ear.

"Yeah?" I ask, instead of answering the phone with a polite "hello."

"Honey, are you on the way home?" My mom asks.

Four.

"Yeah, I'll be there soon," I sigh. I have nothing against my mom checking up on me, but she calls me almost every day I'm out here, and most of the time it just feels a little suffocating.

She's quiet on the other end for a moment, and I know she's thinking about something. I'm not sure if I want to ask, or if I should wait for her to say whatever it is.

"Is everything okay?" she asks. I can hear her biting her lip; a nervous habit of hers that I inherited. "You didn't answer my texts earlier."

Damn it.

I look at my phone and, sure enough, I have three unread texts from her.

My phone has been on silent, but I should've felt it going off when those came in. I hadn't, though. I hadn't been paying any attention.

"Everything's fine," I tell her. "I just didn't hear those come in. I'll be there soon."

She lets out a breath on the other side of the phone, and I know she's a lot more relieved than she wants to let on. Unfortunately, I've become very keenly aware of things like this because all of my family is overprotective and it's hard to not notice after a while.

"Okay. See you in a bit, then."

Five.

"Love you, mom," I say, which is a bit out of the ordinary for me, but I don't really care right now for some reason.

Everything is out of the ordinary for me today. I got into the closest thing to a fight today at school. I made a friend who I'm currently hanging out with. I've been holding a straight conversation for the past couple of hours. Can my day get much weirder?

"Love you, too," she says, and hangs up the phone.

Six.

I plop myself down on the ground before looking up at Chase, who's looking at me like he's waiting for something. I mean, he did just hear my half of that conversation, so I'm sure he knows exactly what I'm going to say.

"Gotta be home soon," I tell him as I drop my phone into my lap. "My parents are kinda overprotective."

He smiles, but it's not to tease me like most of the times he's smiled at me have been. This one is kinder; almost understanding.

It doesn't register for a second why he's giving me that look, though. He thinks I'm worried they'll be irritated when I get home and find out I'm late home because I've been hanging out with a guy. He thinks I mean overprotective in the helicopter-parent way, but also in the way that parents are when their kids hang out with members of the opposite sex.

"Not like that," I say, probably quicker than I should. "They just don't like it when I'm out past dark, and my mom likes to check up on me to make sure I'm alright, is all." And sure, my parents will be upset that I'm hanging out with someone, but not because he's a guy, because he's another person. But I don't see why they need to know about it.

"I gotcha."

He climbs back down from the tree again. This time he doesn't do any fancy jumping from insane heights, though. This time he climbs over the branch he'd been sitting on and hangs from it for a second before dropping to the ground only a couple feet beneath him.

"C'mon," he says, offering me a hand. "I'll walk you home."

"Aww, such a gentleman," I tease. "Bet the girls love you." I wink at him before taking his hand and letting him pull me to my feet.

"Pfft. Now you *really* sound like my sister," he says.

I watch him as he bends down to grab his phone off of the ground. I didn't see him drop it, but, then again, I haven't been the best at paying attention to things today, so I don't know how I would've managed to notice something as dumb as that.

"And, no," he tells me as he stands back up and puts the phone in his pocket. "I'm not on the football team, and I'm not popular." He winks at me and starts walking toward the street. "So, which way is home?" he asks.

"Benford Court," I answer.

I don't give him time to answer before I march off ahead of him.

I'm not overly fond of the idea of him walking me home, but protesting seems dumb. I don't want my parents or siblings to see me with him, but I don't want to make him think I don't enjoy his company. He's the only person I've ever talked to for more than a few minutes. I don't want to get rid of him quite yet.

Before we even get to the end of the street, the silence that falls over us makes me uncomfortable and I turn around so I'm walking backward and facing Chase.

He's looking at the screen of his phone, but I can't tell if he's texting or looking at an incoming call that he doesn't want to answer.

"I have the same phone," I tell him, because conversation instead of complete silence is a good thing, even if it's not always wanted. "iPhone 8, right?"

He looks up at me, but then back down at the phone in his hand. He turns it over and looks at the back before turning it again so the face is up like it had been a moment ago. "I think so," he says with a shrug. He doesn't look anywhere near certain, which I find amusing because it's his phone and you'd think he'd know what model he has.

He puts the phone back in his pocket.

"Sorry, needed to do something," Chase says, sheepishly. "So, where exactly do you live? Benford Court isn't exactly small and I already had to take PE earlier, so if I faint from the effort, just know that I won't be offended if you go on without me."

I snort but am careful not to actually laugh or smile. I roll my eyes. "You're an absolute idiot," I decide.

"Yup, and for some reason, you thought it'd be a good idea to be friends with me." He shakes his head. "You only have yourself to blame for being stuck with me."

I can't say he's wrong, but that doesn't mean I have to agree with him. Sure, I did decide that it wasn't the worst idea in existence to try to be friends with him, and I do only have myself to blame for that, but I also have my perfect excuse regardless of that.

"Here's the thing, though," I say, pointing straight at him. I wait for him to meet my eyes before I continue. "How was I to know that you'd end up being a complete moron? For all I'd known, you could've been a quarterback." I shrug and drop my hand back down to my side. If I've gauged him correctly, my referring back to his earlier statement about girls not liking him because he's not on the football team won't annoy him. He hadn't given me any reason to believe that his lack of girls being head over heels for him is a touchy subject.

"You couldn't have, but now you must accept your tragic fate." He puts a hand over his heart and sighs dramatically, a look of mock despair on his face.

"You should try out for drama club," I say, amused. "You'd do great in anything Shakespeare from what I've seen." I haven't seen much, but what I have has all been very dramatic, so I figure I can pretend I know what I'm talking about.

"Pfft. They'd kick me out in two minutes," he says. "My acting skills are crap."

I shrug. "But it might be fun for your friends, specifically me, to see you fail miserably at it."

Chase rolls his eyes at me, but he's got a smile on his face.

Silence falls over us again, but this time it isn't as uncomfortable as before. The two of us walk side by side, our steps in sync with one another, my stride a little longer than it usually is and his seeming to be a little shorter.

I can't remember the last time I walked quietly with someone else and it didn't feel a thousand percent weird. Fayre and my mom can be alright sometimes, but I don't usually like it when it's quiet. I'm not sure if that's because I'm actually uncomfortable, though, or if it's because I'm expecting whoever I'm with to find it uncomfortable.

I'm almost disappointed when we get to my house and I have to stop walking once I get to the driveway so that I don't pass it up.

So far, I'm liking having a friend, and that's a strange thought to me, but not a completely unwanted one.

"Well, I'll see you tomorrow, I guess," I say, because

now I'm going to be really awkward. How do you say bye to a person and not sound weird? I've never had to say bye to anyone but family members, and at family gatherings and stuff I avoid talking to anyone so that a simple "bye" when people are walking out the door is perfectly fine. I know that method won't do me any good right now, though.

"Yup." He reaches into his pocket and pulls out his phone. "And you also might want this back." He hands me the phone, and I notice the small crack on the bottom of the glass screen. I hadn't seen it when he'd pulled it out. I thought it was his.

"Oh, thanks," I say, taking it and putting it in the pocket of my jacket. "Didn't even realize I left it."

"No problem." He takes a few steps away, back in the direction we'd come from. "See you tomorrow," he says, and gives a small wave of his hand.

"Yeah, see ya," I respond, and wave back, which feels weird and foreign.

He turns and leaves and I stand there for a minute, unsure if I'm supposed to walk away too, or if I'm supposed to wait until he's farther away before I abandoned my post on the driveway.

Chase has only taken about five steps away from me when I decide that going inside before someone catches me standing out on the driveway would probably be better than waiting until I'm eighty.

Chapter Seven

"There you are," Fayre says as I walk through the door and shut it softly behind myself. "Mom's been worried sick." There's relief on her face, though, which tells me mom wasn't the only one who was worried about me. I don't understand why, though. They know I'm out this late all the time. What makes today any different?

"I was just at the abandoned houses," I tell her, my confusion and mild irritation seeping into my tone of voice. I don't mean to sound rude, but it's hard to keep it from coming off like that. I shouldn't be upset. I know they're overprotective. There's nothing more to it than that.

Fayre gives me a look that I can't place. Surprise? Confusion? Does she think I'm an absolute idiot? Her look could be any of those and more. "You were supposed to help mom with dinner, remember?"

"Crap," I mutter beneath my breath, barely loud enough for her to hear me. "I completely forgot about that."

Before Fayre has enough time to say anything else, I practically sprint down the hallway and into the kitchen where I know my mom will be. Sure enough, when I get there, she's standing in front of the stove with a spoon in one hand and the handle of a pot in the other as she stirs.

Her eyes dart up when she hears me come in. "Oh my god, there you are," she says with the same tone of voice Fayre used when I walked through the door. "You were supposed to be home an hour ago. And you didn't answer your phone until I called you. What's going on?"

Her words sound out of order, like she wants a thousand answers at once, which I know she does.

"I'm sorry," I say as I walk over to one of the drawers and pull out an apron. I tie it around my waist, but it's hard with only one hand and my fingers fumble about a thousand times over the course of a few seconds. "I lost track of time, and I left my phone in my jacket so I didn't hear it go off." Half of it's a lie, but the other half is true, and I hope she'll believe me and leave it alone. Even if she doesn't believe me, I just hope she'll know that nothings actually wrong and not press.

My mom gives me a suspicious look, but goes back to what she's working on and doesn't question me any further.

Instead of questioning me, she starts handing me things that I have no idea what to do with. She instructs me to chop up whatever the thing in my hand is and gets back to stirring while I work on that.

Between the two of us, it takes another half an hour to get dinner finished and put on the table. She had been about midway through making it when I came in, which told me she'd been waiting impatiently for me to get home for half an hour before she had decided to get our meal started.

Mom announces to the house that dinner is ready and I plant my hands on either side of my head to keep my ears protected from her screaming. I don't need to be deaf and have a lethal touch. That would just be extra unfair.

I sit down at the table across from mom as my siblings come in and sit down across from each other: Fayre next to me and Daemon next to mom. Dad isn't home from work yet, and won't be until after we've all gone to bed.

I look around the table at each of them as we start eating. I know mom will ask us how our first day of school went, and I'm already trying to find an answer to that that leaves out everything that happened that I don't want any of them to know about. I don't need them to think I got into a fight at school, and I *definitely* don't need them to know about my new friendship with Chase. But, aside from those two things, I have absolutely nothing else to say about my day.

Mom looks up at us, and I bite the side of my cheek instead of the food in my mouth. I know what's coming, but that doesn't make me any more prepared for it.

"So, how was everyone's first day back at school?" she asks, grinning at each of us expectantly. Why does she have to give me that look? It'd be easier to lie to her rather than actually tell her the truth, but I can't do that when she looks so genuinely hopeful that each of us had a good day.

"I've got a date Friday," Daemon says, by way of answer.

Fayre's eyes go wide beside me and she grins from ear to ear. "Yay!" she says, but it's practically a shout.

"Really?" mom asks, but she sounds almost as excited as Fayre does.

"That's too bad, man," I say, shaking my head like someone ran over his bike instead of what actually happened. I don't feel like not being sarcastic right now, though.

"Oh, hush," mom snaps at me, gently swatting at my arm. I know she means it teasingly, but she hits my left arm and it jerks my arm enough to make my shoulder uncomfortable.

"Wow, Than, I wasn't expecting you to be so excited about my love life," Daemon says, his sarcasm matching mine. He raises an eyebrow at me, curious if I'll continue with this little competition he started.

"Definitely," I say, narrowing my eyes at him, the corners of my mouth turning up, but not enough to be considered an actual smile. "So excited I think I might even go as far as to offer to do your hair and makeup."

Fayre snorts beside me, but mom just rolls her eyes at us like we're being childish and dumb, which we are.

"That's nice of you. I was thinking about getting some extensions for my hair and matching my purse to my lipstick. What's your opinion? I'd love to get all the fashion tips I can from you before I go picking out my exact outfit."

"Mm," I say, pretending like this is a serious conversation instead of the monstrous joke it really is. "Black, black, and more black. Just look like you're going to a funeral and you're good." I give him a thumbs up. "And I'm thinking a V neck dress to show off that nonexistent cleavage of yours." I point to his chest.

Fayre is practically doubled over laughing beside me, but I do my best to ignore her. Mom looks amused, but also sick of us at the same time.

Daemon looks like he wants to laugh too, but bites his tongue. "Great tips. I'll definitely take them into consideration," he tells me, then gets back to his food as if nothing happened.

I do the same, Fayre's laughter finally dying down beside me as she gasps for air. She has hiccups by the time she's managed to catch her breath again.

"Well, congratulations, Dae," mom says, getting back to the topic we were supposed to be on. "How about you two? Anything exciting?"

Fayre sighs beside me. When I look over at her, she's got the same dreamy expression on her face that she had earlier. "I met the *cutest* guy," she says, her voice almost giddy sounding.

Daemon's attention snaps up at that. "Name? Number? Height? Age? Average grades in math? Shoe size? Best friend's middle name?"

I want to laugh at that, but I hold it down and end up just choking on air instead.

Fayre glares at him for a moment but then decides it's not worth the argument and rolls her eyes. "Drake. He doesn't have a phone, just an email. He's five foot seven inches. He's fifteen. He says he sucks at math and has an average of a C+. I think he said his shoe size is an eight, and his best friend's *full* name is Carlos Ivan Garcia."

My eyes go wide. I wasn't expecting that at all.

Daemon's eyes look like they're about ready to pop out of his head and I get a strange urge to give Fayre a round of applause for being able to make him look like that.

My mind goes over everything she just listed, trying to figure out what about it sounds strangely familiar. I don't think I talked about this guy enough with her to find anything other than his name familiar, but that isn't it. I feel like I'm missing something.

Sucks at math? No.

"That's impressive, Fayre," my mom says, sounding surprised and also approving at the same time. It's not hard to hear those two things in her voice at the same time, but this is also my mom. Hearing both of those together when it's my dad is a very different story.

Shoe size? Definitely not.

Daemon still looks completely taken aback by the fact that she was able to answer everything without so much as a second's hesitation. I really can't blame him, though. Who asks a person that much on the first day they meet? I don't even know half as much about Chase and we were talking for hours.

Carlos Ivan…wait…

"Carlos Ivan Garcia," I say, holding up a finger as if I've just figured out the secret to life. When I look around the table and see all of them staring at me like I'm a moron, I feel my face heat up and I put my hand down. I clear my throat. "The boy who was her best friend or whatever last year? The one she talked to every day but always referred to as her 'guy friend' instead of actually using his name?"

"Duh," Daemon says, but then he seems to catch on, too. He looks over at Fayre. "So, one of your friends introduced you to his best friend so that the two of you could fall in love and live happily ever after?"

"Pfft," I say, because he's being dumber than usual, and even though I fully approve of it, it's not going to keep me from thinking he's just acting stupid.

Both of us watch as our sister's face turns bright red. It starts in her cheeks, but it spreads up to her forehead, to the tips of her ears, and down her neck.

"You look like a tomato," I say, bluntly, before I can catch myself.

Fayre rolls her eyes at me, but, if it's even possible, she turns a few shades redder.

I've got the same blushing problem as my sister. It's always embarrassed the heck out of me, but it's never bothered Fayre half as much as it has me. She knows this fact, which is no doubt why she thinks it's as stupid as it is for me to open my mouth at all.

"Well, am I wrong?" Daemon asks, but he doesn't sound like he's being serious like usual. He sounds like he's trying to tease her in a strange, overprotective older brother sort of way that I'm unfamiliar with.

"He introduced us because we were talking in the hallway and Drake came over," Fayre says. She's fidgeting with the hem of her shirt, which I pretend not to see because she's more embarrassed about her fidgeting than I am, and I don't intend to make her hate me.

My phone vibrates in my pocket and I frown.

"What?" Fayre snaps at me.

My best guess is that she took my expression to mean I didn't believe her, or that I found something about what she said confusing, when that's really not even close to what I was frowning at.

I shake my head. "Sorry, no. I wasn't making that

face at you." I look down at my pocket. "Anyone know why dad would be texting me?"

"Maybe he's bored at work?" Fayre suggests, seeming eager to change the subject. I doubt she'll get away with it for half as long as she'd like, though. As soon as I find out what dad wants, I'll get back to messing with her, and, if I take too long, I know Daemon will take my place in starting it back up.

I pull my phone from my pocket and turn it on. The text that shows up on the screen isn't from my dad, though. It's from a number I don't recognize.

Hey, Trespasser, I read.

I want to groan when I read it. I doubt I'll hear the end of being a trespasser for a while.

But how did he get my number? I never gave it to him, and it's not like I have any friends he could've gotten it from.

Oh my god, I text him back. *How'd you get my number?*

His response comes in a second later: *You should really put a passcode on your phone.*

The realization hits me when I read his text. That wasn't his phone he was messing with when we were walking to my house. That was *my* phone.

You suck, I text him, and wait for a response when I see the read receipt come through.

I know.

"Oh my god. Than, is that a smile on your face?" Daemon says from across the table.

I look up at him and his dumbfounded expression.

"No," I answer. "It was your imagination because I don't smile. Maybe the corners of my mouth twitched and that overactive imagination of yours decided to over-exaggerate it."

I shrug and type out a response to Chase without actually looking down at the screen: *I don't think that's something you should be so proud to admit.*

"Either way, you just admitted to being happy about something," Fayre points out. She looks excited about the fact that she can turn the tables on me and start teasing me back. She doesn't know who I'm texting, though. She thinks I'm texting dad. She doesn't know I made a friend. So, I don't have to tell her or anyone else anything.

"Found a funny meme," I tell them, and quickly flip to my photos app to pick one out of the seemingly endless selection I have. I turn the screen around so they can see it, and all three of them roll their eyes but look amused at the ice cube with sunglasses on the screen with the words beneath it reading "I'm cooler than you."

I turn my phone around as quickly as I can without being suspicious so that if a response comes in from Chase, I won't have to worry about them seeing it.

I feel it go off as soon as my family can no longer see the screen, but I don't look at it as I shut it off and put it back into my pocket. I'll text him back when it won't be so easy for someone to see that I'm texting some random number they didn't know was in my phone.

Chapter Eight

I wake the next morning to Daemon pounding on my bedroom door. I'm late again, but that's my own fault. I set my alarm to go off forty minutes ago, but I hadn't even hit the snooze button when it started blaring at me. Instead, I just turned it straight off.

"Than, twenty!" my brother calls.

A couple seconds pass and I don't respond, but he must know that I'm awake because, instead of yelling again or pounding on my door, I hear his footsteps retreat down the hall in the direction of the living room.

I let out a groan before I roll over on my bed, letting my feet fall off the end but keeping my top half on. Usually, I'd roll straight off, but with my broken shoulder, that's not the smartest thing to do today.

It's not even seven in the morning, and already I'm feeling the exhaustion from my lack of sleep. It's my own fault for staying up so late texting Chase, but that had only been until about twelve-thirty, and, after that, I'd just been tossing and turning for hours. All in all, I got around 3 hours of sleep in total. And the entire time I'd been getting them, I slept like a rock.

I don't usually toss and turn a lot in my sleep, but I do wake up a lot in the night and I'll stay in a hazy phase somewhere between being asleep and awake for a few moments before the sleep will claim me again. I usually dream a lot, too, but trying to remember my dreams from last night is like trying to find a speck of light in a black void.

My backpack sits on the floor next to the door where I left it last night after getting it ready. I'd rushed through my homework last night and had barely finished it before I texted Chase back, and I didn't stop texting with him for a straight 3 hours.

Slowly, I climb to my feet. I head over to my closet, grab some clothes, change into them, and head out of my room. I almost manage to forget my backpack, but grab it at the last second and sling it over my shoulder.

I can smell the bacon my mom is making long before I'm in the kitchen. Despite the fact that the kitchen counter is covered in different things I could eat, I choose not to grab anything and just get a glass of water instead. I don't need nausea on top of my sleep deprivation.

"Whoa. Ana, you look terrible," Fayre says as I come into the living room where she's gracefully sitting on the couch. Her hands are sitting clasped in her lap. She's wearing a too-short dress that shows off her legs and the curve of her hips. Her shoulders are bare and the neckline of her dress dips down in a V shape.

I raise an eyebrow at her outfit, but otherwise ignore her as I plop down on the opposite side of the couch. I don't need her to be getting a good look at my face. She already noticed that something was off, but if she looks much closer, she'll see my inability to keep my eyes fully open and the puffy bags under them.

My mind is basically dead as I sit there, staring at the wall as though it's the most interesting thing I've seen in ages.

I don't know how long it is before Daemon waves a hand in front of my face and makes me look up at him.

"I said, it's time to go," he repeats, though I didn't hear him the first time he said it.

I nod wearily and climb to my feet. The weight of my backpack feels like it could pull me over at any second, but I manage to keep from stumbling as I walk outside and climb into the passenger seat of the car. I'm dimly aware of the fact that Daemon is driving us today instead of our mom, but I don't think to ask why or even bother glancing at him again to make sure what I saw is correct.

Daemon turns on the radio and flips through the stations. Once he's found something that isn't commercials, he puts the car in reverse and backs out of the driveway.

I lay my head back against the headrest and close my eyes, the slight vibration of the car lulling me to sleep. The upbeat pop song on the radio makes for a terrible lullaby, but somehow, it works as one anyway.

I'm dimly aware of Chase sliding into the seat across from me after the sound of a lunch tray hitting the table passes. I'm hardly paying attention to the fact that he's there, though. The noise he's made is nothing compared to the rest of the kids in the cafeteria, and I'm already in the hazy space between awake and asleep.

"Not used to sleep deprivation, are you?" Chase asks, his amusement apparent in his voice.

His words jolt me out of my sleepy state, but not completely. I'm awake, but I'm not alert or in any state to be doing anything more than lying here with my head on the table.

I groan in response.

He chuckles. "I'd tell you it gets easier to deal with or that eventually you just don't notice it, but that'd be a complete lie and my mom taught me to be an honest person."

"Did she teach you to be a quiet one?" I grumble. "Or was that your dad's job? Either way, someone failed."

I lift my head enough to see over the edge of my arm, but it's not enough to actually see his face. The only reason I can see him is because he bends down so that his face is within my line of sight.

"Nah," he answers. "They left me to fend for myself in that category. However, my sister did try to help with that when she was able to. Apparently, having her big brother around was a huge embarrassment when she would hang out with her friends." He shakes his head like he absolutely can't understand why that would be.

Confusion strikes me, but I do my best to keep it off my face. I don't know what happened to his sister, but he always mentions her in the past tense. I don't think he'd talk about her in such a relaxed way if she died, but what else would give him a reason to talk about her like that?

I want to ask, but I also don't want to pry. He doesn't seem to mind talking about her, but this isn't a deep conversation where I'm asking him what happened to her. This is just him being sarcastic and weird because that's what he seems to be good at.

"Yeah, speaking of embarrassment," I say, pulling myself up off the table as I lift my arms above my head, stretching the sleep from my body. It's painful but I've broken enough bones in the past to know how to mostly get around it. "You're a very big one, and I've got a reputation to keep up."

He snorts a laugh but makes no move to get up. He knows I didn't mean it literally, though. And, even if I did, I doubt he'd leave. I'm the moron who said I wouldn't mind trying to be friends.

"Mm-hmm. And what reputation is that?" he asks. "The girl who never talks to anyone, hates the world and everyone in it, gets bullied because of her mouth, and trespasses on other people's properties for fun?" He smirks at me.

I nod. "What else would it – wait a minute." I glare at him. I almost hadn't caught that last part. "The trespassing isn't advertised," I point out. "Only the mouthy, 'I hate everyone' part is." I can't seem to help but say it like it's the most obvious thing in the world, never mind the fact that he already knows it.

He's seriously not going to stop bringing up the trespassing. I don't think I should've – not that I ever did – think otherwise, but that doesn't make it any less annoying. So, I admit to trespassing on the property that his uncle's company owns. So what? It's not like he caught me doing anything horribly wrong.

"Ah. It's all clear now." Each word is drenched in a thick coat of sarcasm.

I roll my eyes at him.

Maybe I hadn't literally meant that I wanted him gone earlier, but part of me is terrified of the idea that one of my siblings could see us sitting together. I'm not sure I want to deal with them freaking out in the middle of the cafeteria. Or ever, for that matter.

The chances that anyone in my family would take the news of me having a friend well are so slim that I'd rather keep pretending that Chase doesn't exist when I'm at home. Texting him is fine, but I don't plan on ever calling him to talk because that would raise way too much suspicion. And I'd really rather just completely avoid ever telling my family about him at all.

I glance around the cafeteria, but when I do, the first thing I notice is Daemon looking right back at me.

Damn it.

I chew the inside of my cheek as I pull my eyes away from my brother and turn back to facing forward. I don't look at Chase when I turn back, though. Maybe Daemon will think he's just some random new kid who didn't have a place to sit so he sat down across from me because he didn't know what else to do. If I don't look at him or say anything to him until Daemon isn't looking anymore, I should be safe.

"You okay?" Chase moves so his face is within my line of sight again. I know me suddenly ignoring his existence isn't exactly subtle, but I hoped he'd ignore it momentarily.

I can see Daemon making his way over to where we are out of the corner of my eye and have to bite back a string of curse words.

"Overprotective brother alert," I mumble, sighing.

I have no doubt that Chase will think me saying that means Daemon hates me being around guys, but he can think whatever he wants to think, so long as I've made myself clear that my brother won't be happy about the fact that I'm with him.

I do my best to avoid flinching when I feel Daemon set a hand down on my shoulder.

Good lord. So, he's one of those *brothers.*

I almost groan when I realize what I'm in for, but I manage to keep my annoyance contained and instead shrug my brother's hand off of my shoulder. I make a face at him over my shoulder, but he doesn't pay me any attention. Instead, his eyes land on Chase across from me for a second before he finally realizes that I'm his only way to get into this conversation.

"Who's your friend, Than?" he asks, nodding in the direction of Chase as he sits down beside me. I didn't ask him to, and I'm sure he knows I don't want him to, but that doesn't stop him.

I roll my eyes. "Nice to see you, too, Dae," I grumble, and, before I can think it through, I stand up, slamming my hands down on the table, and glare at my brother. "Anyway, great to have you around. Lovely chat we had. Go away."

"Hi," Chase says, interrupting me before I can say anything else. He looks amused when I look over at him, but he suppresses it so that Daemon doesn't have a chance to see it. "I'm Chase," he tells my brother, extending a hand for him to shake.

Daemon gives him a suspicious look, but shakes his hand, anyway. "I'm Daemon," my brother says. He nods in my direction, his eyes not leaving Chase's. "This one's brother."

Chase gives an amused smile and takes his hand back. "Yeah, she's mentioned you."

Yeah, no kidding I've mentioned him. I probably

only said a couple good things about my brother last night when we were texting, but, other than that, most of what I've said regarding him hasn't been anything pleasant. I wouldn't be surprised if Chase thinks I hate my brother at this point.

"You're not helping," I mumble beneath my breath, exasperated. If I could tell Chase to shut up and ignore my brother and then follow it up with shoving Daemon back over to the other side of the cafeteria, I would. Unfortunately, I'd rather avoid the risk of accidentally making skin to skin contact with either of them. It would be hard to, but that's something I'm very rarely willing to risk.

"I'm sure she has," Daemon says, sighing.

I can feel his eyes on the side of my head, which is probably why Chase doesn't seem to think anything of it when he winks at me in response to my irritation. Dumb as he may be every now and then, I don't think he's actually stupid enough to risk misleading my brother into thinking we're anything more than just friends.

Although, I suppose I'm not doing the best in that category as it is. There's no doubt in my mind that because I've done nothing but imply that I want him gone, my brother is going to think that I want to be alone with Chase because I'm interested in him or whatever, no matter how far from the truth that actually is.

"And here I thought I was the only person in this

school who you enjoy tormenting," a girl's voice says from somewhere behind me.

I recognize the voice, but I can't put a face to it until I turn around and see Lauren standing behind my brother.

Lauren's eyes are on my brother, but they switch over to me before flicking to Chase for a split second and then coming back to me again. A knowing smile spreads across her face and, much like how my brother invited himself to sit down, she squeezes between me and Daemon.

I can't tell what she's doing, but I get the feeling her moves are calculated.

"Nice to meet you," she says to me, and I realize that I know exactly who she is, but have never actually properly been introduced to her. "I'm Lauren."

"I know," I answer, before I can stop myself. My cheeks heat up and I duck my head slightly to hide my embarrassment. "I'm Thana."

"I know," Lauren says, but her tone isn't mocking and neither is her smile. She looks mildly amused by me, but she doesn't seem to want to be offensive at all. Not that she even seems capable of it. I don't get the feeling she could be mean even if she tried.

I hadn't known what to expect when contemplating what my brother's taste in girls might be, but I definitely hadn't expected him to fall for one of the girls who I only ever hear nice things about. I don't get told a lot of gossip, but people don't seem to care all that much who overhears them in the bathrooms, and I've never once heard anyone say something bad about her.

Lauren turns so she's facing Chase. "You're the new guy, right?" she asks him. "Chase, but I can't remember your last name." She gives a sheepish smile, the tiniest bit of a blush making its way onto her cheeks.

Chase smiles. "Yup," he tells her. "And don't worry about the last name. I'll answer to just about anything. 'Hey, you over there' is one of my most common names."

Chase watches me out of the corner of his eye, and I know he's waiting for me to lose my hold on my mask, but I don't let it slip. I can feel my face scrunch up like he mimicked yesterday when I suppress the smile, but I shove that thought out of my head as quickly as it appears.

"I think 'absolute idiot' could be another one," I say, smirking at him.

On Lauren's other side, I can hear my brother give a grunt in agreement to what I just said, and if they hadn't been sitting on the same side of the table as me, I might've missed when Lauren gently smacks the side of his leg with the back of her hand.

I don't understand why she seems to be trying to keep him from saying anything rude, but I'm grateful to her for it. I can't hold this against my brother as much as I'd like to, but that isn't stopping it from pissing me off. I understand that I should be careful – and I am – and I understand that he wants to protect me from other people at the same time that he wants to protect other people from me, but I also know that I'm capable of understanding how bad a friendship could be if I'm not a hundred percent careful all the time.

"Is that a smile, Thana?" Chase asks, eyeing me.

There's a glimmer in his eyes, like he's excited to see what I'll do with his challenge.

I shake my head. "Far from it. I was so unbelievably bored with your company, I hoped that making faces at the wall would at least prove to be somewhat entertaining." I crinkle my nose again, doing my best to copy the expression I had on my face a minute ago. "See? Entertainment of the highest level."

He snorts a laugh. "For you or for everyone who sees you making that face?"

"The latter," Daemon says, which catches me off guard. I wasn't expecting him to talk at all, much less to agree with Chase about something.

Lauren laughs beside me. "Wow, you two." She looks over at me. "Boys, am I right?" She shakes her head and nudges my shoulder with hers. It's enough to make me tense up, but I don't think she notices my discomfort. "They know just how to make a girl feel loved." She rolls her eyes, but she looks amused.

I don't know exactly what she means by that, but I also don't care all that much. There seems to be something hiding beneath the surface of everything she says, but I can't put my finger on it. I know she doesn't mean anything offensive by anything she's saying, though, so I don't think much of it other than to acknowledging my own confusion.

Daemon slings an arm around Lauren's shoulders and she leans into him. "I'm stuck with that job now, apparently," he says, teasingly.

Lauren rolls her eyes and playfully pokes him in the side.

I don't know when they became… whatever it is they are, but it happened faster than I thought it would. I didn't think they'd be all lovey-dovey with each other until after their date, but apparently, I'd been wrong.

I've seen so many movies with characters dating each other and their awkward friends who feel like they're the third wheel, and I've never completely understood why it's so awkward for them. The friends never intentionally leave them out or anything, so I don't get why it would be awkward.

Now it makes sense.

Even though there's literally no reason for me to feel so strange about the situation, I do. My brother and Lauren don't seem any different than they did a moment ago. The only change is the fact that my brother now has his arm around her and she's laying her head on his shoulder. I don't think something so simple should make me feel so out of place, but it does.

I clear my throat and stand up. "I… I'm gonna just…" I point toward the cafeteria entrance instead of finishing the sentence. I don't even know what I was going to say at the end of it, anyway.

"Oh," Lauren squeaks, her eyes wide. She grabs Daemon's hand and removes his arm from around her as she sits up straight. "No, no. Don't go." She stands up without leaving time for me to protest. She pulls Daemon up beside her. "Our friends are expecting us back, anyway," she tells me, giving me a smile.

Daemon looks like he wants to protest, but Lauren fixes him with a look. He doesn't seem happy about leaving, but he doesn't say anything as she pulls him away from our table and over to where their usual crowd is.

Chase and I watch as the two of them leave. He doesn't look as confused as I feel, but he does look uncomfortable, which I can't blame him for because that whole situation was very awkward.

I sigh and turn back around to face him. "What was that about?" I say, more to the air in front of me than to him.

He shrugs, but he won't meet my eyes when he does, and I could swear I see his cheeks turn just the slightest bit pink.

I frown, but I don't comment on it.

Instead, we strike up a conversation about how terrible the food is and, before I know it, the discomfort in the air has melted away and I'm left feeling completely at ease as we fall back into what seems to be becoming our usual routine of verbally challenging each other and poking fun at whatever we can come up with.

Chapter Nine

As soon as the last bell rings, I practically fly out of my seat. I maneuver around people, making sure nothing but my bulky backpack touches them when I do. The hallway isn't much less crowded than the classroom had been, but it's far less crowded right now than it will be in a few moments.

I get to my locker before I text Chase back. He'd asked if we could meet at the abandoned property again, which he knew I'd already planned to go to, anyway. But today I have to stop by home for a bit instead of going straight there. I promised my dad I'd help him do some work on his car before I "vanished for the day," as he put it.

Not that I plan to tell Chase any of that. I don't expect him to think I'm strange, but I've grown so used to people thinking of me as something other than normal – which I am, but that's beside the point – that it's second nature to leave certain things out. The fact that I enjoy working on cars is one of them.

I've always loved helping my dad with things. We used to be super close back when I was little, but that changed once I got my curse. Now I have to be careful around everyone, including him, and that somehow ended up making us drift apart.

It happened when I was six. I'd been playing out in the front yard with Daemon and I'd been so excited when I'd caught a lizard all by myself. I went to show my brother, but when I opened my hands so he could see it, all that was left of the little creature was a small pile of grey dust in my palm.

It didn't take us long to figure out what I could do.

I sigh and throw my stuff into my locker before I shut the door.

That part of my past is probably the most painful.

Someone's shoulder bumps mine and a wave of pain washes over me.

I suck in a breath of air through clenched teeth, gripping my arm so hard that I know I'll have bruises tomorrow from it.

Before even looking, I know who the person to walk into me had been. It's just another threat. Mark just wants to hurt me. He's not going to let me forget about that for even a day, especially after I told him to get away from my sister.

"Oops," Mark says. "Sorry, Thana." He sounds

anything but sorry when he says it. He sounds entertained by my current state of weakness, which I'd expected him to be, even before I caught a glimpse of his face.

The look on his face solidifies what I already knew I was in for, though.

Mark walks off, leaving me alone with the raging pain in my shoulder.

Anyone in the hall could stop to check and make sure I'm okay, but I'm glad no one does. If they see me like this, none of them show any sign of it, and I'd rather it be that way than have multiple people I don't know making sure I'm fine. I'd rather not deal with the fear of killing someone while also dealing with the pain and my anger.

Bright bursts of light flash in my eyes as I climb to my feet, using the lockers behind me to steady myself.

Great.

I groan as I pull myself up to my full height and square my shoulders so that I'm standing up straight. Unless one of my siblings saw my encounter with Mark and decides to tell mom or dad when we get home, I don't plan to bring it up. I'm sure they'll want me to go get another x-ray done, and I would much rather avoid that at any and all costs.

I grab what I need out of my locker, and put what I don't into it before I sling my backpack over my shoulder and head out of the school.

When I get outside, the first thing I notice is that

Fayre and Daemon are both mixed in with large groups of kids; Daemon with the seniors and Fayre with the freshmen. If I want to get home anytime soon, my best bet would be to go get both of them, but that's something I'd really rather avoid.

So, instead, I find the car and climb up onto the hood. I set my backpack down beside me and lean back against the windshield. I have to arch my back in an uncomfortable position so that I'm not lying directly on the wipers, but I've done this more times than I can count and have my positioning down so that it's not completely miserable.

The sky above me is clear and the sun shines down painfully bright on my face. I have to squint my eyes to be able to see, but it's so bright that it's basically pointless to keep them open.

After spending a moment or two trying to find somewhere to look where I won't be blinded by the sun's harsh, white light, I give up and close my eyes. It doesn't protect me from the brightness much until I put my arm over my face so that the crook of my elbow is resting on the bridge of my nose, though.

I don't know how long I sit there before someone is shaking my shoulder and telling me to get up. I don't know if I fell asleep or if I just wasn't paying attention, but the person shaking me broke me out of a trance either way.

I groan and sit up. I rub my eyes and blink away the tiredness I feel in every inch of my body.

Fayre is standing in front of me, her pretty blond hair turning gold in the sunlight. "C'mon," she tells me, taking my hand and helping me to my feet before my brain can even register what's going on. "Dad called a moment ago. He said you weren't answering your phone and that you were supposed to help him with the car a while ago."

I have to fight the urge to groan again. As much as I sometimes like to help out when my dad fixes the cars, I'm not in the mood to right now. I'd much rather fall onto a pile of pillows and sleep for a year. I don't know how I managed to stay awake in class earlier, but I doubt I'll be spending much of the ride home fully alert.

My sister pulls me over to the car and helps me inside.

Fully waking up feels next to impossible right now. I'd rather roll over and die. Everything feels weak and my thoughts are blurred around the edges, making it hard for me to understand what's going on in my own head.

"Geez, Than," Daemon says when he gets a good look at me. "How late were you up last night?"

I don't get to sleep early, that's a known thing about me, but I never stay up anywhere near as late as I did last night. 11:00 is usually as late as I stay up during the school year. And, on top of that, I don't usually have much trouble falling asleep. Last night, I did.

"Twelve-thirty," I mumble. My eyes are closed and my elbow is resting on the armrest. My face rests in the palm of my hand, my cheek squished in a way that makes me slur my words. "And then I couldn't fall asleep." The words come out at the same time as a yawn, which makes them near impossible to decipher.

Daemon grunts a response that sounds fairly disapproving, but I'm too tired to be a hundred percent sure or to even pretend that I care.

The sound of Fayre's phone blaring in the backseat sends me into a practical panic less than a moment later. It's just a call coming through, but with how I reacted to it, someone could've blown up a nearby building.

She picks up the phone and starts talking excitedly to whoever's on the other end. She has so many friends that I can't even get a good idea of who she's talking to this time based solely on what she's saying and the tone of her voice. Probably a boy, but I've been terrible at guessing lately, so I doubt I'm actually anywhere close. But, hey, I've got like a one in four chance of being right judging by what seems to be my sister's guy-to-girl friend ratio.

"Than?" Daemon asks, glancing over at me.

It'd be so easy to just keep my eyes shut and pretend I'm asleep. If I did, he wouldn't have to know I'd heard him at all. I could just magically wake up when we get home like I always used to when I was little.

But, for some reason, I can't seem to bring myself to ignore him. I don't know what he wants, and I doubt it's anything good, but ignoring him feels rude and, even though I'd usually be fine with being a complete jerk, I don't have it in me right now.

"Hmm?" I mumble, not bothering to open my eyes. I won't ignore him, but that doesn't mean I need to give him my full attention.

My brother sighs like he's trying to get himself to relax. He's failing at his attempt to seem calm, though. When I open my eyes to look at him, I can see his body is tense and that he's gripping the steering wheel hard enough to turn his knuckles white.

"What is it?" I sigh, knowing now that it's definitely not something I'm going to want to talk about.

"I'm sorry about earlier," he says, so quietly I almost can't hear him.

I stare at him. I wasn't expecting that. I don't know what I was expecting, but that's pretty far from it.

I open my mouth to say something in response, but he interrupts me. "I know you're not dumb and you're not a little kid who needs to be looked after. I know you aren't going to do anything stupid that could hurt anyone, and I'm sorry for acting like I don't trust you." He looks over at me for a second, before he seems to remember that he's supposed to be watching the road. "It's just… you're my little sister. I know you don't need me to protect you or anything, and I know I can't, but I want to. I want to be able to keep you from ever getting close to hurting anyone and to keep you from ever getting hurt by anyone else."

Daemon sighs again, and I don't get the feeling he's

done, but that seems to be all he wants to say right now. I can't tell if it's because he doesn't want to touch another topic, or if it's because he doesn't know how to say whatever it is that's on his mind.

I don't exactly care either way, though. If he doesn't want to say anything else, I'm perfectly fine with that.

"It's fine," I tell him, not meaning it as much as I wish I did. I do my best to make it sound believable, though. I don't think I'm going to forgive him for a while, but that's my problem, not his. He apologized. The least I can do is pretend I've forgiven him.

"It's not, though," he says, seeming to not be done with this conversation even though I so badly want to be. He doesn't seem to notice my desire to escape, though. "I really shouldn't have done that, and I promise I won't again."

Something in his expression looks like pure agony; like he's beating himself up way too much about what he did. I know he probably is, considering how much he's apologizing, but is there really anything I can do about that?

With a sigh, I realize there is something I can say that would most likely make it better for him. And the words wouldn't exactly be untrue either.

"You're my older brother," I state, as though there's something comforting about that sentence. "I think that's what older brothers do. And you didn't say anything wrong, as annoying as it was. I know you only wanted to protect me."

It sounds like some dumb statement out of a movie, which is kind of what I was going for in saying it, but that doesn't make me feel any better about it.

I want my brother to be there for me if he wants to be, but I also don't want him hovering over me like some crazy helicopter parent. If anyone should be responsible for embarrassing me that much, it should *be* one of my parents. Neither of them is that bad, though. They'd love to keep me in the house all the time, I know that, but they don't actually try to stop me because they know that's pretty useless in the grand scheme of things.

Daemon doesn't seem to get that like my parents do, though. He seems to think he can actually protect me from the world and that he can actually protect the world from me. There's no way that's possible, though. I've never touched a single thing and not left my mark, whether it be something living or not. I kill living things, and I turn nonliving things grey or black. It's like my ability wants to strip the world of everything good and beautiful.

"Still no excuse," Daemon responds, shaking his head. He still looks frustrated with himself, but the fact that I told him everything is fine seems to have taken the edge off a bit. His body isn't so ridged anymore, though his grip on the wheel is still tighter than it should be.

No, it's not, I want to tell him, but I keep my mouth shut. We're both still kids, after all. And I don't think that changes once you hit the magical age of 18. We both still have a lot to learn, and I don't think we're going to learn half as much as we want to about the world until long past when we need it.

"Can I go with you to the abandoned neighborhood later?" Daemon asks, which catches me, like, three thousand percent off guard.

My head snaps up and my eyes are wide. I do my best to hide my shock and explosion of fear, but I don't think it works as well as I want it to. He's already looking at me with an expression of complete confusion, and I don't think I'll be able to explain my way out of it without giving him the truth.

"Um… I'd rather you didn't," I say. The truth is something I will avoid at any and all costs. "Sorry," I add, as though that'll lighten the blow at all.

"Y-yeah, okay." He looks hurt, to say the least, and I'm sure he thinks that my reason for saying no is because of what happened earlier, which I guess it could be mistaken as, but that's not the biggest reason for it.

I don't like the idea of anyone going with me. Chase is a different story because… well, I don't know why, but he is. It's been my sanctuary for the longest time, and for some reason, the idea of having my brother go with me doesn't completely destroy that image of it, but it does dampen it.

But, even knowing what him going with me will do, I can't ignore the hurt in his eyes. "Maybe some other time," I tell him. "I just… I need some time alone."

It's another lie, but it's not the worst one I've told. I need time alone, yes, but it's time alone with a friend. I don't know if that counts as the same thing or not, but I'm willing to bet that it doesn't. All I can do is hope that my brother doesn't catch on to how I'm chewing my lip, and hope that he doesn't realize I'm hiding something behind my answer.

I don't think he's stupid enough to completely buy my answer, but he nods his head and at least pretends he does, either way.

Chapter Ten

"Whoa, what happened to you?" Chase asks as soon as I step into the grass that separates the property from the sidewalk.

I practically jump out of my own skin when I hear him. My eyes dart up into the high branches of a nearby tree. That's when I see him for the first time. He's in a dark blue shirt and jeans, which is why I hadn't noticed him until now. He's got a baseball cap on his head and he pulls the brim up so that I can see his eyes.

"You look like death," he says as he weaves himself between branches until he's low enough that he can jump off and land on his feet without hurting himself.

Pfft, funny…

"I'm tired," I snap, never mind the fact that I know he isn't talking about that. I still have grease spots on my face from the car work I helped my dad with. "And that's *your* fault, remember? You're the one who kept me up so late." I stick my tongue out at him before I walk over to the house and sit on the ground against it.

"Nah, that's not it." Chase takes his hat off, his hair falling across his forehead in a sloppy mess. He runs his fingers through it before trapping his hair beneath the hat once again. He comes over and sits down beside me, studying my face. "You look depressed," he decides, looking pleased with himself for having figured it out.

The look fades from his face a second later and he seems to realize that being depressed isn't exactly a good thing.

Truth be told, I am, to at least a small extent. I don't have the best relationship with my dad anymore, and working with him today just solidified what I already knew even more. He's a good dad, but I feel very left out every now and then when it comes to family life. His relationships with Fayre and Daemon are better than his relationship with me, and I can't help but envy them a bit.

I do my best to hide anything that could hint at how I feel, though. I don't want to explain how I feel about my relationship with my dad. I don't want to talk about anything that has to do with my dad. Or my brother, if we're considering everything that I'd rather avoid. I just don't want to talk about my family or any one person in it at all.

"Is everything alright, An?" he asks, resting a hand

on my shoulder so that I'll look up at him again. "And is it alright if I call you that? Don't exactly know how you feel about nicknames." His laugh is uncomfortable, but it's there all the same.

I nod. "And I'm fine," I tell him, leaning back against the building. "I'm just really tired."

"Alright."

He doesn't look like he believes me, but he's not dumb enough to ask me again. I want to thank him for letting it go, but I doubt that would be the best thing to do. If I thanked him, that would only make me seem more suspicious.

The silence that falls over us isn't uncomfortable, but I'm aware that it's there either way. I don't know what to say to fill it, though, and I'm not sure if I even want to. If it were any other day and I'd stayed up as late as I had last night, I most likely wouldn't be here right now. I'd most likely be at home, sleeping. And, even if I had chosen to come here still, I'd probably be sleeping in the field.

"So, what's your favorite movie?"

It's so random and out of nowhere that it takes me a minute to process exactly what an answer to the question would even be.

I shake my head, clearing the confusion slightly when I do. "Um... I don't know... maybe The Fault in Our Stars? It was good at least. I haven't seen many movies, to be honest. My siblings usually go to the theater, but I don't go with, and there's only a few that they don't go to see that we all watch at home."

Chase snorts a laugh. "Not the best, but it was alright. Not my usual cup of tea," he explains. "Why do you avoid the theater? Not a fan of popcorn?" He smirks at me, amusement sparkling in his eyes.

I roll my eyes, suppressing the smile that wants to plant itself on my face. I lean my head against the building, a yawn escaping me before I can stop it, and close my eyes. "I hate people, remember? I've been told that movie theaters are full of them and that in itself is enough reason for me to never go into one."

"Wait. You've *never* gone to a movie theater?" he asks, absolute surprise in his tone.

I raise an eyebrow, but the thought of opening my eyes feels like it'd be harder to do than run a marathon. "Didn't I just say that?" I ask, my voice hardly above a whisper.

"Not going with your siblings and not going at all are two very different things," he tells me matter-of-factly.

I shift, trying to find a better and more comfortable position as I rest my arm over my face, the crook of my elbow against the bridge of my nose so that the bright light from the sun can't keep destroying my ability to sleep. I know that I'm not supposed to be a nocturnal animal, but seriously.

"Stupid building," I grumble under my breath as I shift again. "And they're close enough. I don't think it's required that I make perfect sense all the time."

"Uncomfortable?" Chase asks, and I can hear the smile on his face. Let him think my discomfort is amusing all he wants. It's not like he's trying to sleep and someone who's supposedly his new friend won't shut up beside him.

"Very."

I let out a breath and shift again. I can hear Chase moving beside me, but I do my best to ignore his existence. He doesn't exactly annoy me, but I'd much rather he be quiet and let me sleep. I know that's not why we met up here, but I can't seem to help but want nothing more than to close my eyes and lose myself in the endless abyss that is my mind.

"I promise I'm not trying to make this extremely awkward, but…" I wait for him to finish, but he doesn't. Instead, less than a moment later, he shifts closer to me and puts an arm around my shoulders, pulling my body against his.

The gesture is so unexpected and makes me so uncomfortable that the simple act of breathing feels impossible. Thoughts race through my mind as a flood of panic washes over me. What if he touches my skin by accident? What if there's a hole in my jacket and he somehow touches my shoulder? What if I *kill* him?

My mind works so fast that I don't even understand how it's possible. I can feel everywhere the fabric covers my body. *Nowhere, aside from my face, is exposed and my hood is up, which would make it a lot harder for him to accidentally touch me. He's wearing a T-shirt, so there's fabric covering him, too. If I were to shift, the chances of my skin touching his are near impossible unless I actually try.*

The thoughts don't comfort me as much as I'd like them to.

That, and there's a small part of me that doesn't want to move away from him. There's a small part of me that wants him to keep his arm around me. There's a very small, very *stupid,* part of me that likes this.

I sigh, feeling defeated, as I carefully lean into him.

What would my parents say if they knew I was being this stupid? What would Daemon say? What will *I* think of this later? I'm going to regret this, and I can't shake the feeling that I will.

I pay an enormous amount of attention to every movement I make until I'm comfortable against him, but also facing away from him so that I can't hurt him.

"Any better, or am I too scrawny?" he asks, laughing. He says it so casually that I wonder if I should feel anywhere near as uncomfortable about this as I do. He doesn't sound like he's uncomfortable at all, so why do I feel like if I started shaking, I'd fall apart?

Him and scrawny don't exactly fit together, but I don't understand why the thought of that makes my face hot.

"You make a good chair," I say, by way of answer, instead of something I'll regret. Even just staying silent would be too uncomfortable for me to bear.

Chase laughs beside me. "Glad you approve."

Even through my jacket, I can feel the warmth of

his skin. It's an odd comfort, but one I've never felt before. It's comforting to know he's alive still and that I haven't managed to kill him in the time we've spent like this, but there's something else, too. Something I can't put my finger on.

It reminds me slightly of my dad and the way he used to let me lay on him when I was little. This is completely different in a way, but the reminder of a time when I actually felt like my dad's little girl and not just another kid on this plant is enough to break me.

Before I can stop them, tears are running down my face. They're silent, and I know Chase can't see them and won't be able to unless he looks at me, but it still freaks me out. I don't cry in front of people. I don't cry unless I absolutely can't help it.

It takes longer than I want it to, but I manage to get the tears under control before Chase can see. It only takes me a moment or so, but it feels like an eternity.

"You know where there's a lot of really comfortable chairs?" Chase asks a moment later, seeming to want to go back to our original conversation. "At the movie theater. I seriously can't believe you've never been."

I groan, but I'm amused. "I'm sure there are," I say, rolling my eyes. I shift again, pressing my body closer to his so I don't feel like I'm having to hold my own head up when I'm supposed to be using him for that.

"C'mon. You've never wanted to go?"

"Not really," I answer, but that's not the complete truth and I know he can hear that in my tone of voice.

"Okay, fine. Yes, I've wanted to go a couple of times. But now I'm just being stubborn."

"Never would've guessed," he teases. "So, when can I take you to the movies? You made the mistake of admitting that you've never been and that you want to go, and I'm now your friend, so I consider it my responsibility to make sure you go."

I roll my eyes and snort a laugh, but don't actually laugh or smile. It's hard to pretend I'm not freaking out, though. Especially with his arm around me and his warmth seeping through my jacket and the sound of his heartbeat in my ear.

"Are you asking me out?" I tease, because the only way I escape uncomfortable conversations is by making jokes. I turn so he can see my face and wiggle my eyebrows at him.

His cheeks turn pink at that and he looks like he did the first time I caught him here, singing the sappiest love song I've ever heard. "I'm forcing my friend to go to the movies against her will," he says.

He looks like he's doing his best to come off cool and collected, but there's something in his expression that reminds me of the discomfort I'm still feeling.

"Pfft. Good luck with that," I tell him as I lie back down against him.

"Don't believe I'll be able to get away with it?" he challenges, and I can practically see the glimmer in his eyes again.

I do believe he'll pull it off, but that's because I'm

not completely against the idea of actually going. If I seriously didn't want to go, it'd be impossible for him to ever get me to the theater.

"We'll see," I respond, though I know that's nowhere near the answer he was expecting. "Can I sleep now?"

"Yeah, alright," he says, sighing in mock exasperation.

I smile as I close my eyes, but he can't see it.

A moment passes before he rests his cheek on the top of my head. I can hear him let out a breath before he goes still. I can only guess that he's doing his best to get some sleep, too.

All I can think about as I drift off is how glad I am that I have the hood of my jacket up.

Chapter Eleven

"An?"

I wake to Chase shaking my shoulder gently. It's cooler out than it had been before and the sun is starting to sink below the horizon. I can hear the cicadas chirping from somewhere not too far away.

"Hmm?" I manage through a yawn. I blink twice, but close my eyes again a second later as I shift closer to him. I can't help but like the feel of his arm around me, holding me. I feel safe, even despite the fact that I know I shouldn't because *he* isn't.

I push the thought of his skin turning pale and grey out of my head before my mind gets a chance to run away with the thought.

"Your phone," he tells me. "It went off twice and then like, another fifty times in the time it took me to wake you up." I can hear the amusement in his tone, but I'm far less amused by the situation. He doesn't know exactly what this means for me. I really don't want to have to explain myself to my parents, but I doubt I'm going to have much of a choice.

"Damn it."

I pull my phone from my pocket and find 12 texts, all from my mom. My eyes flick to the time at the top of the screen, which reads 7:04. She's gonna kill me, that's all there is to it. If Daemon doesn't get to me first, that is.

"I'm dead," I say, my voice deadpan. I drop my hand to my side before slipping my phone into my back pocket. It takes me a second, but I manage to clamber to my feet a moment later. The process is slow, and it's miserable, but I don't end up knocking my shoulder on anything.

Chase gets up a second after me. I can feel a pang of disappointment rush through me at the fact that I can't stay here with him. It's stupid of me to feel like this, but I can't seem to help it. I like being with him more than I like being with anyone else. I like being with him more than I like being by myself too, which is saying something.

"I'm sorry," he says. "I should've woken you up sooner. You just looked so peaceful and I didn't know when you needed to be home so-"

"It's fine," I interrupt. I zip up my jacket and fix the hood so that as much of my face as possible is covered. "I've just gotta get home. It's my own fault. I should've set an alarm or something. Or not slept," I add, clicking my tongue thoughtfully. "That probably would've been the smartest thing."

Chase smiles, but he still looks like he feels bad, which makes me worried I'll hear another apology out of his mouth. I think I heard more apologies from him the first time I met him than I'd ever possibly need to hear in a lifetime.

"I've really gotta go."

I turn to leave, but Chase jogs up alongside me before I can get very far.

"So, what's today's topic for the road?" he asks, as I lengthen my stride so I'm in line with his. He shortens his slightly when he notices my change of pace. "I can't exactly get your number every day, so I need some form of entertainment."

I roll my eyes before turning to look at him. He's giving me a look that I can't place when I meet his eyes. It's something warm and caring, but deeper than I can see, like if I were to walk off of a cliff into whatever he's feeling, I'd never stop falling.

Before I can get a chance to figure out what exactly I'm seeing in his eyes, he turns away from me and looks straight ahead.

I clear my throat awkwardly when I realize that answering would probably be a better thing to do than ignoring him and trying to figure out what I couldn't place in his expression. "I mean, technically you could, but I think that'd get pretty boring pretty quickly. And also," I pull my phone from my pocket and wave it in front of him, "I finally got around to putting a passcode on it."

I wiggle my eyebrows at him teasingly as I put my phone back, and he laughs.

"Smart, but the damage has already been done," he says, winking at me.

A retort is on the tip of my tongue, but I push it down. I'd rather joke about how I've screwed up by letting him into my life than tell him as honestly as I can that I'm glad he's here. I think that's something that goes unsaid as it is, but after earlier, all I can picture is how unbelievably awkward I'd feel after saying something so openly.

"I've learned my lesson," I respond.

We turn onto the cross street that my house sits on and walk the rest of the way in silence. I don't know what to say to him to break it, but he doesn't seem to know either. I guess this is another reason I don't have friends. I can't hold a conversation if I feel uncomfortable, and most of the time, I do. Chase has been the odd exception up until now.

I'm not necessarily uncomfortable right now, though. This doesn't feel like a normal awkward silence. It just feels distant, like both of us are thinking about something and are distracted.

"Well..." I say, stopping in the driveway and turning to face Chase. "I'll see you tomorrow."

Chase nods, but he looks like his mind is elsewhere.

"Is everything alright?" I ask, but I don't know where exactly the question came from. He doesn't look not okay, and, usually, that's not something I ask people because I hate when people ask me that same thing.

He shakes his head, like he's trying to clear it, and looks at me. "Yeah, sorry." He smiles, but it doesn't quite reach his eyes, which tells me that something is definitely bothering him. "I'll see you tomorrow."

He looks sad as he turns away and starts down the street in the direction we just came from.

I want to call out to him. I want to say something funny so he'll smile, or laugh, or something. I just want the sadness I'd seen on his face a moment ago to go away. I want him to be happy. I want to fix it, even though I don't know what "it" is.

Instead of saying or doing anything, I watch him go. He's a few houses away before I head inside.

I let out a breath that I feel like I've been holding in for the past hour as I sprawl out on my bed. Mom and dad weren't exactly happy that I was home as late as I was, but I hadn't managed to get into any trouble when I told them, yet again, that I'd lost track of time and that I hadn't heard my phone go off.

They didn't look like they completely bought my lie, but they didn't press either, so I figured they just thought I was being rebellious and coming back late to push the limits but not late enough that I would actually get in trouble. I played it off like that's what I was doing, but that's not even half of the truth of it. I'm pretty sure they suspect something more, but they haven't yet given me any reason to think that they do.

Everything from earlier with Chase is running through my head. I haven't known him long, and yet it already feels like we are the best of friends. I'm relaxed with him somehow. I never would've let anyone else put their arm around me like he did, even if it did make me a little shifty and nervous. But I'd been nervous because of my touch. I hadn't been nervous because I didn't want him anywhere near me. It was strange and different and I liked it.

But then, when we'd been on the walk home… what'd that been? I don't get the feeling he's mad at me or that he doesn't want anything to do with me all of a sudden or anything, but I do get the feeling he's hiding something from me. And maybe it isn't any of my business, but isn't talking about things part of what being friends is?

Sighing, I climb to my feet and head into the bathroom. I pull my jacket off and hang it on the towel wrack. I look half dead, which isn't any different from usual, but it's worse today. I don't think I've ever been tired enough to look this terrible.

I turn the faucet on and let the water pool into my hands before splashing it on my face. I don't really have to "splash" it, though. Water doesn't work for me like it does for normal people. It becomes still as ever when I touch it. I can stand in the tub and no ripples will form around my ankles if I let it fill up. The water still goes down the drain and it still drips off of me, but the lack of ripples in the water is the most obvious difference.

When I rinse my face off, though, I feel more like I have to smear the water on before I towel it off. It feels more like I've poured grease onto my skin than anything else. It slowly drips off of me if I let it, but I get too impatient to wait and just use a towel to dry it off instead.

There's a light knock on my door as I work on drying my face.

"Who's there?" I call, but my voice is muffled horribly by the towel, so I'm not sure if whoever's there can even hear me.

"Your sister," Fayre's voice answers. She sounds impatient.

I take a look at myself in the mirror before I leave the bathroom to get the door. I still look dead.

Fayre is leaning against the doorframe when I get the door for her. "Is it my job to clear the table tonight?" I ask, raising an eyebrow. I can't think of any other reason why she'd be here.

"Nope." She pushes past me and heads over to my bed, plopping herself down before laying back and admiring the blackness that is my ceiling. "That's my job and I just finished."

"So… what'd you want?" I don't mean for it to

come off rude, but what is she doing here? I don't talk with her or Daemon much, and I'm definitely not used to them seeking me out when I'm already shut up in my room for the night.

Fayre sits up and gives me a suspicious once over before she turns onto her side, propping herself up on an elbow. "Who's the guy?" she asks, wiggling her eyebrows at me.

My stomach flips over on itself and I feel like I'm going to wretch. I catch myself before I can give any indication about how extremely nervous her comment just made me. "What guy?" I ask, playing dumb.

"You know exactly which guy I'm talking about, Thana." She rolls her eyes at me like I'm the dumbest thing she's seen since crustless bread.

There's no way I'm getting out of this one, I realize, but, of course, that's not going to stop me from trying. "Uh-huh. 'Cause I know so many guys." I give her a look that I hope gives the impression that I think she's being dumb.

Fayre just mirrors the look I had on my face a moment before. "Exactly, you only seem to know one. So, you should know exactly which one I'm talking about. Unless you just happened to forget about the guy you were sitting with at lunch and who you've walked home with for the past couple of days."

I internally groan as I walk back into the bathroom and grab the brush off of the counter. I start running it through my hair to get the tangles out before I look at her in the mirror. I know there's no way I'm getting out of this, but I really wish I could. I just hope I look calm and collected while I do my best to come up with some sort of excuse. "He's a transfer student," I tell her, which isn't the biggest lie I've told today. "He doesn't seem to get that I don't want people around."

"Mhm, sure."

She looks like she wants to say something else, but, instead, she just starts fiddling with the hem of her shirt, refusing to meet my eyes. Now I really know something's on her mind. I'm not oblivious to people's nervous habits.

"What is it?" I ask, setting the brush down on the counter before tying my hair up so that it stays out of my face. I go back into the room and sit down at my desk instead of on the bed next to her. I don't want to risk being close to her. I can't hurt her.

She purses her lips thoughtfully before she lets out a breath, her shoulders sagging when she does. "Drake has a girlfriend." She looks so defeated that I get a strong urge to punch the guy, even though I don't think I should.

"Oh," I say, instead of letting something like "I'm so gonna kill him" slip out. "How'd you find out?"

Fayre makes an attempt at a laugh, but it's a pathetic one and it just comes out as a puff of air between her lips. She's staring at her hands in her lap and doesn't seem capable of looking up. "Saw them kissing in the hallway after Spanish."

Now I really want to kill him.

"Was it… that bad?" I ask. And then, because I'm heartless, "I mean, you two just met yesterday, right?"

I can feel the sting that my own words should cause my sister, but Fayre just looks like she hadn't expected anything else from me. Apparently, I've gotten so good at hurting people's feelings that she doesn't even notice it anymore.

My sister shrugs. "I guess my hope just got squashed, is all." She says it like it's nothing, but I know that's a lie. I just don't know how to comfort her like she needs. I *can't*. I couldn't give her a hug right now even if I wanted to. It'd be too easy to touch her.

"I'm sorry," I tell her, as though that could help anything.

"It's fine," she says, which is the same lie I've told Chase about a thousand times in the past few days that I've known him. I can see the start of tears in her eyes when she says it, though. Not enough to fall, but enough to be visible in the light of my room.

I open my mouth to say something, to try to comfort her, but nothing comes out. Saying "sorry" over and over again isn't going to help anything. And, if she's anything like me, it'll just drive her insane.

"Anyway," Fayre says, wiping her eyes with the backs of her hands before she straightens and looks at me. "The guy you've been hanging out with. Who is he?"

"His name's Chase," I answer, immediately

regretting the words after they're out of my mouth. My next words are through clenched teeth, as though even my jaw is trying to keep me from saying them. "I met him last week. He's the reason I have a broken collar bone. I almost ran him over with my bike and had to swerve into the ditch. And then he saw me at school, and yeah…"

I leave the sentence hanging in the air, not sure what else I can add to make it sound more complete. I shouldn't have even told her that much. The fact that I almost hit him and had to make a reckless move and swerve into the ditch doesn't sound half as bad as it used to, now that I've befriended him. I hadn't even wanted to tell my parents that much last week. This is a whole new level of "no one can know" and I just let all of it slip to my sister.

"Please don't tell mom and dad," I beg.

"I won't," she says, smiling. She looks like she just found a romance book at the library and can't wait to get home so she can pop it open and read.

I groan. "It's not like that at all."

But right after the words are out of my mouth, I can't help but think of earlier and how Chase held me while I slept. How he moved closer to me and put his arm around me to help make me more comfortable on the ground. How he stayed there even after he'd woken me up.

I shake my head, clearing the thoughts. He'd said he didn't want to make it awkward. Doesn't that mean he didn't want to make me think he likes me as something more than a friend? I think that's all the proof I need to make me believe this is nothing more than just a friendship.

Fayre laughs like she's never heard a joke funnier than what I just told her. I don't find it half as amusing, but that doesn't mean me saying so would change her mind about the situation. My sister is so boy-crazy and so completely in love with the idea of any love story that there's literally nothing I could do to make her see the truth when it comes to this.

"Whatever you say," she tells me, but I know she doesn't believe me at all.

I give her a look. "Fayre, he could never be anything more than a friend, even if we did feel that way about each other."

She sighs. "I know."

I don't remind her that Chase and I shouldn't even be friends.

Chapter Twelve

The days that lead to Friday seem to all blur together. Chase and I sit at the same table during lunch, we hang out at the abandoned property, and we text for a few hours after I've finished my homework. He seems to always be free before me, and I can't figure out when exactly he gets his own homework done, but my best guess is that he does it around the same time I do.

I avoid Daemon to the best of my ability, but it seems harder than it should be. He still seems to want to come with me to the abandoned property, or at least to do something with me, but I'm not particularly keen on the idea of that. It'd be nice to spend time with him, I guess, but I don't want to hear anything about my friendship with Chase, even if he doesn't know half as much as Fayre does after Tuesday night.

Fayre doesn't ask again about Chase, but I can see her watching us from across the cafeteria each day, and I could've sworn that her face was pressed up against her bedroom window watching for me yesterday when I came home.

She's watching me from where she sits with a group of friends right now. After a moment passes though, she gets back to her friends. Apparently watching me and Chase talk isn't as entertaining as she hoped it would be.

Watching her, however, isn't anywhere near as boring as I wish it were. "Mark is with my sister again," I grumble to Chase as I half-heartedly push my food around on my plate.

I want to talk to him and joke around in that way I'm able to do with him where every response is a challenge to what the other said. It feels like a mind game with rules I don't always understand, but I enjoy it. Doing that would be much more entertaining than watching my sister and Mark out of the corner of my eye while trying to not make it too obvious that I'm not actually facing forward.

"Can you keep an eye on him?" I ask, which I don't feel like I should, but I do, anyway. "I don't trust him, and I don't want to be suspicious because I don't want…" I don't finish the sentence, but I think Chase knows exactly what I mean. I don't want to say it and sound like some pathetic girl who can't look out for herself, though. I've never been that and I will never be.

Chase nods. "They're just talking right now."

"Alright."

He watches me for a moment; like he's trying to find something in my expression. I don't know what he's looking for, or why he's looking at me at all, but it makes me feel weirdly self-conscious. I look back down at my plate, hoping my discomfort isn't as obvious as it feels.

"You and your siblings, you guys watch each other's backs, don't you?" he asks, but it doesn't sound so much like s question as it does a statement that requires an answer.

I look back over my shoulder at Fayre, who's smiling widely at Mark, a guy she should never be talking to if she knew what was good for her. I turn back to Chase. "Yeah." I sigh. "That's one way of putting it."

He smiles. "Well, there's obviously some overprotectiveness there, but on a whole, you guys watch out for each other."

I can't say he's wrong, but I don't know how to respond to that. Yes, we do, I suppose, though I've never really paid much attention until now.

Something sad comes over his expression and I want to say something, anything, to make it go away. Is he upset because I didn't answer? I seriously doubt that's it, but it's the only thing I can think of.

I open my mouth to respond, hoping that will help, but he interrupts my attempt. "My sister and I used to be like that," he says, but it sounds more like he's saying it to himself than to me.

I watch him, seeing if he wants to say anything else. He said that much, which makes me think he isn't completely against talking about whatever happened, but he doesn't look like he wants to say much more. "What happened?" I ask, my voice barely above a whisper. I want to know, but I get the feeling I need to be careful about it.

"I haven't talked to her in over a year," he explains. "And then my dad and I moved here, and she stayed back in Virginia."

More questions form on the tip of my tongue: what happened? why hadn't they talked in so long? why was she still back in Virginia yet he was here? But I keep my mouth shut.

Instead, I reach across the table and cover his hand with mine. I don't know what I'm doing when I do it, but it feels right, and he doesn't pull away, so I take that to mean I haven't done anything wrong.

He smiles at me from across the table, but it isn't his usual bright, full smile that lights up his whole face. This is a small, simple one. It's sweet, kind, and gentle. It reminds me somehow of the smile my mom gives me sometimes, but different at the same time.

I can feel my face mirror the smile that's on his. Something in me feels different when the smile touches my lips. It feels warm and caring, which shouldn't surprise me as much as it does because I know I care about him.

I look away a second later and take my hand back, getting back to the food in front of me.

"I saw that," Chase says after a minute.

"Saw what?" I ask innocently.

He smiles at me from across the table and his laugh comes out in the form of a breath as he shakes his head.

It's raining outside by the time school gets out. It's been raining off and on all day, but it's stronger now than it's been so far. When the bell rings, I can see it outside of the classroom and hear the drops when they fall against the window. Once I'm in the hallway, I can't hear it anymore over the sounds of people talking over each other and hurried footsteps.

I move through the hallways as fast as I can, doing my absolute best to stay out of the crowded areas. My phone goes off twice in my pocket, but I don't dare to check it until I'm outside and everyone else is safe.

Everyone outside is standing under any form of protection from the rain that they can find. I don't even bother to try and find something to cover myself as I run across the lawn. My sling is in my backpack, which is waterproof, and I keep my arm held against my stomach to keep it still so that I don't have to pull it out.

By the time I get to the car, I'm wet, but not yet

sopping. I pull open the door and climb in as fast as I can before I throw my backpack on the floor at my feet.

I scan the front of the school. I can't see Fayre, but Daemon is standing with a large group of friends: four girls I don't recognize, Lauren, five or six guys I've never met, and then him. They're all standing beneath the slim awning of the roof. Every couple of minutes, one of them leans around another one to talk to someone on the opposite side of the group.

All of them laugh at something someone says. Daemon puts an arm around Lauren's shoulders and she leans against him, still laughing. It looks so natural when they do that; like there's not even a thought involved. They were like that when they sat down with me and Chase at the beginning of the week, too. I just hadn't been so aware of it because all I'd really been able to focus on was how awkward I felt.

I sigh and pull my phone from my pocket while I wait. With my luck, I'll be sitting here for another twenty or so minutes before either of my siblings even realizes that we have to go home at some point.

I have two unread texts from Chase.

This rain is crazy.

Guess we won't be meeting up today after all.

Well, I'll still be going because my days with the place are already numbered, but I doubt he's referring to me being there or not.

Guess not, I text him back, then put it back in the inside pocket of my jacket.

I do my best to push down the feeling of disappointment. I'd expected he wouldn't want to come if it's raining, and it's not like he doesn't have a good reason. Not many people want to hang out in the rain for multiple hours.

Fayre and her friends come out of the school a moment later. My body feels stiff as I look over each of them. I can feel myself relax when I see that Mark isn't one of the people she's with, though. I vaguely recognize a couple of them, but I'm clueless as to what their names are.

For being so upset about that Drake guy of hers having a girlfriend, she's definitely either calmed down a lot or has an amazing poker face when it comes to her true emotions. She shoves a boy who looks vaguely familiar with her shoulder and he stumbles forward a step, which makes both of them laugh. It looks as easy as Daemon and Lauren make dating each other seem.

Is that how I act with Chase? Or have I not known him long enough for things to flow like that between the two of us?

Fayre hugs a few of her friends goodbye – including the boy she shoved a moment ago – and then goes over to where Daemon is standing with his friends. I can see her say something to them as she maneuvers around them to get to our brother, but I'm horrible at lipreading and have no clue what exactly it was she said.

She says something to Daemon when she gets to him and gestures back toward the car, which I guess means she's telling him it's time to go, before she waves goodbye to them and sprints over to the car.

My sister climbs in the back seat behind me. "I don't like the rain," she informs me as soon as the door is shut.

I snort a laugh, but it sounds more like a breath of air coming out of my nose than an actual laugh. "I like it when I'm not soaked to the bone and have to spend the ride home in a car."

Daemon kisses Lauren, smiles at her, then waves to everyone before he jogs over to the car, his head ducked to stay as dry as possible.

Before I have time to register what she's doing, Fayre stands up behind me and reaches over me, hitting the lock button. She grins at me wickedly in the rearview mirror and I can't help it when I smile.

Daemon gets to the car, tries to pull the door open, realizes it's locked, and says something neither of us can hear through the window.

Fayre laughs maniacally in the backseat as Daemon pulls his keys from his pocket and unlocks the door before climbing in.

"Fayre, you are now responsible for doing my laundry," he tells her as he closes the door behind himself. Both of us watch her in the rearview mirror as she grabs her side and falls over on the backseat. Daemon smiles, shaking his head, and puts the key in the ignition.

He backs the car out of its space and starts off down the road.

"Than, you want me to drop you off at the abandoned part of the neighborhood?"

Confusion bubbles up inside me, but I ignore it. He's probably still trying to make up for being weird about me and Chase hanging out. It's been making me uncomfortable, but I can't say I don't want to take him up on the offer.

"Uh, yeah, if you don't mind?" I answer, but it sounds like a question more than anything else.

"I wouldn't offer if I minded," he says, and smiles at me.

A few moments later, Daemon drops me off at the abandoned property by the same house I usually spend my time near. I don't have a raincoat because I left that at home this morning, but I don't really care that I don't have it. The only reason I wear the raincoat when in public is so that people don't see the water against my skin, but I don't have to worry about that since Chase isn't here.

It's rained enough already that there are large puddles all over. I left my shoes in the car along with my backpack because my brother offered to pick me up later if I want him to. My phone is inside a Ziplock bag, so I can call him if I need him and not destroy it in the process.

I walk around the property, enjoying the feel of the cool rain against my face. There are five houses still standing in total. Two of them are brick, and the other two are wood. The house at the end of the block has a small shack behind it that's falling apart even more than any of the houses are.

I walk the length of the whole thing, running my hand over each of the houses. I can't feel much through my gloves, but I can feel enough and I've learned how to distinguish different surfaces through them after years of not being able to take them off.

When I get to the house at the end of the block, I run my hand over it just like I did with all of the other ones, but midway through walking the length of it, I freeze.

What was that?

I squint at nothing in particular and listen again.

Chapter Thirteen

My heart races in my chest as I look around. I could've sworn I heard something. Something that sounded distinctly like music, but there's nothing there. I'm far enough away from the other houses that I shouldn't hear anything, even if someone's blasting it from a speaker in their backyard, but I could've sworn I heard something.

Just when I decide that I'm crazy, I hear it again. I frown and remove my hand from the side of the house before I follow the sound of the music.

It's coming from…

My eyes land on the shack that's falling apart behind the house.

Slowly, and as quietly as I can manage, I make my way over to it.

The first thing I notice when I get to it is that the

door is slightly ajar. It's never been like that in all the years I've come here. Someone's playing a guitar inside, and it sounds like the intro to a new song.

There's a window on each side of the shack, but the one on the left has absolutely no glass anymore, and the one on the right does. I take my chances with the left side, and work my way around to it, keeping my head ducked low so that I can't be seen unless whoever's inside is actually looking for me. Judging by the fact that the music hasn't stopped, I'd say they don't know I'm here, though.

"I'm no superman, I can't take your hand and fly you anywhere you want to go."

My heart does a flip in my chest and my jaw practically drops. I almost want to laugh, but I put a hand over my mouth and keep any sound from escaping.

Slowly, I peak into the shack over the window's edge, and that's when I see him.

Chase isn't facing me. He's facing the window on the other side of the shack. I'm glad for it because it means he won't see me unless I make a sound. He's sitting with his legs crossed beneath him on the dirt floor of the shack, his guitar in his lap.

I listen to him play and sing. It's the sappiest love song I've ever heard, but it's sweet, too.

It takes me a minute to realize he's singing the same song I heard him singing the day he caught me trespassing for the first time.

"If you're the one for me, like gravity, I'll be unstoppable."

He sings it gently, his eyes fixed on something outside the window. It sounds so perfect, but not like he's rehearsed it a thousand times to make it that way, more like he's in love with whoever he's singing it to. Which would be the window in this case.

His voice rises and falls as he sings the lyrics, his fingers strumming the cords. I've never liked love songs, but I find myself getting lost in this one; the guitar, the lyrics, his voice. It all makes me feel something I've only ever felt a few times when listening to music.

Chase's song ends and he lets out a breath; like he didn't want it to end just as much as I didn't. He sits there for a moment, holding the guitar still and looking out the window.

I smile. Could I get a better opening?

"Nice song," I say, resting my elbow on the edge of the window.

Chase's shoulders stiffen and his whole body goes rigid. I almost want to laugh, but I manage to keep my amusement off of my face. I don't think I should feel so much fulfillment from destroying his moment, but I do.

"You… weren't supposed to hear that," Chase says, looking over his shoulder and back at me. His face is bright red, and I can't help but wonder how much redder he'd turn if I could come up with some ways to torment him about it.

"I know." I smirk at him teasingly.

I tighten my grip on the window before I jump through it, tucking my legs so I don't hit them on the metal frame. I land as close to flawlessly as I can with my hurt shoulder, but the jolt of my feet hitting the floor still sends a wave of pain through me, anyway.

I suck in a breath through my teeth, but do my best to ignore it when I notice Chase giving me a worried look. I'm not going to let my stupid collar bone ruin this opportunity to make him look like the brother of a cherry.

"So," I say, "what's the song from?" I can hear the strain in my own voice, but I play it off like it's not there at all as I walk over to him and sit down across from him. His face is still just as red.

"A movie I like," he answers, setting his guitar down in a case beside him. He hasn't looked me in the eye once, and I can't decide if I think it's hilarious, or if I'm waiting for him to finally look at me so I can be even more amused when he does.

"Is it as cheesy as that song?" I ask, doing my best to keep from smiling. I haven't smiled so much in so long that I think I'm getting close to breaking my face.

"*Maybe*," he says, stretching it out in a way that makes it obvious that it is. If it's possible, he's even redder. A minute ago, it was just his nose, cheeks, and forehead that were red. Now it's spread to the tips of his ears and down his neck.

"You're cute when you blush," I tell him, but before

the words are even out of my own mouth, I can feel myself frowning at them. Where had that come from?

I've never told a guy he's cute before. I've never even really talked to any guys besides him. I'd never had the chance to because the few times I did think a guy was cute, it would've been extremely weird for me to say anything about it at all.

"You're cute when you smile," he says, as if that's an answer.

I can feel my own face heat up for some reason at the words. I've also never blushed because of something some guy said to me. Unless it was my brother or dad because they'd embarrassed me somehow, that is.

Chase smiles, his eyes sparkling. "Now we match."

"I hate you," I say, bluntly.

His smile widens and he winks at me teasingly. "I know."

It's still raining outside of the shack, but I can't seem to hear it over the sound of my own breathing and the slow *drip, drip, drip* of the water that's falling from my hair. A small puddle has started to form next to me from it, and it's suddenly become very interesting.

I look around the perimeter of the small shack. It's not sitting off of the ground, but there are so many holes in the sides just above the ground that water is starting to leak in. If it rains too much, it'll flood the shack easily.

I clear my throat. "So, how'd you learn the song?" I ask.

Chase shrugs. "Taught myself. I like to play but haven't taken lessons in years. I tend to just learn random stuff when I feel like it."

I nod. I don't know what I'd been expecting as an answer, but it hadn't been that. "How long did you take lessons?" I ask, glancing at the guitar again. He's plucking at the strings. He looks as uncomfortable as I feel. "You had to have taken them for a while to be able to play like that. It doesn't exactly look easy."

He looks at the guitar, runs his hands over it, and picks it up. "About three years," he tells me. "And it's not that hard. Here." He passes the guitar to me, and I take it as gently as I can. It feels big and awkward in my hands and I don't know exactly where to grasp it.

I look at the guitar in my hands, then back up at Chase. "Uh… I have no clue what I'm supposed to do with this," I say, sheepishly.

Chase smiles. "Turn it like this." He moves it so that the back of the guitar is against my stomach, then moves to sit beside me. "Put your fingers like…" he takes my left hand and positions my fingers over three different strings, "this. Now press down hard and strum all the strings."

I do as he tells me, but it sounds like shit compared to his playing a few minutes ago. I cringe at the sound of it and Chase snorts a laugh beside me.

"Well, that was supposed to be a C, but I think you created a whole new note instead." He looks at my hands for a second, checking the positioning, before he seems to figure out whatever the problem is. He rolls his eyes, muttering something beneath his breath that sounds suspiciously like "Chase, you're a moron."

"Your gloves," he says. "That's why the sound's weird."

I feel my breath catch in the back of my throat at the thought of taking off my gloves. "Here," I say, handing the guitar back to him. "I… can't take my gloves off." My words are barely above a whisper and I can't seem to make myself look up at him.

He takes the guitar back, but his movements are slow and I can see the confusion on his face. "Why?" he asks. It's not even the tiniest bit rude when he does, he's just genuinely curious and confused, but it still makes me cringe and want to leave, anyway.

There's no way I can tell him the truth. I could never tell him the truth, even if I wanted to. But I have to tell him *something*. Why don't I take the gloves off? Do I hate germs? Do I have some sort of crazy disease that spreads through touch? Do I have skin cancer?

"I've got really bad eczema…" I lie, still unable to meet his gaze.

Of all the stupid things you could say…

Great, so now I have eczema. And I'm going to have to remember that I have eczema in case it ever comes up in conversation again. And I should probably do some research on eczema too, because I have barely any idea what it is or what it's like to have it.

"Oh." He doesn't look confused anymore, which

tells me he believes my lie. "Is it painful or something?"

"Just embarrassing," I blurt, because I have nothing better.

Great, now he's gonna think I'm super self-conscious. I internally groan at my own stupidity.

Now he looks mildly confused again. Apparently, he isn't completely oblivious to the fact that I'm not all that self-conscious. "Alright," he says, as though I just told him my mom wants me home by five and not something that doesn't exactly fit very well with what he knows about me.

His expression is impossible to read, which isn't something I'm used to with him. I can't even tell if he's uncomfortable or if he's just bored with the fact that I'm here.

I chew my bottom lip.

Drip, drip, drip.

Can the water dripping from my hair be any louder?

"Do you know any other songs?" I ask, doing my best to start another conversation that'll put an end to the silence.

Chase shrugs. "A couple."

I want to ask him to play another. I want him to play something I'll get lost in again. I want to hear him strum the guitar, and his voice when he sings. I don't know how to tell him that without making this whole situation about a thousand times more awkward, though.

"Have you written any?" I ask instead, because I

figure that's less awkward than asking him to play another for me.

"… sort of," he says carefully. "I don't have any lyrics for it but I wrote out a melody a while ago. It's not perfect, which is why I haven't given the lyrics a try yet, but yeah." He picks up his guitar and looks over at me. "You wanna hear it?"

I nod, probably too quickly, and the hint of a smile forms at the corners of his lips.

He picks up the guitar again and puts it in his lap – like he'd had it when I found him a bit ago – before he starts playing a melody. It's not long, maybe twenty notes before it repeats again. He plays the melody twice before it changes to something similar, but slightly different. The chorus is a simple melody that couldn't possibly sound any more perfect. It's slow and gentle and, somehow, he's managed to come up with something that sounds like a love song that I don't actually hate. The rift is easily my second favorite part after the chorus. It's a bit faster, but somehow, he's managed to do that and keep the same feeling in the song at the same time. After the rift is another chorus, and a slow, sweet-sounding ending.

I'm left feeling both sad and happy at the same time. I don't think he intended for it to be that way, and I'm sure it won't be once he's come up with lyrics, but I like that, at least for now, I can't completely decide if it's supposed to be happy sounding or sad.

Chase is looking at me expectantly by the time I'm

finally able to shake my head and come out of the trance the song put me in.

"That… that's amazing," I tell him. "I love it."

He smiles and puts the guitar back in its case. "I'm still working on it. And I've been saying that for the past couple of months, but I think I'm getting closer."

I think about it for a second. It sounded practically flawless to me, but I suppose that's because I'm not the one who's been working on it. He probably notices every small thing about it that doesn't sound quite right because he's the one who wrote it.

"Can I offer a suggestion?" I ask, realizing there was one thing I noticed that sounded the tiniest bit less than perfect.

He nods. "Please."

"What if, in the bridge, instead of that one high note toward the end, you went lower instead?" I say, my eyes on the guitar in its case.

I don't necessarily feel like I have a right to be offering my suggestions, considering that I've never written any music or even played any. It makes me feel uncomfortable that I have an idea, especially because I'm not sure if it'll be good or terrible.

"Huh." Chase picks up the guitar again and plays the bridge, changing out the note I was talking about to a lower one when he does. When he finishes it, he looks up at me. "Well?"

I bite my lip and shake my head. "Better how it was before, I think," I tell him, even though I'm not quite sure what I think. It doesn't sound much different and it could work either way. But I don't like the idea of saying that I like my own idea better than the way he played it before, even if they don't sound much different in the long run.

"I liked it better," he says with a shrug.

"Seriously?" I ask, confused because I really wasn't expecting that for some reason.

He frowns at me. "Yeah...?" It sounds a lot more like a question than an answer, but I take it as the latter either way. "You have any more suggestions?" he asks. He looks like he really thinks I'll be able to help him make his song better. I don't think there's any way I could help him as much as he seems to think I can, though.

I shake my head. "Not really," I answer, sheepishly.

"Is everything alright?" he asks me.

He looks genuinely concerned, and it makes me weirdly nervous. Did I say something offensive? Am I not acting just as normal as usual? I'm pretty sure I'm not acting that much different from how I usually act.

I nod. "Yeah, I'm fine."

"Okay. You just seem a little quiet today, is all," he explains.

"I'm sleep deprived, which I blame you for. But other than that, I'm fine." Aside from feeling really weirdly awkward for some reason, I was, anyway. "Hey, look. It stopped raining," I say, in a desperate attempt to change the subject.

"No kidding," he says, looking amused. "It stopped about five minutes ago."

Oh…

Great, so now I'm feeling awkward and it's showing. Can this situation get any more complicated and uncomfortable? There's got to be a way to make myself seem normal, even though that feels impossible.

I watch Chase as he puts his guitar away and stands up. "C'mon," he says, offering me a hand to help me up. I take it, and he helps me up to my feet.

"Where exactly are we going?" I ask, raising an eyebrow at him. There's not really anywhere to go but the rest of the property, yet he seems like he has something in mind, which I don't understand at all.

"You'll see," he tells me. He glances back at me, but when he does, I catch a glimpse of something in his eyes. It reminds me weirdly of the look Fayre had on her face earlier when she locked Daemon out of the car, but I don't have enough time to decide if I'm crazy or not.

Chase doesn't let go of my hand as he pulls me toward the door. He sets his guitar down before he pushes it open. I can hear water trickling down from somewhere, and, before I have a chance to realize what's happening, water is pouring down from the roof of the shack and Chase has pulled me under it with him.

The water pours all over me and it feels like I'm standing beneath a small waterfall. It beats down on my head, my neck, and my shoulders. It feels like the water is only hitting a bruise when it comes down on my collar bone, which is much better than I would've expected it to feel.

By the time the water stops, Chase is laughing like he just saw the funniest thing in the world. And the funniest thing in the world that he was laughing at was probably the expression I had on my face when he pulled me under the water with him.

I blow out a breath of air, the drops of water that had been on my lips flying off of my face. I can feel my hair sticking to my forehead and cheeks. I really hope he can't tell how slowly the water is moving against my bare skin.

"I hate you," I say to the space in front of me, my eyes still closed.

I open my eyes to see Chase still standing beside me. He's still laughing, but not as hard as he had been a moment ago. "You have good reason to," he tells me, smiling at me with an expression I'm unfamiliar with.

Before he has time to realize what I'm doing, I hook my foot around his ankle and pull, sending him sprawling backward into the puddle of water at our feet. He lands on his back, but what I'd forgotten about was that he's still holding my hand. When he falls back, I fall with him. I land on top of him with a thud, muddy water splashing up onto my face.

I groan at the pain in my shoulder and grab my left arm with my right hand as Chase laughs. When he notices why I'm not joining in, his expression changes to something worried. He puts a hand on either of my shoulders and sits up, holding me with him.

"Are you okay?" he asks. He doesn't sound amused anymore.

I let go of my arm and steady myself against the ground with my hand. I nod my head. "I'm fine," I tell him, but my voice is strained again.

It takes a second for the stab to ease to a dull throbbing, but it's faster now than it was earlier in the week.

"You're sure?" He runs his hands up and down my arms, like he's not sure what to do to help, but he wants to.

"I'd tell you if I wasn't," I assure him. "And, also, I think this might be a clue that I'm perfectly fine."

A smile forms on my lips as his expression turns to confusion. I grab a handful of the mud beneath my hand and smear it across his face, laughing when I do.

"Whoops," I say. "I missed a spot." I run my muddy hand over his cheek, and my laughter starts up again.

It's been so long since I last laughed, I'd forgotten what it feels like. It's like a warm happiness is spreading itself throughout my body, starting in my chest and moving out in all directions. It's the best feeling I've had in forever.

I pull my hand back and study his face, having to suppress another bubble of laughter that's doing its best to surface. He wipes away the mud from his eyes with his shirt and gives me a look like he isn't amused, though I can still see the familiar glimmer in his eyes that tells me otherwise. "That's so not fair," he accuses me. "I was worried about you."

He splashes me with the water from the puddle we're still in and I laugh again as I shield my face.

"I like your laugh," he says, and that same nervous feeling I've had all day decides to dance around in my stomach again, making me feel like I'm gonna throw up.

I study his face for a second. "I like you covered in mud," I tell him, sticking my tongue out teasingly.

"Aww, thanks."

He smiles at me and we stay there for a second. His expression changes to confusion a moment later, though.

"Huh," he says. "The mud looks grey on your face somehow."

My heart does a flip in my chest and, as quickly as I can, I stand up. I pull the sleeve of my jacket over my hand and wipe at my face until I'm almost positive that all of the dirt is off. I can't have him noticing that. He didn't seem to, but he can't know. I shouldn't have even risked him seeing the water earlier. He hadn't, but I was lucky this time. And he had seen that the dirt was grey. Maybe he didn't think much of it this time, but what if something like that happened again? What if I'd had more on my face than just the bit of mud that had been in the water? Would he have figured it out then?

"What's wrong?" he asks, standing up with me. He studies my face, and I do my best to suppress all of the fear I'd felt a moment ago. I doubt I've hidden it as well as I should've, but it's the best I can do and he doesn't point out the fact that it had been there.

He lifts the hem of his shirt again to wipe more of the mud off of his face, leaving a decent amount of his stomach bare. All I can think of is what it would be like to see his skin turn to grey beneath my touch. That's all it would take: my skin against his and he'd be dead. It could've happened when I let him put his arm around me, but I was careful then. I wasn't careful this time, though. I could've killed him when I fell on top of him, and I hadn't even given it a second thought until now.

"It's nothing," I respond. "I was just… supposed to be home earlier today than usual and my brother offered to pick me up and I forgot to call him."

"Oh. Okay, I gotcha." He doesn't seem to think much of my answer. He seems to take it for what it should mean: that I forgot about something I could get in trouble for.

I pull my phone from my pocket and call my brother. The plastic bag is cool against my skin, but I can tell it's turning to a dingy grey beneath my touch. Luckily, Chase takes the moment I'm on the phone to get his guitar from the shack.

Daemon picks up on the second ring. "You're ready to come back already?" he asks. "Seems early for you."

"Not really," I lie, to make this go as fast as possible. "Can you pick me up in five?"

I can hear him hesitate, and I wonder if he's putting any of the pieces together, but he doesn't say anything about it when he responds. "Yeah, sure. I'll be over in a few."

"Thanks," I say, and hang up the phone before he has time to say anything back.

Before Chase can get a chance to see, I stuff my phone back into my pocket.

My head is spinning with possibilities. He could've seen what I can do. He could've put it together and realized what I'm capable of.

"My brother will be here in about five minutes," I inform him. My voice doesn't waver with the fear I feel rushing through every inch of me, and I can't help but be glad that it stays so well hidden. I don't know how long it will last, though.

Chase nods, and the two of us start toward the front of the property so that I can wait on the sidewalk for Daemon to show up.

"So… what're you doing here?" I ask him, realizing that we weren't supposed to meet up today. He'd even been the one to say it. "I thought you didn't want to come because of the rain?"

Chase shakes his head. "No, I still planned to come. I thought you wouldn't want to come because of the rain. I guess we both just assumed the same thing, but about the other person." He smiles over at me.

There are still streaks of mud on his face, but it's nowhere near as bad as it had been a moment ago. He's cute even without a blush or mud on his face, I realize, which makes the queasy feeling come back again.

"Yeah, I guess so," I agree.

"Hey, are you free tomorrow, by chance?" he asks.

I look up at him. "Yeah…?" I say, confusion dripping from my tone. "Why?"

"Because I need to take you to the movies because you've never been in a theater before, and that is a crime," he answers. "That and this one theater is half-priced on Saturday, so if we go tomorrow, we don't have to pay as much for me to drag you in there." He winks at me teasingly.

"Oh wait," I say, hitting my head with the palm of my hand. "I just remembered I'm busy after all. I forgot I have to take my unicorn to the salon to get his mane and tail styled for the upcoming Hooves and Horns fashion show."

Chase snorts a laugh beside me. "So, I'll pick you up at five?"

I sigh. "*Fine.*"

He laughs beside me, and I can't seem to help it when a very much unwanted smile forms on my face.

Chapter Fourteen

Daemon pulls up in front of us a few moments later. His expression is completely confused at the sight of me and Chase standing here, covered in mud. I'm sure he's less aware of the filth than he is of Chase, though.

"You ready?" he asks me through the open window. He's not looking at me, though. He's looking at Chase, which is making me uncomfortable. I really don't want him to pull any of his overprotective brother business right now.

"Yes," I answer, but there's an edge to my voice. It's enough to pull his attention to me, though. I turn to face Chase. "See ya tomorrow." I smile, but it's not as easy to do as it was earlier.

"Bye," he responds, smiling.

I climb in the car, setting my jacket down on the seat

before I sit on top of it. The seats are leather, so I'm not terribly worried about destroying it, but I will need to clean it when we get home. Daemon didn't ruin them earlier after Fayre locked him out of the car, but he still wasn't as wet as I am right now.

My brother puts the car in drive again and starts on the short drive home. I can hear all of his unanswered questions despite the fact that he hasn't said a word, but I don't want to answer any of them. I don't want him to know about the times I've met up with Chase here without anyone else knowing, or about how many times I've almost touched him. I know I'll have to tell him at some point because that's how things always end up, but I want a little more time to pretend they didn't happen at all.

Somehow, we manage to drive the whole way home and Daemon doesn't ask any questions I don't want to answer. He doesn't say anything to me at all, though, which means he's definitely not happy about the situation. I consider that to be his problem, though. Chase and my friendship with him are mine.

Daemon pulls the car into the driveway and parks it behind my dad's truck. He turns off the ignition but doesn't make a move to get out. That's enough to tell me I should make a break for it, but I stay put and accept the fact that I can't escape this. Even though I don't know exactly what "this" is yet.

My brother lets out a breath. "You know how dumb hanging out with him is, right?" he asks, which is like a fist to the gut, but I pretend like it didn't just send a wave of pain through me.

"I know."

"Then why are you with him all the time? What happens if you touch him, Than?" Daemon doesn't sound like he's trying to guilt me into anything. He just sounds genuinely confused. I think that's the worst part.

"I don't know," I confess. I can't meet his eyes, but I can feel him watching me; waiting for me to say something else. "I just want a chance to have a friend. I know I shouldn't want that because of what I can do to him, but I do. And I know it's stupid, but I don't know how to stop wanting it. I want even more to be normal every time I see him. I get to see you and Lauren, and I get to see Fayre with all of her friends, but I don't have anyone. I get that I have you two, but that's not the same thing. I just… I need someone who isn't scared of me."

Daemon looks taken aback by my words, and I realize only too late what exactly I said. I want to take them back, but there's no point in doing so. They're the truth, even if I don't want them to be.

"I'm not scared of you, Than," he tells me. "I'm scared of your ability, and I'm scared for you and everyone who could be hurt by it. Fayre, mom and dad, and I know how to be careful. We know we can't touch you, but people like Chase? They don't. Yes, we're scared of what you can do, but we're careful because of it. People who don't know, they're the ones who could get hurt much more easily."

I know he's right, but I don't want to listen. And besides, what does it really matter? It's not like I could ever tell Chase the truth, anyway. The only way I can keep people completely safe is to stay away from them altogether. I don't know if I can do that forever, though.

What is staying away from people going to mean when I'm an adult? What does it even mean right now? I can't do that. I have to go to school, and when I'm an adult, I'm going to have to go to work and maybe even college. There's no way I could forever stay away from people completely.

I sigh and, instead of answering like I know he probably wants me to, I get out of the car and head inside.

My brother comes in behind me but he doesn't make an attempt to start up our conversation again.

Fayre is sitting on the couch inside, watching a show with the volume down so low I can barely hear it. She's hardly paying attention to whatever it is, though. She's texting at the same time, but she seems way more interested in her phone.

Mom is cooking dinner in the kitchen, which is a bit earlier than usual, but if nothing else, that means I'm home early enough to avoid getting a call from her saying she wants me home at 5 instead of the usual 7.

I don't know where my dad is, but he's somewhere

in the house because his truck is parked outside. He tends to get off earlier on Fridays than any other day of the week. It's like they try to give him an extra-long weekend or something.

Fayre says something to me as I walk past, but it's so quiet I can't hear her clearly and I'm not exactly in the mood to talk anyway, so I pretend I didn't hear anything and keep walking. I've got to clean up the car before I can do anything else, which is annoying, but at least it gives me something to do with myself. It'll be better than sitting on my bed and thinking about all the ways I could kill Chase if I wanted to, or even if I don't.

Everyone eats in silence. The only sound I can hear is forks hitting plates and the occasional glass being set down. Mom already did her usual "how was everyone's day" thing where she asked each of us and made us answer with more than two words, but no one seems to have anything to say now that it's over.

I still need to ask my parents about going with Chase to the movies tomorrow, but I'm not sure if I want to ask it here or if I want to ask them later. I don't want to hear what Daemon will have to say about it, so, so far, I've kept my mouth shut.

He hasn't talked to me since the car ride earlier, only glancing up at me every now and then, as if to remind me that he doesn't approve of the choices I've made.

It's getting exhausting, but I don't feel like arguing with him about it, or even admitting that it's driving me crazy.

A few more minutes pass before I give up. I set my fork down and look up at my mom, who's taking a sip from her glass. She sets it down before I make any attempt to talk.

"Can I go to the movies with a friend tomorrow?" I blurt, before I can decide against doing it.

Every sound stops and I'm keenly aware of everyone staring at me, but I keep my eyes on my mom instead of acknowledging it.

Her eyes are wide, and it takes her a moment to form a response. "Um, sure," she says. She doesn't sound upset by the idea of it, just surprised that I'm actually asking if I can do something with another living being.

"Thana, are you sure that's the best idea?" my dad asks carefully.

Here we go...

"I'll be careful," I say quickly. "I'll avoid being too close to anyone and I'll dress like I do for school. It can't be any worse than being crammed into a school hallway."

He seems to think about my words for a second, but he doesn't look entirely convinced. "You have to be extremely careful," he tells me, leaving no room for argument.

I want to groan, but I keep myself from doing it.

They've been telling me this for as long as I can remember.

The most annoying part is that I know they're right. I do need to be careful, it's just that I can't help but still be annoyed that I can't just be normal like my brother and sister. I want to be able to go and only have to worry about my dad being overprotective because I'm going with a guy, instead of him being worried that I'll accidentally kill someone because I'm not being careful.

Daemon covers the overprotective part, yes, but it's not just that. There's always the layer of him being worried I'm going to screw up. There's that layer to all of them, and I hate it with a passion.

I know full well that a screw up could mean someone's life, but I've carried that weight around for most of my life and have never made an attempt to be a normal kid. I want the chance to try.

"I know," I say.

My mom and dad share a look, and I can see the worried expression they both have on their faces, but, eventually, they look back at me, and my dad nods. "Alright," he says, but he still doesn't sound like he wants to let me go.

"Is your friend picking you up?" my mom asks, standing up with her plate in hand. I hadn't even noticed that she'd finished eating.

I nod my head. "At five."

"Okay," she says, then disappears into the kitchen.

Everyone else finishes up one after the other and

follows after her. I can hear the clatter of dishes in the sink, and then they all vanish to various places in the house; Daemon goes to his room, my dad goes out to the garage, and my mom stays in the kitchen to clean up.

Fayre is the only one who stays with me at the table.

"*So,*" she says, drawing the word out. "Is Chase the one taking you to the movies?"

I groan, laying my arm down on the table in front of me before I drop my head against it. "Yes, I'm going with Chase," I answer. "And no, that doesn't make it a date."

"Are you sure it doesn't?" she asks, wiggling her eyebrows at me teasingly. "It sounds awfully suspicious to me."

I definitely should've waited until after dinner to bring up the movies. It would've saved me from this.

"Last I checked, you hang out with guys all the time and don't consider every time a date," I retort, picking up my dishes and taking them into the kitchen. I drop them in the sink and my mom gives me a half-smile. I leave before she gets a chance to say anything about tomorrow, and head to my room.

Fayre is waiting for me when I get there, though. She's got her nose in my closet and is flipping through my clothes, muttering under her breath and frowning a lot while she does.

I roll my eyes before I walk into my room and sit on the bed. "Don't you have enough clothes to pick from?" I grumble, dropping my face in my pillow so that my voice is muffled.

She snorts. "Like I'd ever come to your room for alternate clothing options."

I can hear her flip through three more before she takes one off. The next thing I know, a hanger hits my leg. I sit up, looking at the shirt that's on my bed, and I groan again. "Please don't tell me you're doing what I think you're doing."

"*We're*," she says, emphasizing the heck out of it, "picking out an outfit for you to wear tomorrow."

I glance at the shirt on my bed. It's a black button-up dress shirt, and probably the nicest thing I own. "I haven't worn that in years," I scoff. "I think the last time I put that on, we had a funeral to go to."

"All you've got," she says, chucking a pair of jeans at me. She spins around right as the jeans collide with my face. "Okay, so the jeans and the shirt and… oh."

"That wasn't a good 'oh'," I comment, peeling the jeans off.

She sighs. "Never mind," she tells me. "We'll have to come up with something else. I… forgot about the gloves and jacket."

Something twists in my gut at her words.

When did I start wishing so much to be normal? It never bothered me this much until I realized how hard it is to have something as simple as a friend. But what do I care that my sister can't dress me up like a Barbie doll and love what she sees me leaving the house in?

I've never wanted her to in the past, and I *definitely* don't want her to right now, but it still hurts. It feels like I'm missing some vital part of the experience that is having a sister.

"Here," Fayre says, knocking me out of my trance. She's holding out a plain black T-shirt. "Put this on with the jeans, but tuck it in and leave your jacket unzipped."

I raise an eyebrow at her. "Right now?"

"Right now," she responds.

I sigh, take the shirt and jeans from her, and head into the bathroom to get changed. I strip from the clothes I changed into less than an hour ago before changing into the new ones. When I look at myself in the mirror, I don't look much different from how I usually look. A little more stylish, maybe, but not unlike me and not anywhere near what my sister had seemed to originally be hoping for.

"Well?" I ask, coming out of the bathroom. Even if it's only a slight bit more stylish than usual, I'm not feeling all that comfortable at the thought of wearing this to the movies tomorrow instead of a plain, untucked, wrinkled shirt.

Fayre smiles at me. "You look beautiful," she tells me, and I don't hear anything but how much she means it in her tone of voice.

Chapter Fifteen

Fayre is sitting with me in my room when five o'clock rolls around. She made me wear the jeans with the tucked-in T-shirt because, apparently, there's no way I'm getting out of letting her dress me even though I'm the world's worst model.

Chase texted me a couple minutes ago to let me know he's on the way and I warned him that my parents will want to meet him. He told me he'd come to the door so he could say hi, which is why I'm in my room right now and not waiting on the porch. The easiest way to do this is probably to let either mom or dad get the door, have them call me out, and then I can just leave and not have to do any awkward introductions. I think they're all smart enough to handle that on their own.

The knock comes on the door less than a moment

after the clock on my phone changes to 5:00. I listen to my mom answering the door, saying a polite "hello."

Fayre is smiling so wide next to me that I bet the world's best long-jumper couldn't jump the length of her smile. She's jittery and keeps hopping up and down.

My mom calls my name and I get up. Fayre, who's had herself glued to my side for the past three hours, gets up with me and follows after me as I head to the door.

Chase smiles at me when he sees me and my mom looks like she's doing her best to suppress her nervousness.

"Hey," I say, my expression matching his. I can hear Fayre take in a breath when I smile, and I can almost hear her gushing about it to my mom as soon as I leave. Mistake number one, and counting.

"Hey. You ready?"

"Awkward" could be written on a sign with blinking lights and hung over both of our heads and it would still be less obvious than it is right now.

I nod. "Yup." I turn to my mom. "We'll be home by about eight," I say, then, to both her and my sister, "Bye."

Chase says a polite "goodbye" to both my mom and sister, telling my mom that it was nice to meet her and all that stuff, which she seems to think is absolutely adorable or something, then we both leave.

The door closes behind us and I let out a breath. "I'm sorry about that," I tell him. "They make it like we're going out on a date or something." I blush at the words as soon as they're out of my mouth and have to duck my head and let my bangs fall over my face to hide it.

"It's fine," he says, but something about his tone sounds tight, like even though he's saying it is, it really isn't anywhere near fine. I hope my mom didn't take on what's supposed to be my dad's job and grill him like a freaking steak.

"I'm still sorry."

"Don't be," he says, laughing uncomfortably. "Seriously." He nods in the direction of the driveway, and I notice for the first time that there's a car there and that we apparently aren't walking to the movie theater. "My dad's the one driving us. Get ready for the most uncomfortable car ride *ever*."

"I've had a lot of awkward car rides," I assure him, but even before the words are out, something has wrapped itself around my stomach and squeezed it so tight that I'm starting to wonder if it was a good idea to have eaten lunch.

"I don't know," he says, looking like he doesn't fully believe me. "Every single one of my friends who's ever ridden with him didn't have anything positive to say about the experience." He gives me an apologetic look. "I guess I could've driven now that I've got my license, but I wasn't sure how you or your parents would feel about that so…"

He looks so awkward and uncomfortable that I almost want to laugh.

"You're cute when you're flustered," I tell him, the words slipping out before I can catch them.

Chase laughs. "Is this just a competition to see who can complement the other more?" he asks teasingly as he opens the car door for me.

"Obviously." I roll my eyes at him, a smile tugging at my lips. I stare at the door for a second, unsure what to do, then realize that the only thing I can do is climb into the car, so I do.

"Well, in that case…" He smiles and leans over so his lips are next to my ear. "You're always cute," he whispers. When he stands up, he nods toward his dad and raises his eyebrows as if to tell me that he didn't want his dad to hear it.

I can't help it when I laugh even as my heart races in my chest at a speed that shouldn't be possible and my face turns red.

So, I'm not the only one who refuses to say certain things in front of their family.

"So, you're Thana?" Chase's dad asks me from the front seat as soon as Chase closes the door. He's turned so that he's awkwardly facing me but also not enough for him to be turned around in his seat.

I get a good look at him for the first time and whatever inside of me that had been nervous a minute ago decides that freaking out might be the right course of action. It's not because he's the same guy I saw sitting in the restaurant however long ago, even if I wish I could blame the fact on that, it's because it makes it more real. I heard him and the other man, his brother from what I've put together, talking about the plans for the property. Even though I know it's not his fault at all, it still eats away at me. He's working for the company that's taking the only good thing that's ever happened to me away.

"Yeah," I respond. My throat feels tight and my one-word answer comes out sounding like I'm choking on it. I can't seem to look up and meet his gaze. My eyes stay focused on my gloved hand in my lap as I play with the hem of my shirt.

"You haven't been introduced to many of your friend's parents, have you?" he asks, sounding amused.

I look up at him for a second, then shake my head. He has Chase's smile, but his eyes are blue instead of brown. There are other small features about him that he doesn't share with his son, but I can't put my finger on what exactly all of them are. I look back down before I really have the chance to figure it out, though.

"Don't worry," he assures me. "I'm not as scary as I look."

Scary is the farthest thing from the description I would give him with his messy hair and round glasses, but I'll let him think whatever he wants.

The door on my left opens and Chase slides into the seat beside me before closing it again. He looks at me, then at his dad. "Are you torturing her already?" he groans, throwing his head back for emphasis.

Blindly, he searches for the seatbelt and pulls it over his lap.

I snort a laugh and do the same.

"What else would I be doing?" Chase's dad asks, but he winks at me in the rearview mirror as if the fact that he wasn't tormenting me is some kind of secret between the two of us.

Chase gives me an apologetic look as his dad pulls the car out of the driveway and starts toward the movie theater. It's only a few minutes from our house. It's closer than the school is, and most of the time my siblings walk because of that, which is why I'd assumed we'd be doing the same.

The first thirty seconds of the car ride are an awkward quiet that no one seems to know how to fill. But, before anyone is able to figure out how to get rid of it, Chase's phone goes off. He pulls it out and looks at the screen before silencing it. I have enough time to make out the contact before it disappears from the screen: *Mom.*

I want to ask, but I keep my mouth shut.

"Still ignoring her?" Chase's dad asks from the front seat.

Chase doesn't answer him. Instead, he looks out the window at something that's apparently much more interesting.

I want to ask, but it doesn't seem like it's my place to. I know after what he told me about his sister that his mom isn't dead, but I still don't understand what exactly happened.

"She misses you," his dad says when Chase doesn't answer.

"I don't want to talk about it," Chase snaps at his dad.

It's the first time I've seen him angry at all, and it's not just a bit upset either, this seems a lot deeper than just a mild inconvenience. His hand is clenched into a fist at his side and his knuckles are white. He runs the other hand forcefully through his hair, as though that'll somehow help calm him.

He glances over at me and his cheeks turn red when he does. "I'm sorry," he tells me, as though he just got mad at me and not something I don't even understand. "It's just…" he starts, but whatever his explanation is, it dies on his lips.

"He doesn't like to talk about the divorce," his dad finishes. "Or his mother, or his sister."

My eyes widen at the word "divorce." Of course that's a thing that happens, but I hadn't even considered it a possibility. It makes a lot more sense than them being dead like I'd originally thought they might be.

"It's hard enough without it being brought up all the time," Chase snaps at him. It's a jab, which tells me that Chase not wanting to talk about it probably makes his dad more desperate to get him to. I know because my family does the same thing to me a lot.

His dad doesn't say anything else, just gets back to looking at the road.

Chase lets out a breath and slumps against his seat, looking like that conversation was enough to exhaust him for the rest of the day. He closes his eyes and takes in a breath before letting it out slowly.

It only takes another minute or so for us to get to the movie theater, but it feels like an eternity. The silence is overwhelming in a way that makes it impossible to sit still and not feel like you're doing something wrong. It claws at your insides until you're coming up with random things to say that make no sense to anyone but you, and then you have to stop yourself from saying them out loud so that you don't embarrass yourself.

Instead of parking the car, Chase's dad takes us to the front of the theater and stops for a second to give us time to get out.

"I'll be across the street," he tells us, pointing toward the same fast-food restaurant that my mom took me to after I broke my shoulder. "I'll pick you two up at about seven forty-five or so."

"Cool," Chase says as the two of us open our doors and climb out.

"Thank you for the ride," I say, and his dad smiles at me in the rearview mirror. I manage to force my own smile before I close the door behind myself.

The evening sun is bright and blinding as it reflects off of the white parking lot. I shield my eyes and walk around the back of the car to where Chase is still standing, talking to his dad through the open car window.

He stands up when he sees me come around, says bye to his dad, and the car drives off, leaving us alone in front of the large building.

"C'mon," he says to me, putting on his own fake smile. He seems to think he's fooling me with it, but I can see right through his attempt to look happy.

We walk into the building and go over to the ticket booth thing where a woman sits behind a computer. There are four electronic signs over our heads, flashing the names of different movies I've never heard of.

I pull my wallet from my pocket as Chase tells the woman what we're here to see. I can't hear what he says, but I can hear her tell him that the cost is $18.47.

I nudge his shoulder and hand him a five and four ones.

Instead of taking it like I expect him to though, he gives me a confused look and pushes my hand away before handing the woman a twenty.

Something about the gesture makes another knot form in my stomach. I have no idea what I'm supposed to say after that, but he's quick to kill my moment of discomfort.

He bumps my shoulder with his teasingly. "You can buy the snacks," he says, winking at me.

I roll my eyes. "I could've sworn that I hate popcorn," I tease as the woman hands him two slips of paper and his change.

"It'll be in theater three," she informs us, then gestures for the people behind us to step forward.

Chase grabs my arm and pulls me out of the way before I can realize what's happening. It takes me a minute to realize he's not still standing next to me. I jog to catch up with him and match my stride to his. "Popcorn isn't the only thing they have here," he says. "And I don't know of a single person who doesn't have a weakness for chocolate."

I snort a laugh. "And what if I'm one of those weirdos?" I challenge.

"Then I will turn you to the dark side." He wiggles his eyebrows at me and I laugh.

He leads me over to the snack bar, which has enough junk food on it to supply even a teenager for a minimum of a year. I think I just found my personal version of heaven.

Chase grabs a couple of bags of M&Ms for the both of us, then leads the way to theater 3, which is on the left side of the building and around a few turns. Judging by how fast Chase spots it, I would've thought he'd been here a million times. But that isn't possible because he only moved here a little while ago.

We find our seats up in one of the top rows. The theater is empty except for a mother and her daughter, which I find kind of odd considering it's a Saturday evening.

"I have one very big problem with M&Ms," I confess as I open up the bag. My voice is barely above a whisper because the room is so quiet and something tells me I shouldn't kill the silence.

He looks over at me with a worried expression, like he thinks he might've missed somewhere in there that I'm actually allergic to chocolate.

"I only like the brown ones," I explain, which makes him laugh. "I'm serious! I can't eat chocolate that looks like it's actually strawberry flavored." I pull out a red one and make a face at it.

Chase takes it from me and pops it in his mouth. "Problem solved," he tells me.

"There's a lot more 'problems' where that one came from." I pour a few into my hand and show them to him. "See? This weird multicolored chocolate is evil."

He shakes his head at me. "If you say so."

"You don't by chance think you can eat almost two bags worth, do you?" I ask, nodding at the M&Ms in my hand.

"Is that a challenge?"

"If it means you'll eat the weird ones."

He laughs, taking the M&Ms I'm holding out of my hand.

I pour another few into my hand and sort out the brown ones as the lights dim all around the large room and the movie starts.

I groan when I hear the music start. "You brought me to the theater to see Frozen?"

Of all the movies he could bring me to see. It's not that I don't like this one, it's that I've heard too much about it and heard Fayre singing Let It Go too many times.

"*Maybe*," he answers, drawing out the word.

I shake my head, smiling.

As the movie plays, I sort out the M&Ms, eating one every now and then and handing the rest of them to Chase. I'm halfway through the bag and the movie is about five minutes in when I hear him let out a breath beside me.

"I'm sorry about the car ride," he says, giving me a sheepish look. "And that I haven't told you about the whole, divorce thing. I don't like to talk about it."

A sad smile forms on his face as I look at him. There's an amount of sadness in his eyes, but it's not as bad as it was earlier. He still looks upset, but nowhere near as upset as he did in the car. I pour the remaining M&Ms I have in my hand back into the bag before I reach over and grab his hand, lacing my fingers through his.

He looks down at our hands, then back up at me. His smile is more genuine this time, but the sadness in it isn't gone. I don't know what I should say, but I don't get the feeling I need to say anything at all.

"Thank you for bringing me," I say, as the sisters sing contradicting lyrics to a song in the background.

Chase meets my eyes for a second and smiles, squeezing my hand gently.

"*Make one wrong move and everyone will know.*"

I smile back.

Chapter Sixteen

I lie in bed, staring blankly at the ceiling above. Fayre and Daemon are in the living room, doing their usual Sunday evening thing of binge-watching some dumb show. They've gone through so many different shows in the past couple of years that I've completely lost track of what they're working on getting through now.

Chase and I didn't meet up at the abandoned property for the first time today because he had some stuff going on with his dad, but we've been texting pretty much since the sun was above the horizon. He said Sundays are usually a day his dad sets aside for "father-son bonding time," or in other words, a day when they go out to an arcade or bowling alley or whatever they feel like and don't come back until mid-afternoon.

We've spent most of the day talking about strategies for how he can beat his dad at certain video games. They didn't help him all that much when they got to Pac Man, though.

I haven't bothered to go to the abandoned property today, but mostly because it's been raining off and on and I've spent a decent amount of time watching random shows with my siblings. I talked to mom earlier for a bit about the shopping list for her trip to the store tomorrow, but nothing really exciting came up in that conversation. Unless you want to count my mom going on a tangent about how much they charge for squash. That was pretty entertaining, if nothing else.

Even with mom's complaining about the price of squash, I haven't been able to get yesterday out of my mind. Chase hadn't let go of my hand the whole time the movie had been playing, and I hadn't made a single move to pull away either. I liked the warmth of his hand and the feeling of his fingers intertwined with mine. But it also bothered me in a way I couldn't place. I shouldn't like the feel of his touch. I shouldn't *want* to touch him at all, regardless of the fact that I was wearing my gloves. It's too dangerous for me to get used to something like that, but even more so for me to *like* it.

A loud rock song blasts on my earbuds, and I do my best to lose myself in it. Maybe if I can focus on my music, I can forget about the Chase thing for a bit. I know it's a worthless attempt, but it's the last idea I have to distract myself from the world.

The world doesn't seem to want that for me, though.

A tapping sound starts on my bedroom window and I bolt up in bed, sucking in a breath through clenched teeth at the pain it causes in my shoulder. It stops a second later, and my best guess is that my dad is outside mowing the lawn or something and something hit the window.

Slowly, I lie back down, turning up my music even more to block out the world.

The tapping starts up again a second later, and, despite the fact that my music is louder now, I can still hear it just as clearly.

"The heck?" I mutter, squinting at the black curtains, as though staring at them long enough will make them become invisible and show me what's disturbing my peace.

After a moment, I give up and climb to my feet. I make my way over to the window and pull the curtains open.

I yelp and take a step back, the curtains falling back into place. It takes me less than a second to step back up to the window and pull the curtain out of the way again. I pull open the window. "What are you doing here?" I snap, as I step out of the way and Chase climbs in.

"Your dad sent me around when you didn't respond to him yelling for you," he answers, looking amused.

I pull on the earbud cords and they fall from my ears

and into my hand. I can still hear the music playing. I pull my phone out and turn it off before putting my phone and earbuds in the pocket of my jacket. "There's a door," I say, pointing at it.

He shrugs. "The window sounded more entertaining."

"Jerk," I mumble beneath my breath as I plop myself back down on my bed like I'd been a moment ago. "So… what're you doing here? I thought you were out with your dad?"

"I'm here to kidnap you," he answers, matter-of-factly.

"I don't think kidnappers stop at the door," I point out, but it's hard to keep my face completely straight.

"Kidnappers stop at the door when they need parental consent."

I raise an eyebrow at him. "Parental consent to do what? Disturb my peace?"

"As I said," he pulls a ring of keys from his pocket and tosses them in the air before he catches them in his other hand, causing the keys to jingle against each other, "I'm kidnapping you."

The car ride isn't long, but Chase makes me keep my eyes closed, anyway. Within the first five minutes, I already feel like my dinner is going to make a second appearance. I've never actually thrown up from being car sick, though, so I suck it up and deal with it.

I can feel every movement the car makes beneath me. Every time Chase brakes, makes a turn, changes lanes, or does anything, it feels like a fist gripping my stomach and squeezing just the tiniest bit harder which gets me just the tiniest bit closer to throwing up all over the dash.

"Are we almost there?" I groan, leaning my head back against the seat. "I don't know how much more of this I can take."

Everything inside of me screams at me to open my eyes, but I push the urge away and keep them closed. I don't know where he's taking me, and he doesn't seem to want to tell me for fear of "ruining the surprise" or whatever, but I seriously doubt anything he could be surprising me with could be worth this.

"Almost there," Chase assures me. "Just another couple turns and then you can open your eyes."

A couple more turns takes longer than I want it to, but I don't complain again. As soon as he parks the car, though, my eyes fly open like I just woke up from the worst nightmare I've ever had.

My eyes widen at the sight in front of me. I've seen this place plenty of times before, but I'd be lying if I said I ever gave it more than just a passing glance. It's not the real thing, and it's never meant anything to me because of that, but Chase remembered. He remembered what is probably the dumbest thing I've ever told him.

When they started remodeling this area and making it fancier, they added a giant manmade lake. There's a trail that goes around it, but in one section, there's a small patch of sand at the water's edge that's been made to look like a beach. It's tiny, and it's cheesy with its rainbow beach umbrellas. It's never appealed to me until now.

I turn to Chase, dumbfounded for a reason I can't even explain.

"Surprise," he says, smiling at me with something I can't place twinkling in his eyes. It reminds me vaguely of amusement, but I know it's not. "It's nowhere near the real thing, but it's the best I can do on short notice. It's also blue, even if that's just from the dye."

"My favorite color," I whisper, but I don't know if I'm saying it to him or to the air in front of me.

I feel strange; like I'm watching my life play out through someone else's eyes. It feels more like I'm watching a movie than sitting right here myself. I don't even understand my own emotions fully. I feel them, but they don't feel like mine, and I don't even know what they mean.

"You okay?" Chase asks, and I realize I've been quiet for longer than I probably should've been.

"I just…" I shake my head, clearing the foggy feeling. My face feels hot and I can't seem to look up to meet his gaze. "You didn't have to do this." My voice sounds strained; like I'm about to cry or something even though crying is probably the last thing I could do right now.

He shrugs. "But I wanted to, and I did."

I watch him as he pushes open the car door and gets out. I'm not sure what to say to that, or if there even is anything I could say to it. He gives me a look, as if to ask if I'm coming or not, then shuts the door.

Slowly, I push open the door and get out, too. Every movement feels stiff, like my joints have rusted in the time I was sitting in the car, and now that I'm out, they have no clue what their job is anymore.

I close the door and take a few tentative steps forward so that I'm standing in the sand. It feels strange to walk on it, like I'm sinking deeper and deeper with every step, even though I know I'm not. My first few steps in the sand are wobbly; like I just learned how to walk this morning.

Chase laughs from somewhere not far off when I almost lose my balance and end up bent over forward with my arm out to the side to keep myself from landing face-first in the sand.

I glare at him. "It feels weird," I snap, as though that's a good enough excuse for why I look so pathetic.

"You're cute when you're frustrated," he says, amusement glimmering in his eyes.

I roll my eyes. "I'm not frustrated," I argue. "I'm determined to figure this out." I take a couple more steps, this time without tripping over my own feet and without losing my balance. "And also mildly irritated," I add. "But that's not the same as frustrated."

Chase snorts a laugh as he comes over to where I am. "It's close enough to the same thing, but I'll let you have that one for now." He puts an arm around me, careful to avoid hitting my left shoulder when he does, and leads me away from the umbrellas to an open area by the water's edge.

I want to shove him off and tell him I don't need his help to walk, but the stupid part of me that likes his closeness butts in and makes me realize that I don't want to shove him away at all. If anything, I want him to stay there and never step away.

I match my steps to his, watching each of my footfalls for no apparent reason. I can feel when my ankles get close to giving out and making me stumble, and I don't need to watch my steps for that, but I'd much rather watch and not have to look up at Chase. Even though he's seen me blush plenty of times before, I'd rather hide it as much as I can.

The only thing I wish I knew is why exactly I'm blushing. I have no good reason to be.

"Look up," Chase whispers, leaning closer to me when he does.

I do, and as soon as my eyes land on the sight, a smile forms on my lips. I never thought something manmade could be so pretty.

The shopping center is lit up with strings of lights that are strung between buildings and hanging over the open space where a small park-like area is set up and a bunch of kids are running around, chasing each other. The reflection of the lights glistens off of the water's surface like stars in a clear night sky.

I move away from Chase and kneel at the water's edge. I run my hand through the water, my glove making ripples that spread out the farther they go and smear the perfect picture that had been reflecting off of the surface a moment ago.

I can hear Chase sit down beside me, but I don't look up. I keep my eyes trained on the water. In the dark, I can't see the blue dye like I can in the daylight. It looks almost black.

"This is beautiful," I breathe, looking up at the shopping center again. One of the kids laughs as she tags another girl she'd been chasing. They both turn around and their game starts over again, but the girl who had been chasing the other last time is now the one running away.

"Every bit," Chase agrees.

I glance over at him, and he's looking at me. My cheeks heat up, but I smile teasingly at him and push down the nerves I feel in my stomach. "Everything right down to that mess of hair on your head," I tease.

He rolls his eyes at me. "It's not that-"

Before he can finish, I move over so I'm right next to him and ruffle his hair until it's a tousled, tangled mess.

A laugh escapes me and Chase just sits there with an expression that's both amused and looks like he thinks he should've seen that coming and couldn't understand why he hadn't on his face.

"Mhm, and you say I'm the jerk."

My laughing dies down a second later, and I'm able to answer. "You are, but I never said I wasn't one, too." I try to give him a teasing smile, but, instead, I find myself smiling because of genuine happiness and not just to spite him.

I look up and meet his eyes, and for the first time, I realize just how close he is. His face is only a few inches from mine.

I suck in a breath and sit back. I could kill him. I can't be that close to him. I can *never* be that close to him. I shouldn't even be here with him at all if I want to keep him safe. I shouldn't be near him *ever* if I don't want something bad to happen to him.

But the thoughts ebb away the longer I sit there, chewing on my bottom lip and awkwardly staring at the sand on the ground between us.

I want to be close to him, and the part of me that wants that is what wins out again, even when I fight it. I move closer to him again and lay my head on his shoulder. Less than a moment passes before he puts his arm around me and pulls me closer. It feels normal somehow; like this is just how things are supposed to be.

"Thank you," I say. "For bringing me here."

Chase rests his cheek on top of my head. "I'm glad you like it," he says.

I don't know how long we stay like that. It feels like a few seconds at the same time that it feels like hours. The moment is like something from a movie. It's peaceful and perfect and dumb in a way that makes me love it more.

But there's a small part of me that wants so badly to kill it. Not even because I know I shouldn't be here, but because I want to ask him something that I know won't sit well with him.

"Can I ask you something?" I ask, sitting up so I can look at him. My voice is hardly above a whisper, but I know he heard me.

"What's up?" There's something nervous in his tone; like he knows exactly where I'm going with this.

"What… happened? With your parents? And your sister?" I keep my eyes trained on his when I ask, watching for the tiniest bit of a flinch, or any sign of frustration or anger, but nothing comes. He's not mad at me for asking, he just looks sad.

Chase lets out a breath, looking away from me, and runs a hand through his hair, as though that will help him somehow get his thoughts together. He doesn't look back up at me when he talks. "Nothing…" His voice is tight, and it's clear that he's not trying to avoid the topic when he says it. That's his actual answer. "They didn't fight. Neither of them cheated on the other. It was literally nothing. They just… somehow quietly agreed that they didn't love each other anymore and that splitting up would be the better thing to do.

"We hardly saw my dad as it was. This is the first job out of state, but he's been doing jobs in other cities for the past few years. The company would pay for him to stay at a hotel for a few months. We'd see him every other Sunday and every now and then we'd call him or whatever, but that was really it. I guess… I guess they just got used to the idea of being without each other."

I watch him, unsure what I'm supposed to say or if I should say anything at all. He doesn't seem to not want to talk about it, considering how much of an answer I just got from him, but I don't know how much I can ask before it's prying.

I bite my lip. "What about your sister? You said you haven't talked to her in a long time."

Chase takes in a breath and lets it out. "It's just…" He runs his hands through his hair again. "The paperwork and everything took a while to go through, and my parents were trying to figure out what they were going to do with us. Before they filed for the divorce, I'd started going with my dad every now and then. I liked to see what he was doing and I liked to be able to spend more time with him. I called home every night, but Viv always seemed to feel like I was choosing dad over them, even though she never outright said it.

"When I asked if my main address could be with my dad and I found out that she wanted to stay mainly with our mom, it kind of… broke our relationship in a way. And, since our parents made it happen, and since now I basically always stay with our dad and she's basically always with our mom, it's kind of taken away any reason for us to really talk."

"Damn…" I mutter, not knowing what else to say.

"I think it's pretty dumb now, and she's probably come around to think so too, but... I don't even know what I would say to her. I want to talk to her so badly, just to hear her voice, and tell her how much I miss her, but..."

I can see the start of tears in his eyes, and when he sees me looking, he wipes them away with the backs of his hands. When he sets his hands back down, I grab his left one in mine and lace my fingers through his, giving a gentle squeeze. "But what?" I ask, unable to help it when I do. I should keep my mouth shut and not butt into something that isn't my business, but I can't seem to help but ask.

He sighs, holding tight to my hand like it's a lifeline of some kind and he doesn't ever want to let it go. "Just... what would I even say?"

A smile forms in the corners of my lips. "Chase?"

He looks up at me. "Hmm?"

"Don't take this the wrong way, because I'm not trying to be a jerk, but pull out your phone, dial her number, hit the call button, and wait for her to answer. And, when she answers, the first thing you do is say whatever comes out of your mouth."

He smiles back at me and shakes his head, like the idea is amusing but not something actually possible. He sighs. "It just feels really hard," he explains.

I wish I could tell him that I know exactly how that feels. I wish I could tell him that every moment of my life feels really hard, but that even when things are hard, sometimes you have to do them anyway. A couple weeks ago, I never would've thought I'd ever sit on a fake beach in the middle of the city with a boy who means more to me than he ever should.

I want to tell him all of this, but I press my lips together and keep my mouth shut.

I squeeze his hand again. "That just makes the end result even more worth it."

Chase stares straight ahead for a second, and I start to think that he didn't even hear me, but then he nods. "Alright."

I frown at him. "'Alright' what?"

He pulls his phone from his pocket. "I'm gonna call her."

A smile forms on my face as he puts in the passcode, then dials her number and hits the call button. I watch him as he lifts the phone to his ear and waits. I hear a chime on the other end, and then some muffled words being said, which I can only guess is his sister answering.

A moment later, though, he sighs and pulls the phone away from his ear. "I got an answering machine, but it wasn't even for her. She must've gotten a new number since the last time I called her."

He sounds so defeated when he says it; like he's too late to fix things with her now that he knows she has a new number. It makes me even more desperate to come up with something that'll fix this.

My eyes snap up when the realization hits me. I feel

dumb for not having thought of it sooner. "Your dad," I say, and he looks over at me with a confused expression on his face. "Your dad will probably have her number."

Chase nods. "He should. He calls her a decent amount and I doubt he goes through my mom to do it. I'll ask him about it when I get home. I seriously doubt he'll answer his phone at this hour."

Without giving it a second thought, I climb to my feet. He's giving me a confused look when I meet his gaze, but I just roll my eyes at him and stick out my hand to help him up. "C'mon," I say. "I know how fear works." I smile at him teasingly, knowing he gets exactly what I mean.

He takes my hand and climbs up to his feet. "So, you think I'm going to chicken out, do you?" he challenges as we walk back over to the car.

"I think most normal people do," I say, giving him a look like I think he's a moron for implying that he won't.

"And something about me makes you think I'm normal?" He raises an eyebrow at me, but there's a smile on his face.

"You're here with me," I say, by way of answer. "Nothing about you is normal."

He rolls his eyes at me, chuckling softly. He swings our hands back and forth. "Then I like not being normal," he tells me. I can't place what I see in his eyes when he smiles at me.

He holds my hand until we get back to the car.

Chapter Seventeen

The car ride is quiet, but it's not uncomfortable. I can tell Chase is thinking about what he'll say to his sister when he calls her.

I'm honestly amazed he even wants to do it. I'd meant it literally when I said he should call her, but I'd thought he'd take it as a joke and maybe think it over tonight or something, and maybe in a few weeks he'd decide that he wanted to. I didn't think he would want to do it right away. But, then again, I can only know what I would do in the situation, and I'm not him.

I watch out the window as he drives. It's been a long time since I've gone anywhere but to school and back in a car. And that's not even at night. I know exactly where we are, and I recognize the area well enough because of how much I used to like going places with my mom, but, in the past few years, that's changed, and I forgot how pretty it is to be out at night.

The lights on buildings illuminate everything in a soft orangish glow, and the stars sparkle in the dark sky above.

"I'll be quick when we get there, I promise," Chase says, which snaps me out of my trance. There's a red tint on his cheeks. "I didn't mean to cut short your first time seeing a fake beach." He smiles at me teasingly, but there's something in his eyes that tells me he's being more serious than not.

I snort a laugh. "I'm the one who brought it up in the first place," I retort.

He shrugs, glancing at me before he turns back to the road again. "We can go back if you want. We're already most of the way to the house, but I can grab her number from my dad and we can go back. I don't have to call her tonight. And the whole purpose of me kidnapping you wasn't for you to sit there, bored out of your mind while-"

"Sure," I interrupt, before he can ramble on any more about it. "And stop feeling guilty about it." I smack his arm with the back of my hand, biting my lip to keep the smile that wants to form on my lips off of my face.

"Is it really the best idea to abuse the driver?" Chase asks, smirking at me playfully.

I groan. "*Fine.* I guess I can wait until we get there."

It only takes a couple more minutes to get to

Chase's house. They're renting the house a few down from mine, and I'm surprised that I hadn't even noticed the fact that the house is no longer empty. I've walked by it each day on the way to the abandoned property and back, yet, somehow, I've been oblivious. I noticed when the "for rent" sign had been put up in the yard a few months ago, but apparently when it came down wasn't as important.

The house is grey with white trim around the windows. The driveway leads up to the doors of a closed garage, and, near the top of the driveway, a stone path leads to the front porch. The porch is small and closed in on three sides. One of the sides is a raised flowerbed with nothing in it but dirt and a paint can, and the other two are blocked by the door and the side of the house. The porchlight blinks creepily every couple of seconds.

It's not a perfect place by any means, but it seems weirdly peaceful.

Chase parks the car, takes the key out of the ignition, and turns off the headlights so fast that it looks more like one fluid motion. He pockets the keys before he turns to me. "I don't know exactly how long this is gonna take because my dad might already be in bed. You wanna come in?"

There are no lights on inside, so I take it that he's probably right.

I shrug. "Sure, I guess," I say, even as my head screams at me to do anything but. I can't help but feel like something bad is going to happen if I go in, but what bad could possibly come from it? They have a pet cat that Chase hasn't mentioned who decides to play with my shoelaces? I've got my hood up, I've got my gloves on, and I'm not going to touch anything or let anything anywhere close to me.

It'll be fine.

I follow Chase up to the front door and watch as he puts the key in the lock. Once he's got it unlocked, he turns the knob and opens the door, and when he does, the porchlight decides it wants to go out.

I flinch at the sudden darkness, even though I can still see.

"Stupid thing," Chase mutters.

I watch as the silhouette of his arm reaches up before he knocks on the wall beneath the light. Whatever he hits, it makes the porchlight happy because it turns right back on.

"Sorry about that," he says to me, once the light is back on. "It's been like this since we moved in, but my dad hasn't figured out what the actual problem is yet, so…" He glares at the light instead of finishing his sentence.

I snort a laugh. "Sounds like fun."

He gives me a look. "Mhm, yeah. That's *definitely* how I'd explain it."

Chase opens the door again and flips on a light that makes the whole entry room visible before he walks in. I follow after him, and my eyes widen when I get inside.

It smells like paint, but not super strong; like maybe that can in the empty flower bed has been sitting there for a few days. There's a walkway that leads back into a kitchen, and to my left is a bright, open living room with a carpeted floor. There's a couch that could easily seat six that's facing a television on the wall, and there's a dining room table to the right of it where the carpet turns to tile again. There aren't any pictures hanging on the walls or anything, though there's a lot of open space where there could be. But, even despite the fact, somehow it has a homey feel to it. It's comforting and somehow pretty at the same time.

"Wow," I breathe, taken aback by it for some reason.

Chase wrinkles his nose. "Yeah, the paint smell is terrible."

I laugh. "That's not what I meant. I meant, wow as in, it's nice in here." I gesture at the living room to make my point, but it's awkward because I have to do it with my right arm.

"I suppose it's not that bad," he says, shrugging a shoulder. "My dad did the decorating, and he says he's not quite done yet, but I get the feeling it's just going to go downhill from here. I seriously doubt I get my lack of decorating skills from my mom. She specializes in interior design."

I snort a laugh. Maybe it was going to go downhill, but, for now at least, it definitely didn't look bad by any means in here.

He gestures at the hallway that leads off to the right up ahead. "I'm gonna go find my dad. He's probably in his room either working or sleeping. I'll be right back." He turns to leave, but only gets a few steps before he stops and turns back around. "And you can sit down or whatever if you want. You don't have to stand in the doorway the whole time, I promise." He gives me a teasing smile before he leaves.

Despite the fact that he told me I can go sit down, I stand in the doorway and watch him leave. Once he's gone, though, I can feel the discomfort settle itself over me like a weighted blanket slung over my shoulders. It's a crushing feeling and makes me wish I could crumple myself up into a ball on the floor and not come off as completely insane when Chase comes back if I did.

It doesn't take long for standing in one place to feel like the most awkward thing I could be doing right now.

Letting out a breath, I take a few tentative steps forward, making sure the floor won't fall out from beneath me or anything before I shift my weight fully onto my lead foot. When I've taken a few steps and a sinkhole doesn't appear out of thin air, I decide that going over to the table and sitting down might be the least uncomfortable thing to do.

I can hear Chase knock on a door down the hall, but I can't see him even when I sit down at the table. I take it his dad answers the door, because I hear voices talking but can't make out what exactly they're saying.

I wring my hands in my lap awkwardly as I study the contents of the table. There's a manila folder placed in front of the chair across from me. It has no form of identification except for a circular orange sticker. Beside it, there's a closed laptop that's plugged into the wall on my left. The cord is suspended in midair about a foot off of the ground. A phone is sitting face down on top of the computer.

It's all so neatly organized, like the folder and the laptop never move from this table, so they have to be nicely placed to compensate for not belonging on a shelf.

"Ah! Person," a voice says from somewhere in front of me and my attention snaps up. Chase's dad is standing in the hallway entrance looking like he just saw a ghost. He leans his arm against the doorframe and then puts his forehead against his arm, letting out a breath. "Geez, you gave me a heart attack."

Chase is standing a few feet behind him and I can see when he rolls his eyes at his dad's reaction.

When I turn my attention back to Chase's dad, I realize for the first time that he's not wearing normal clothes. He's wearing a plain white T-shirt that looks like he's worn it a lot over at least a couple of years, a pair of fluffy pajama pants with smiley faces on them, and fluffy blue slippers that look suspiciously like Cookie Monster from Sesame Street with googly eyes that rattle slightly with each step he takes.

I have to bite my tongue and look away to suppress a laugh.

"Chase, you couldn't have warned me that we had company before I came out and ruined any chance I ever had at making your friend think I'm actually an adult?" He doesn't sound mad; he sounds genuinely curious.

I almost choke on my own laughter, but manage to cover it up with a cough.

Both Chase and his dad are watching me with amused expressions. I can feel my face heat up about a thousand degrees.

"Nah," Chase says. "Where would be the fun in that?" He's watching me with a look I can't place. The amusement is still there, but there's a glimmer in his eyes, too. It's the same one I see sometimes, but I still haven't figured out what it means.

Chase's dad looks between the two of us. "Ah," he says, as if Chase's answer was the most obvious thing in the world. He comes over to the table and grabs the phone off of the laptop before he tosses it to Chase, who catches it clumsily. "You can copy the number, or you can just call her from there. Either way."

"Well, we were gonna head back out, so I'll snag the number and I'll call her in the morning," Chase tells him as he unlocks his dad's phone and taps it a few times, pulling out his own phone in the process.

His dad looks absolutely confused by what his son just said, but I honestly can't blame him that much. I'd be completely confused, too.

"*Okay...?*" his dad says, but it sounds a lot more like a question than anything else.

I stand up, pushing the chair back when I do. It scrapes across the floor loudly and I cringe. "Call her now," I say. "I live just a couple houses down. I can walk-"

"No, it's not that big of a deal. And you said you wanted to go back," Chase argues.

"But I want you to call her as soon as you can because you want to talk to her. It's already getting late, and if we go back, it'll probably be too late to call her then."

"But-"

"I have a solution," Chase's dad interrupts, holding up a finger with a triumphant grin on his face. "Chase, call her, tell her whatever you need to, and set a time to call her tomorrow so you two can talk more. Make it brief, and the two of you can go back out on your date or whatever. Sound like a plan?" He looks between the two of us, but I keep my head down.

My face is hot and I don't want either of them to see me blushing for a second time already.

"I guess…" Chase says, but he sounds very unsure of his answer.

I nod, making sure my head stays low enough that they can't see my face clearly. "Sounds good to me."

Chase sighs. "Alright, I'll be right back." He turns to his dad. "Don't scare her."

His dad gestures down at his pants. "In my smiley face jammies?" he asks. "Even *I'm* not that good."

Chase gives him a look before he disappears down

the hallway. I hear the door to a bedroom close, and that's when I realize that conversation is something I'll probably have to do.

"Geez it's late," Chase's dad says, and walks off in the direction of the kitchen. "I need coffee if he's gonna make me be awake at this ungodly hour. You want any? We've also got tea and water if you're not a fan of coffee."

It's only 9:00, but I'm also not the person you talk about when you talk about getting to bed early. "No, thank you," I answer, sitting back down at the table. "I'm not really thirsty."

"Alrighty."

It feels like less than a minute before he's back, holding a steaming mug of coffee that he sips every now and then. He sits down at the table across from me, moving his laptop and setting it down on top of his folder to make room for his mug.

"Thank you," he says after a moment.

I stare at him like he's got three heads. What's he thanking me for? I didn't come over and cut his lawn or anything. "Um…" I say, because conversations are definitely my talent in life.

He smiles at me over the rim of his mug. He pulls it away from his lips and sets it down again. "I haven't seen Chase happy since before the divorce. He used to avoid being home a lot, and when he got home, I wouldn't see him because he'd hide in his room. He still isn't home a lot, but I take it he's with you because, when he does come home, he's singing dumb love songs under his breath like he used to. And a couple days ago, I heard him playing his guitar again." He smiles, but his eyes aren't focused on me or on anything in particular. "He hasn't played that thing in years." He shakes his head, but the wistful smile is still on his face.

I purse my lips and look away and down at my hand in my lap. "He didn't tell me about that," I confess. "I caught him playing it a couple days ago, but he didn't tell me he hasn't played in a while. He sounded so good, I thought he'd just avoided telling me he likes to play because of his whole thing with cheesy love songs."

Chase's dad laughs. "He does have a thing for those, doesn't he?"

I nod, not sure what else to say. My mind has drawn a blank on conversation topics. I could say something about how much I like the room, or I could be offensive and tell him how bad of a headache the paint smell has started to give me, but I can't seem to make any words form on my tongue.

"Are you sure I can't get you a drink or anything?" He looks like he feels as awkward as I do, but like he's trying to play it off as though he's completely comfortable.

I shake my head, but it's probably too quick and forceful when I do. I hope I haven't given him a good reason to be suspicious of me. "No. I-I'm really okay," I stutter. "Thank you, though."

He frowns at my response, but the expression quickly fades. He studies my face for a second, then something flickers across his expression that looks like recognition.

Alarms start to blare in my head, but I force myself to ignore them and act normal.

"You're the girl I saw at that restaurant a while ago," he says, nodding to himself like he's pleased that he made the connection. He looks back up at me. "What in the world happened to that hamburger you were eating?" He laughs like it's a joke and he didn't just make every hair on my arms raise in panic while adrenaline decided to surge through me like a dam just broke.

I laugh too, but it sounds forced, even to me. "They must've burnt it or something," I answer, rolling my eyes like I can't believe they would do such a thing. "I asked for them to toast the hamburger buns, but they seemed to char them instead because it came out all grey looking." The lie rolls off my tongue as well as every other lie I've had to tell to hide my secret.

He doesn't even look suspicious when he shakes his head in astonishment. He takes what I said like there's no other possibility. But, to him, there probably isn't. Of all the things most people have seen, a girl who can turn things grey with her touch is most likely not one of them.

Chase comes back just then, and I couldn't have asked for better timing. Everything in me eases at the sight of him coming back and the fact that I can get out of this conversation without feeling completely awkward.

He comes over to the table and hands his dad his phone. "I'm gonna call her again tomorrow at about seven," he informs him, then turns to look at me. "You ready to go?"

I nod and stand up, hoping it's not too obvious that I'm in serious need of a getaway.

Chase's dad stands up, too.

"Well," he says, looking at me. "It was nice talking to you, Thana." He smiles at the both of us. "You two enjoy the rest of your evening, and I'm going to do what old people do and sleep."

I bite back a laugh. "It was nice talking to you, too," I manage. "And I love your taste in pajamas."

Chase's dad squints his eyes at me like he's trying to figure me out. After a moment, he nods his head. "I like this one," he says to Chase, then leaves us alone and heads down the hallway.

Chase rolls his eyes. "Sorry," he tells me. "My dad is weird."

I laugh. "C'mon," I say, grabbing his hand and pulling him toward the door. "Am I allowed to ask how the call went?"

He nods. "It was fine. I told her I miss her. She said she misses me, too. We completely ignored the whole 'I'm mad at you for staying with this parent instead of this one' thing, and it was totally fine. I don't know if we'll talk about that tomorrow, but I don't get the feeling we need to really, and I'm fine with that." He glances over at me and smiles. "Thank you."

It's the second time someone has said that to me in the past hour, and I have no idea what to do with it.

"I'm glad it worked out," I tell him, and I can feel a smile form on my face.

I give his hand a gentle squeeze before letting go so we can get into the car.

Chapter Eighteen

"Thank you for kidnapping me," I say, giving Chase a teasing smile when I do.

He's standing outside my bedroom window, his elbows resting on the ledge, and I'm sitting on the floor in my room with my knees pulled to my chest. It's a little after midnight, but my parents know I'm home and that he's still here, and I haven't gotten in trouble yet. We got back about half an hour ago, but we've been talking since. I don't want my parents to get around to being upset, though, and I really do need to get some sleep before school tomorrow.

"I'm glad you had fun," he says, glancing in the direction of the driveway. "I should probably get going. I'm not technically supposed to be driving after midnight until I'm eighteen, even if it's just down the street." He winks at me teasingly.

I can't help it when I laugh. "That's not a good thing at all," I point out.

Chase smiles at me, then shrugs. "Well, I mean, it's not like I'll even be driving past anyone, so I think it'll be fine." He climbs to his feet and I follow a second later. The process of me climbing to my feet versus him is a lot slower in my current one-armed state of being.

"Thank you again for convincing me that calling Viv was a good idea." He grins at me, looking amused like he thinks it's funny that it took me asking about it for him to think it would be a good idea to talk to her.

"I'm glad it worked out," I tell him, my smile matching his. "I'll see you tomorrow."

"See ya," he says, and walks off in the direction of the driveway.

I watch him go for a second before I close the window and pull the curtains shut. I can feel the smile on my face even before I throw myself back on my bed, my body sinking into the mattress.

The night replays in my head like a movie on triple speed, pausing momentarily at moments that make my stomach feel tight at the same time that they make me smile. Everything is so vivid and clear, like I'm still there, even though I know I'm not and that, even if I want to, I can't actually relive any of it.

We'd gone back to the fake beach, and we'd sat out there until they'd turned the lights in the shopping center off and left us in the dark with only the moon and stars for light. We'd spent maybe an hour or so finding patterns in the stars before he'd brought me home.

Everything my mind chooses to linger on couldn't be anything less than perfect, but then I start thinking about my conversation with Chase's dad.

It felt like a riddle I couldn't quite grasp the meaning of. What had he meant when he'd thanked me? He'd said that since Chase and I have become friends, Chase has been happier, but that could easily have nothing to do with me.

And the guitar… he said that Chase hasn't played it in years, but what did that have to do with me? He'd said it as though it fits perfectly into the picture, but, to me, it didn't. Maybe Chase plays his guitar when he's happy, but that has nothing to do with me. From what Chase told me, the divorce didn't happen all that long ago, so he must've just wanted to pick it back up only after he'd gotten used to the idea of it. I didn't see where that had anything to do with me.

My thoughts switch back to Friday when I'd caught Chase playing his guitar in the shack. There'd been real feeling in it when he played and when he sang, but how hard is it really to get lost in something like that? It's music. It's supposed to draw you in and make you never want to leave.

I don't see how him playing his guitar is a result of him being happy. It seems more like his happiness is a result of playing his guitar.

The feeling had stayed in his music, even after he

switched to show me the song he wrote. The way the notes flowed into one another, and the way the melody seemed impossible for anyone to not be captivated by it.

I sit up and look out the window as Chase's song plays in my mind and I hum along to it beneath my breath. I get all the way through it before I repeat it again.

"*Soft as the rain falls, from the sky,*" I sing, so quietly that the words are barely more than a breath. I don't know where it comes from, but I don't make an attempt to stop it.

"*There's a feeling, locked away deep inside*
"*Am I the reason it hides?*"

I climb up off my bed and walk back over to the bathroom to get changed and ready for bed. I pull my brush out of the cabinet before I run it through my hair, humming unknown lyrics beneath my breath until I get to the chorus.

"*I know nothing can last forever,*
"*That's just not how this cruel world works,*
"*But if it could, oh if it could,*
"*Could we be something beautiful?*
"*Could we be something I've never dared to dream possible?*"

I sing it like a lullaby, matching the slow, soft tune to the one Chase played for me a few days ago. It's not perfect, and it sounds a lot more like something from a musical than something you'd hear on the radio, but it flows nicely, and even if I'll forget it in a couple hours, it feels nice to sing it, anyway.

"You're the key,
"And even if I don't want it,
"You unlock the feelings inside of me,
I sigh, setting my brush down and pull my hair back and away from my face.
"You sing the song of my heart,
"Though I still haven't figured it out,
"When did you start?"
I shake my head as I pull my jacket off and hang it over the wrack, stopping my train of thought and killing whatever the next lyrics I had before they can even form on my tongue. I strip from my clothes and change into an old, baggy black shirt and sweat pants before I brush my teeth and leave the bathroom.

My bed creaks beneath me as I lie down and make myself comfortable beneath the covers. The lyrics that died on my tongue still haven't come back to me, but I think over the ones I just sang. When had I turned into some lovey-dovey girl? It had to be Chase who was doing this to me.

I never liked any kind of sappy love songs, and that's all I've ever heard him sing. I doubt it's a coincidence that I'm singing the same thing all of a sudden.

Sleep doesn't come quickly at all, but the last time I look at my clock before I drift off, it reads 2:00AM.

Chapter Nineteen

Thursday comes in what feels like the blink of an eye. The days pass in the same routine as usual, and though my parents don't seem to want me hanging out with Chase, they've seemed to warm up to it more since Saturday.

A bird sings up in a tree not far off. The wind blows past, doing its best to pull my hair with it. It's warm out, much warmer than it's been in the past few weeks, but not as hot as some days in the middle of summer can get. The breeze is probably the only thing that keeps it tolerable, though.

Chase strums a song I don't recognize on his guitar a few feet away from me. He's got an earbud in his left ear, and the other one hangs down in his lap. His phone is sitting in his lap with the screen on, showing the album cover for a song that he keeps turning back to the beginning over and over while he tries to figure out the notes.

I listen to him play as I watch the chirping bird fly back and forth in the tree. It looks young, but I mostly guess that because of how playful it seems. It's hopping from branch to branch and flying to higher ones before flying back down.

"Okay, I'm done now," Chase says, setting his guitar aside and pocketing his phone and earbuds. He gives me a sheepish look like he feels bad that he's spent the last few minutes not talking to me, never mind the fact that I told him it was perfectly fine.

"You finish it?" I ask, nodding to his guitar that he put down on his other side.

"Yeah," he answers. He plucks at the strings, creating a rhythm I've never heard before. I can't tell if he's just playing with it, or if it's another song he's been working on learning. "Took a couple days, but that was the last of it."

I sit up, pulling my thighs against my stomach and chest and resting my chin on my knees. "Can I hear it?" I ask.

His cheeks turn the slightest bit pink, but after a second, he nods, pulling his guitar into his lap. "Just don't make fun of my inability to sing."

I snort a laugh. "Alright. But just this time."

He strums the strings of the guitar, putting his hand over them to make the sound stop suddenly before he plays the same notes again. He refuses to look at me while he plays, his eyes staying locked on his hand as he strums. "*I can feel you coming from a mile away, my pulse starts racing from the words that you say.*"

He looks up at me, and his cheeks are still a bit red, but when my eyes lock on his, they're all I see. Something in my chest tightens and my stomach feels weird.

There's something in his eyes again. It's the same thing I can never place, but it's somehow captivating. It makes my breaths feel short; like I'm gasping for air before sinking back beneath the water in a pool.

"*You don't have to try too hard; you already have my heart.*"

He sings it to me like he was singing to the window when I caught him in the shack last week. He sings it to me like it's meant for me, despite the fact that I'm pretty sure I've heard it in one of the movies Daemon and Fayre watched together at some point.

"*Don't say goodnight, you know, you had me at hello.*"

I'm chewing my lip, and I know I'm chewing it too much because I can already taste blood, but I don't think I can stop. My heart is hammering in my chest, adrenaline is working its way through every bit of me and I feel like I'll be bent over vomiting in a few seconds unless my stomach decides to relax.

Chase finishes the song, but I hardly notice. His eyes are locked on mine and I can't seem to look away.

"I like that song," I tell him, but my voice is hardly above a whisper. My words come out shaky; like I'm shivering from the cold even though it's 90 degrees out.

He smiles. "I'm glad."

We're quiet for a second, but I still can't seem to look away from him. His eyes are dark, so dark they could be black in the right light, yet they're somehow beautiful even with the lack of color.

"There're flecks of blue in your eyes," Chase says, so quietly I almost don't hear him. It's not the first time someone's managed to think they see color in my eyes even though that's not possible. Fayre thought she did a few years ago, but when she looked later, she said it must've just been a trick of the light. And that's all this is, too.

Despite the fact that I know it's not possible, and that he's just seeing things, I smile.

And, before I realize what's going on, something about the moment changes. He's leaning in closer to me and I'm leaning in closer to him and my eyes are closing. I can feel his breath against my face and I know what's about to happen. He's going to kiss me. And I know that can't happen, but I can't shake myself from the trance. I can't smack myself out of it and realize that this shouldn't be happening. I *want* to kiss him.

Something brushes against my lips – the wind maybe? – and it throws me back into the real world.

My eyes snap open and I throw myself back and away from him.

I can't kiss him. No matter how much I want to, I *can't.*

My heart is hammering in my chest and my breaths

are coming in fast, shallow gasps. This is a different kind of feeling now, though. This isn't the giddy, nervous excitement of a crush I shouldn't have on a boy I can never be with. This is fear from the horrifying realization that should never have come to me like this: I could *kill him.*

I stay there long enough to see that he's fine. That he didn't touch me and that what I felt had to have been the wind.

Then, faster than I've ever managed before, I climb to my feet and I run.

I don't look back over my shoulder and I don't think. I just run as fast as my feet will carry me.

If Chase says anything, I don't hear him, and even if he did, I don't think I could hear it over the sound of my pulse in my ears, anyway.

I have to get away from him.

I can't be anywhere near him. I have to get home, where everyone knows what I can do, and how to keep themselves safe from me.

By the time I reach the house, my legs can barely support the weight of my body. There's a stitch in my side, and every time I take in a breath, a stab of pain runs through me.

Tears are running down my cheeks when I push open the door, but I don't know how long they've been falling. They could've just started, or they could've started when I ran off and left Chase behind with no explanation whatsoever.

Chase…

The look in his eyes before I ran off flashes in my mind. The surprise in his eyes, the hurt… But the worst thing to see was the fear. He knows what almost happened was a mistake, even if he doesn't know why. He knows what this means, even if I can't tell him why.

I run to my room, ignoring my sister when she calls after me, asking what's wrong.

No one else saw me, but even if they had, I don't think I'd even care.

I lock my bedroom door behind myself before I slump against my bed, burying my face in my pillow.

It isn't until I'm alone in my room that the sobbing starts.

It's not a gentle sobbing that's easily contained and quiet. This sobbing is violent and pathetic. It makes my throat burn and shakes my whole body each time I heave in a breath that comes out a second later in a shaky breath.

I bury my face deeper into my pillow, hoping that will help muffle the sound of my crying, but I doubt it helps as much as I want it to.

When I finally calm myself down enough, I sit up. My pillow is covered in snot and tears, but I don't even care. I shouldn't care. I shouldn't care about anything that has to do with me.

I could've killed him…

He could be dead right now because of me.

Because, somehow, for some stupid reason, I'd

thought that if I never admit to the fact that I have feelings for him, somehow that'd keep him safe.

But there's no way to keep him safe. Not if he's around me.

I could've killed him. He could be dead…

But he's not…

He's not because I got lucky and the feeling of the breeze against my lips had snapped me out of it. He's okay because of pure luck and nothing more.

He's alive, he's alive, he's alive.

I repeat it over and over again in my head until I believe the words. Until they sink in and I'm no longer terrified.

And he'll stay that way…

Chapter Twenty

Chase texts me so many times that I have to put my phone on silent and leave it hidden in my closet so that I can't hear it. I'd contemplated blocking his number, but the thought had brought on another crying fit along with the realization that I really have to let him go.

He showed up last night, asking my parents if he could talk to me, but I hadn't answered and I'd shut my blinds so that he couldn't come in through my window again. I'd heard his footsteps, and I'd held my breath until I'd heard him leave.

I haven't told anyone anything about what's been going on. Fayre tried to get me to spill last night before bed, but I couldn't even bring myself to tell her.

Daemon knocks on my bedroom door and my attention snaps up and into the real world. "We leave in ten, Than," he calls to me.

"I'll be right out," I respond, swallowing down the wave of fear that washes over me at the thought of going to school.

What am I going to do at lunch? He'll find me there, no doubt, and it's not like I can grab my lunch and go hide in the bathrooms. I doubt he won't be waiting for me to do just that.

I know what he thinks is going on. He thinks I don't like him like that and that he freaked me out because he totally misunderstood something, and that's what I *need* him to think. If I tell him that's not the reason I ran off, I'll have to tell him what the real reason is, and I can't do that.

Before Daemon gets a chance to give me the five-minute warning, I sling my backpack over my shoulder and head for the door.

My phone goes off in my pocket for the 10th time this morning, Chase's ringtone blaring so loud that I'm pretty sure it woke up half of Canada. Or maybe that's just me because I've been dreading the sound of it for the past three minutes since his last text came through.

I haven't dared look at anything he's sent. I don't want to know what he's saying. I don't want to lose my head again and think that maybe everything will be okay if I'm just careful, because what happens when "careful" isn't good enough?

"Eat up quick," mom tells me when I get into the dining room. "Don't wanna be late."

"I'm not hungry," I say, my voice raspy because I'd

been crying not fifteen minutes ago. I hope they can't see the redness in my eyes.

Mom frowns at me. "Not hungry?" she asks, looking completely confused. "Thana, you didn't eat dinner last night. You must be starving by now." She comes over to me and puts her hands on my shoulders, careful to avoid hitting my broken shoulder even though I'm past the point of a gentle touch hurting anymore. "Honey, are you okay?"

One.

"I'm fine," I answer, stepping out of her reach. "Just don't have much of an appetite lately, is all."

"Are you sure?" she presses. "You're not going on a hunger strike to lose weight or anything, are you? Because, honey, you're beautiful."

Two.

I sigh. "No, mom. I'm really just not hungry." I hike my backpack up higher as my phone goes off in my pocket again. "I'll be out in the car," I tell them, and before anyone has a chance to respond, I leave.

As soon as I'm outside, I delete the texts without looking at them and power my phone off before shoving it back into my pocket.

Instead of going to lunch at all, I hide in the restrooms until everyone has filed inside the cafeteria and the doors are closed. When I'm fairly sure the coast is clear,

I sneak out and find a spot to sit before I lean against the wall and slide down to the floor, my knees pressed up against my chest.

I can hear the sound of people talking in the cafeteria even from where I sit in the hall, but I can't make out what anyone's saying. Even when I'm inside there too, though, I can't seem to make out a word of anyone else's conversation.

Anyone else's…

I sigh and lean my head back.

When Chase gives up trying to contact me and realizes that there's no way we can ever still be friends, things will go back to the way they used to be. I won't have any friends or anyone to talk to at lunch, just like it's always been.

Despite the fact that I know this is how things need to be, it's still enough to make tears form in the corners of my eyes.

I blink them away before they can get the chance to have any real effect as the doors to the cafeteria open and two figures slip out.

They walk down the hallway toward the school's entrance/exit, but I can't make out their faces or anything that could distinguish them from every other person in this place with the harsh afternoon light shining through the doors ahead of them.

Fayre's laugh is what makes me realize who I'm watching.

My body tenses and I struggle to make out the face

of the person she's with. I'm pretty sure it's a guy, but is it that guy Drake she was talking about or…

Mark opens the door for my sister and holds it open for her to pass through, smiling at her in a way I don't like.

Where are they going?

Once they're outside and I'm positive they didn't see me, I climb to my feet and follow after them. What is Fayre doing? Is she stupid?

Something deep in me rages like a wildfire of anger and I clench my hand into a fist at my side.

I can't believe that she outright ignored me. Does she think I was just being overprotective of her and that's the only reason I wanted her to stay away from Mark? Did she see my outburst at the store and think it was for no good reason?

I jog down the hall and push open the door. The sunlight is blinding when I get outside, and the heat hits me in a sudden wave that makes me nauseous. I swallow down the feeling and follow the sound of my sister's voice until I spot her and Mark around the side of the school.

She'll kill me if I go over there, I know that much, but there's no way I'm not going to stay here and watch either way. I don't trust him, and I don't feel like I'm being overprotective by not wanting her around him.

He's tormented me for the past three years, and never once in that time has he given me any reason to think that there might be something nice beneath all the cruelty. He can ruin my days at school all he wants. He can shove me around and tell me how worthless I am and try to make me hate my life more than I already do, but he's never going to get to me as much as he wants to because he doesn't know the truth. He doesn't know what really scares me and he'll never know.

If Fayre opens up to him, though, he will know how to hurt her.

I hide behind the building, poking my head around the side just enough to be able to see. They could still easily see me if they looked, but they seem too interested in whatever the conversation they're having is.

They talk for a few minutes, but it doesn't take Mark very long to get touchy enough with my sister that I contemplate interfering. He touches her arm, running his fingers across the skin beneath her shoulder, and I can feel myself cringe when he does.

A feeling of disgust crawls up my skin and makes me shudder.

My sister doesn't seem anywhere near as disgusted as I feel, though. She looks like she likes it. Her cheeks are pale pink, and there's a nervous smile on her face. She won't look up to meet his gaze, but she's not pulling away from him either. She looks flattered and happy, if anything.

Mark keeps finding new places to touch her; her hair, her cheeks, the curve of her hip. I don't understand how she hasn't pushed him away yet.

I don't see even the tiniest bit of disgust or surprise on her face until he does exactly what I've been waiting for him to do, and kisses her.

It's not anything more than a peck, but it seems to take Fayre aback. Her cheeks are bright red, and somehow, she still doesn't seem to know where this is going. She looks like any girl should after her first kiss: happy.

Mark seems to see that as his opening, just when I realize that I shouldn't still be standing here. He presses her back against the wall of the school and kisses her again, this time it's nowhere near just a peck, though.

I'm up on my feet as soon as I see my sister push his shoulder, making an attempt to get him off of her. Instead of taking the hint, or even acting like he noticed it, he moves and kisses her neck, his hands moving up the front of her shirt.

I break into a run, but they aren't close to me, and it feels like they're a hundred miles away from where I am. I want to scream at him, but I can't even get words to form on my tongue.

"No," Fayre gasps. Her eyes are wide and her voice is hardly something I can hear. "Let me go." A sob makes her voice hitch and tears start to fall from her eyes.

Something breaks inside of me at the same time that a new fire ignites itself. "GET OFF OF HER!" I scream.

Mark looks up at me, and right when he does, Fayre

kicks him in the stomach and shoves him to the ground. Before he even realizes what's going on, she runs off.

I freeze in my tracks as she runs past me, tears streaming down her face. I want to hold her. To comfort her. I want to sit with her until she can't possibly cry anymore.

But that's not the sister I am. I've never been and I'll never be able to be because I *can't* sit with her. She'll go back inside and she'll find Daemon, and he'll be able to sit with her for as long as she needs him because that's something he can do.

And I have something in front of me that I can do, too.

Mark climbs shakily to his feet, his breaths coming in short gasps, but I don't care how much pain he's in. I step up in front of him, grab him by the shoulders, and shove him back against the brick wall of the school with every ounce of strength I possess.

I want to hurt him. I want to rip him apart limb by limb and watch him die slowly. I want to break every bone in his body so that all he is, is a worthless sack of flesh on the ground. I want to watch him turn to grey dust like every other living thing I've ever killed.

It would be so easy, too. All I'd have to do is take my glove off.

Take the glove off…

"Thana?" Mark's voice is strained and surprised; like

he completely forgot I'd been the one who shouted just a second ago.

"Yeah, that's right, it's me," I growl. I shove him harder against the wall, pinning him in place. I want to burn his entire being, starting with his skin and ending with the worthless excuse for a heart in his chest.

Just take off the glove…

He glances in the direction Fayre ran off in and I can see the fear in his eyes when he looks back at me. "Look, I'm sorry… I like your sister and I took it a step too far and-"

"Bullshit!" I shout in his face. I want to claw out his organs and grind them under the heel of my shoe while he watches. "I saw you! You aren't sorry about that! Were you sorry about it the last time you harassed a girl who's three years younger than you? Were you sorry the last time you hurt *me?*"

Tears are running down my cheeks; hot and angry.

Take. Off. The. Glove.

"Look, I'm sorry, okay?" he says, but I can tell he isn't at all. "Let me just go apologize to her and this can all be over." There's a cocky air about him again, just like he had at the store. He's not outwardly saying anything, though, and I can tell he's still scared of me even though I'm a lot smaller than him and he could easily beat me in a fight.

Take. It-

I shake my head, shoving the thought away before I actually do something I never could.

"What's the matter?" I taunt, my voice dripping in venom and hate. "Now that you don't have your mob with you, are you running away from me? All I am is just a little broken girl, Mark." I want to make him mad. I want to turn this around and put him in the same situation I've been in for years. I want him to feel what it's like to be at someone else's mercy, and I know I can if I do it right. There's still fear in his eyes.

A second after the words are out of my mouth, though, something dangerous flashes in his eyes, replacing the fear that had been there a moment ago.

Faster than I have time to process, our places are switched and he's the one shoving me against the wall. A stab of white-hot pain ignites in my shoulder, but I bite my tongue to hide any sign that I felt it.

He presses his forearm into my neck, crushing my windpipe and making my breaths come in short gasps. His long-sleeved shirt is soft against my skin. I almost wish it wasn't already black so he can see just what I can do to people.

"Not so tough now, are you?" he hisses.

He's so close to me I can feel his breath on my face, warm and vile-smelling. His eyes keep darting from side to side, focusing on my left eye and then on my right.

"You think I'm scared of you?" I wheeze, my voice pathetic sounding. It gets my point across, though. He presses his arm harder into my neck and everything in me screams to cough, as if that will help. I hold it in, even as tears start to stream down my face from it.

"Awe, don't worry," he whispers. "We'll fix that."

He grazes my cheek with his fingers, the touch so light it feels like a feather against my skin.

"NO!" I scream.

My eyes go wide and I shove him away, but the damage has already been done.

Even though he's not touching me anymore, the grey is spreading through his body, starting at his fingertips and moving out in every direction.

Mark takes multiple steps back, staring at his hand in disbelief as bits of grey dust float away in the breeze. "Wha-what did you do to me?!" he screams, panic in his eyes.

I can't even answer. My silent tears turn to sobbing as I watch.

I've killed him.

Mark keeps shouting at me, saying he knew there was something wrong with me, that he knew I was something evil, but I just sit there, a pathetic mess of tears on the ground.

Before his body is even completely grey, he's lying dead in front of me. It continues to spread until he's a heap of dust in the grass, and I'm unable to do anything but sit there and watch as the realization hits me over and over again.

I killed him, I killed him, I killed him…

Chapter Twenty-One

I don't go back into the school and I don't go home. Once I manage to stop crying and the last of the dust that was Mark's body has floated away on the wind, I go straight to the abandoned property. The sun is beating down hard on me and sweat drips down my forehead, but I hardly notice it.

Everything feels numb.

I lost the only friend I've ever had because I could hurt him, but he has to think that it's his fault, and I have no way to change that because no one can know my secret. And then... then I killed Mark...

Even with the pain in my shoulder, I force myself up into the branches of the old oak tree. I've climbed it so many times that the movements are automatic, even while I'm only climbing with one arm and only using my other elbow as a brace.

I maneuver my way around and between the branches until I come to the same spot I always sit in. It's one of the higher branches of the tree, near the middle of the large, bushy part. It juts out straight from the side, and though it looks frail at first, somehow, it's able to support my weight.

The hours pass slowly, and I don't move. I have nowhere else to go, and no one to talk to. I can't tell anyone about what happened today. Not even Fayre, who was there a moment before I…

Daemon might be the best person to tell, but I can't risk him freaking out on me. I'd rather keep the possibility open and the outcome undetermined. It's less painful to think that everything will be okay if I do tell him than it will be if he freaks out.

Sooner than I'd like, 2:45 rolls around and I know I have to leave before Chase shows up looking for me. I don't know how long he'll want to spend trying to talk to me about the almost-kiss, but if I were in his position, I don't think I'd leave him alone until at least a week of nothing has passed. I hope he's not as persistent and stubborn as I can be.

I climb down from the tree and start toward home. I left my backpack in my locker, and what I should do is text one of my siblings to grab it before they leave, but I haven't even dared to turn my phone back on because I don't want to see how many texts I've gotten from Chase.

By the time I get home, the car is already back in the

driveway, which means Daemon and Fayre are back from school. I don't see my dad's truck, though, which means that both he and my mom are still at work.

I unlock the front door and push it open slowly. I know Daemon won't be happy with me for disappearing and not texting, especially with what happened with Fayre, but I don't want to hear it right now.

Unfortunately, that looks unavoidable. As soon as I poke my head into the house, the first thing I see is Daemon sitting on the floor. He's watching me, which means my disappearance is the only reason he's taking up residence in the entryway.

"Is Fayre okay?" I ask, before he gets the chance to say anything to me. His long legs are taking up the entirety of the entryway, trapping me. I won't walk over him because if I trip and fall, I could hurt him or destroy something else.

"Far from it," he responds, climbing to his feet. "She ran into my class, crying. She's lucky my math teacher has a heart."

He's eyeing me with a look I've only seen on my mom's face. It's the "Thana, you're in serious trouble" look, and I hate it with a passion. I have to take it, though, because if I don't, I'll have to crack and tell him the truth.

I don't make a move to say anything, but he looks lightyears away from being done with me.

"She said Mark… *harassed* her, and that you were out

there when it happened and that's the only reason she got away from him, but you vanished after that." His arms are crossed and his look is anything but pleased. "Where did you go? We couldn't find you anywhere at school and you wouldn't answer your phone. You weren't even at the abandoned property when we checked, so where the hell were you?"

He runs a frustrated hand through his hair, and the gesture reminds me so much of Chase that the numbness I've felt since earlier breaks and sends a newfound wave of grief over me.

Tears are pouring from my eyes and my breaths are coming in gasps before I even have time to attempt to stop them.

Daemon is looking at me like I'm some sort of foreign creature, which only makes the feeling worse.

"I killed Mark," I sob, my voice shaky and uneven. "He tried to hurt me and he touched my face and he's dead."

Daemon's watching me, but he doesn't look like he has a clue what to say. Instead of saying anything, though, he comes over to me and wraps me up in a tight embrace. I bury my face in the front of his shirt as he holds me.

I feel better, but the tears start falling more for some reason and the sadness is even harder to keep under control. Before I know it, I'm telling him everything.

"He was kissing her and touching her, and she looked so scared and she was crying, and I couldn't keep my mouth shut," I say, the words flowing out of me like the tears from my eyes. "I pinned him against the wall and I taunted him because I wanted him to know what it feels like, what he does to people, and he got angrier than I've ever seen him. He was choking me and trying to scare me, and he touched my face and I... I killed him..."

I want that to be all I say, because I didn't even want anyone to know that much, but what happened yesterday starts to slip out, too.

"That could've been Chase..." I whisper. "He tried to kiss me, and I wanted him to kiss me so I didn't even think about it, and I snapped out of it and he didn't, but that could've been him. I could've killed him like I killed Mark and it would've been all my fault because I didn't even think."

"Than..." Daemon says, his voice gentle, but I hardly hear him.

"I never should've even become friends with him. I never should've talked to him because now he has to think that it's his fault that I'm not answering his texts. He has to think I hate him because he tried to kiss me, but I wanted him to, and he can't even know that because I can't ever talk to him again and-"

"Thana." Daemon's voice is less gentle this time, but I don't freak out because he snapped at me. I stare him straight in the face, his eyes locked on mine. I can feel the warmth of his hands on my cheeks, making me look up at him.

I'm frozen in place, paralyzed by a fear a hundred times stronger than what I felt earlier when Mark touched me.

This is different. This is my brother.

Daemon's eyes stare into mine, horror-struck. He's only there for a second before he takes a step back and looks at his hands.

I close my eyes as soon as he pulls away. I can't bring myself to watch him die, too.

Why can I do this to people? Why am I such an evil creature?

"Than?" Daemon's voice is scared, and it stabs my heart in a way I haven't felt before. It hurts my entire being in a way that shouldn't be possible.

Why do I have to be like this? Why can't I just be normal?

"Than."

The sound of my name on his lips again makes me look up. He should be gone by now. Mark didn't last this long. He was already dust.

When I look up, Daemon isn't dead, or even dying, though. Everything about him looks the same. He's staring right back at me with the same expression I feel on my own face; joy, confusion, and shock.

He's alive.

I didn't kill him.

Daemon rushes back over to me and wraps me up in another hug before pressing a kiss to my forehead, which he pulls away from looking just as normal as ever.

"Than, I can touch you," he breathes, holding my face in his hands again. There are tears in his eyes now, too.

I've never seen my brother cry before. I didn't think it was possible. It doesn't seem real, this moment and everything I've ever known.

I can touch my brother.

The realization doesn't feel real. It feels like a lie someone is telling me so that they can rip my heart out again. I can't help but feel like, in a matter of a few seconds, he'll drop dead at my feet.

He doesn't, though.

He touches my cheeks, my forehead, my nose; all the loving, teasing ways that I've seen him touch Fayre before but have never felt.

And it feels real.

I can touch him and not be afraid.

I'm crying again, but the tears don't feel like they're ripping my heart out. They feel like they're putting the tiniest bit of me back together again.

Daemon smiles at me, cupping my face in his hands again. "I can do this now," he says, laughing slightly. He wipes the tears from my cheeks with his thumbs and his smile widens in what looks like disbelief and pure happiness.

The look only makes me cry more.

My brother hugs me again, and I hug him back.

I can hug my brother and not be scared.

"Okay, so what happened?" Daemon asks. He's sitting next to me on the couch as I play with a hair tie on my wrist.

We agreed that we can't tell anyone about what we found out. It'll have to stay our secret. We can't risk anyone knowing that he can touch me because no one can get used to the idea of me being touched. If they do, what happens if Fayre or my parents try to touch me, too? We don't know why Daemon can touch me, and we can't risk that anyone else might get lucky and not die if they make the same mistake he did.

"I ran away," I answer, the feeling of shame making my cheeks warm. I can't look up at him when I say it, and my voice comes out as a whisper.

Daemon doesn't seem phased by my discomfort, or by the fact that I killed another human being. He looks like he's shut off his emotions for my sake. Like he thinks that being indifferent to the fact will somehow make it easier for me.

"What about his clothes?" he asks. There's a hint of worry in his eyes now, but it's the first time I've seen it since we finished talking about the possibility that I could still kill Fayre or our parents.

"I… they're still outside the school," I say, cursing my own stupidity when I realize what I've done.

"Damn it…" he mutters beneath his breath.

It's the first time I've heard him swear in a long time.

"Okay, we can work with this," he says, but he still looks worried. "Fayre said you guys were on the side of the school. No one really goes over there because everything interesting is in the back and people tend to hang out in the front more often than not. But we still can't risk anyone finding the clothes there, so come on."

Daemon climbs to his feet and gestures for me to follow.

Reluctantly, I do.

The last place I want to go is back to school, but I don't think I have much of a choice. We need to get Mark's clothes and burn them or something so that no one ever finds them. I could easily be found if the wrong people got their hands on them, and, even if I am technically responsible and even if I do feel like it's my fault he died, I didn't kill him intentionally.

But I can't help but think that maybe that'd be the best thing for me. If I got caught by the police or something and arrested because of a murder, and they threw me in a cell for the rest of my life where I'll never be close enough to ever touch anyone again… wouldn't that be better for everyone?

"Stop it," Daemon snaps at me, grabbing my hand and pulling me toward the door. "Nothing bad is going to happen and *it's not your fault.*"

It's the first time he's said the words to me, and I thought it'd help a lot to hear them from my brother. I thought him telling me would make me believe them.

But I don't. If anything, it makes them harder to believe.

My brother pulls me out the door and to the car. He doesn't let me go until he realizes that he has to so I can get in on the other side.

I get in on my side as I hear Daemon's door close. I sit carefully in the seat beside his as he starts the car and puts it in reverse to back out of the driveway.

The first few minutes in the car are quiet. I don't think either of us knows what to say about the situation. Daemon seems to be thinking about it but not voicing any opinions, which I'm okay with because I'm not sure if I even want to hear them.

"Your blood," he says after a moment, as if he's just figured out the reason for life on earth.

"Huh?" I ask, because I don't think I have a reason to not be confused.

"Your blood," Daemon says again, glancing at me for a second before looking back at the road ahead. He looks mildly excited; like he thinks he might be on to something instead of the dead-end I'm sure it is. "Your blood is the only thing about you that never turns black or grey, right?"

I nod. It's not something I've ever thought much about, and I'm not sure how it applies here, but he's not wrong.

"What if that's why I can touch you? Technically speaking, we have the same blood. And not just because of family bonds or whatever, we actually do, to some extent. What if I can touch you because I have the same blood in my body?"

I shrug in response. "Maybe."

I don't know what else I'm supposed to say to what he's suggesting. If he's right, then I should be able to touch everyone in my family. That's never something we'd dare to try though, so he might be on to something and he might be right, but that doesn't mean we can ever risk it and find out.

It's quiet again, but it doesn't last half as long as the last silence did.

"So, what were you doing outside, anyway?" he asks. He doesn't look at me this time, instead focusing his eyes on the road.

I sigh, blowing a slow breath through my lips as I sink deeper into the seat. "I was avoiding the cafeteria," I answer, not sure if I know exactly where this will lead, or if I can get out of it when I want to. "I saw them come out and followed. I know I shouldn't have, but… I'm glad I did."

I swallow. As hard of a fact as it is, it's the truth. Mark didn't deserve to die, there's no doubt in my mind about that, but Fayre is my sister, and she comes before anyone else. I wouldn't be able to live with myself right now if he'd done something to her and I'd been oblivious.

Daemon doesn't seem to have anything to say to that. Instead, he just keeps driving until we get to the school.

He doesn't seem as happy about the silence as I am, but he doesn't make an attempt to break it again. I know he probably wants to ask about what happened with Chase, but I'm glad he hasn't brought it up. I know I won't be able to not explain more at some point, but, as of right now, I don't think I could even if I wanted to.

I've never seen the school at night before, and I'm not sure if I prefer it when there's a bunch of kids bustling around everywhere who I have to avoid, or when it looks like the perfect place to film a horror movie.

"Creepy," I mutter as Daemon pulls into a parking space and turns the car off. He gives me a look I don't know what to do with, then opens his door and gets out.

I follow after Daemon, even though I'd rather stay in the car. I don't want to go back to that spot, ever. I *killed* someone back alongside the school. I didn't just hit someone or call someone an ass and mean it. I *killed* him.

The sound of the word isn't hitting me like a thousand-pound weight anymore. It feels untrue. How could I have possibly done that? It doesn't feel possible, even though I watched it with my own eyes.

"Than," Daemon calls. He's already ahead of me by a decent amount.

I jog to catch up with him.

He's not standing far from where it happened. A

few more steps and he'll be standing right where I was when Fayre ran past me.

When I get to where he's standing, I don't even look at him. My eyes land straight on Mark's clothes on the ground. There are still a few flecks of dust in the grass and, when the wind blows, a few more get picked up and carried away.

I thought I'd feel some amount of relief if we found the clothes, but I don't. I feel nothing.

Daemon's body has gone rigid, but I know he doesn't want to admit that just the sight of clothes on the ground is terrifying. I don't pose a threat to him anymore, but that doesn't mean I couldn't still kill every other person on this planet.

It takes my brother a second, but he steals himself from whatever the emotions are that he was feeling a moment ago. He marches over to the clothes, picks them up, and comes back over to me a moment later.

"Come on," he says, offering me a half-hearted smile.

I can feel myself break just a little more inside when I do my best to match it.

Chapter Twenty-Two

The rest of the week and the weekend pass slowly. I can't go to the abandoned property because there's no doubt in my mind that Chase will be there. Going there is the only thing I truly want to do that feels like it would distract me at least to some extent. I can't risk seeing him, though.

He stopped texting every other minute Saturday evening, but I still heard from him on Sunday, even if I didn't actually read the texts.

Fayre comes and talks to me every now and then, which is fairly unusual for her, but I get the feeling it has something to do with what happened last week.

She still doesn't know I killed Mark, and neither do our parents. I don't know how long it's going to be until I get around to telling them, but Daemon promised he wouldn't say anything until after I've broken the news to them.

A soft knock comes on my bedroom door. "Ana?" Fayre's voice calls. She's quiet; like she's afraid to wake the beast that's asleep in the cave. "Are you up?"

Lucky for her, she's not actually waking me up this morning.

"Yeah," I call back, poking my head out of the bathroom for a second before retreating behind the doorframe again.

I can hear her open the door and come in. She closes it softly behind herself and walks over to my bed, her footsteps light against the floor. She's been quiet since everything happened. She doesn't talk as much and her eyes stay downcast; like she's afraid of everyone she looks at. I wish I knew what to do to help her.

"One sec," I tell her, toweling my wet hair until it's a damp mop on my head that I'm able to sling over my shoulder. I get dressed in jeans and a baggy T-shirt that's been sitting in a drawer for somewhere around three years. I pull my jacket on and pull the hood up before grabbing my gloves and slipping my feet into a pair of sneakers.

Fayre crinkles her nose at my outfit when I come out. "You're wearing that?" she asks, eyeing my shirt with a mildly disgusted expression.

I look down at myself. "What's wrong with it?"

She smiles, a bit of her usual sparkle lighting her face

up. "Chase is gonna be there," she says, her voice high and teasing.

The sound of his name feels like a stab in the gut.

I haven't told Fayre about what happened with Chase either, though, so she has no reason to suspect that something so dumb could hurt so much. And, because she doesn't know already, it somehow makes me more reluctant to explain my reasoning, or even let what I'm feeling show.

"And I'm supposed to care what he thinks?" I challenge. I stick my tongue out at her playfully.

"Most people care even if they don't need to," she points out. She climbs to her feet and heads over to the door. "Breakfast is ready, by the way. And Dae is driving us to school again."

"I'll be right out," I say.

She nods.

Watching her expression go back to something painfilled is like another stab to the gut that's meant to finish me off.

The bell for lunch rings and I wait for everyone else to get out of their seats before I follow. Everyone's rushing through the hallways outside as I stare out the window. Once the last of the kids in my class are up and out, I get up and leave, too. I don't need to be coming up with an excuse for what I'm still doing here when I don't even fully know.

Chase won't see me right now. He's probably already in the cafeteria with how close his class is to it.

I trudge through the hallway, keeping my head low, and avoiding the most crowded areas. Instead of going to the cafeteria, I go straight to the closest restroom and lock myself inside of the farthest stall.

My stomach grumbles in protest, but I can't risk getting lunch today.

Sighing, I slump against the wall. I slide down it until I'm sitting on the floor. There's an air vent blowing down on me, making my hair dance at odd angles in front of my face. I shiver and pull my jacket tighter around myself.

I hug my knees to my chest and lean my head back against the wall before I close my eyes, welcoming sleep with open arms.

The bell ringing is what wakes me up.

I sit up groggily and stretch the sleep from my body. It felt good to sleep for a while, but now I really don't want to get back up and go to class. Unfortunately, school doesn't really give you much of a choice about when you can and can't nap.

The door to the restrooms opens as I climb to my feet, and I can hear two girls talking in hushed voices. Once the door is shut behind them, they're no longer quiet.

"They're thinking it has something to do with that girl he was with," one of them says to the other.

They're not far enough away from the door to see

me clearly unless they're really looking, but I climb up on the toilet seat to avoid being seen, anyway.

"The freshman?" the other one asks in response. Something clatters on the countertop as she talks.

I have to suppress a groan. I've been in the restrooms enough to see how many girls fix up their makeup midway through the day as if they don't have to go straight to class after lunch.

Great. Now I'm going to be stuck here listening to gossip *and* late to my next class.

"Yeah, Fayre, I think her name is," the first one says.

My attention snaps up.

Why are they talking about my sister?

"She's the last one he was with, from what I heard. Elena said she saw them leave during lunch and that he didn't come back in. She came back in bawling her eyes out, apparently. No clue what that's about, but no one has seen him or heard from him since."

My stomach drops to the floor.

Mark. They're talking about Mark.

The second one clicks her tongue. "Weird," is the only thing she offers as a response. "So, who do you think you're gonna go with now?"

Well, that was a fast topic change.

"No clue," the first one tells her. "Got my eye on the new guy, though. Maggie said his name's Chase, and he is *so* cute."

The two of them laugh as something grips my stomach and bile rises in the back of my throat. I swallow it down.

"Well," the first one continues. "If that Fayre girl doesn't steal him too, that is." I can practically hear her roll her eyes when she says it.

"I wouldn't be so worried about Fayre," the second one says. "Her sister, the goth freak, seems to have somehow gotten her hands on him. I'd be more worried about her than a freshman like her sister."

That's it…

I jump down from the toilet seat and unlock the stall door. The two girls are staring right at me when I come out.

They look familiar, but I can't say I know who they are.

"Don't talk about my sister," I tell them, my voice calm and confident. I want to scream at them to shut up, but my fight isn't in me today. "Talk all you want to about me, but don't talk about Fayre."

I hike my backpack up on my shoulder and push past the two of them toward the door.

"Who's gonna stop us?" the first girl calls to me, but I ignore her and leave.

I pose no threat to her, whether or not I want to be one. I could take her easier than I could take Mark, but it's not even worth it. She's just a jealous girl who thinks she has a right to the heart of any boy she wants.

They can think whatever they want about me, and even Fayre, but they'll never know the truth about what happened that day. If Fayre decides she wants to tell anyone at some point, that's her business, not mine. But they'll never know what happened afterward even if they do find out what he did to Fayre.

I get to class three minutes late, which is enough to earn me a warning from the teacher, but nothing more.

When I snap out of my trance, I'm standing in front of the abandoned property.

Daemon had agreed to let me walk home when I'd caught up with him and Fayre after school. I told him I wouldn't be back any later than five, because I might do some walking around. But, instead of walking around aimlessly, my feet had led me straight here without even a second thought.

I look around quickly, but Chase isn't here yet, if he's coming at all.

The tension in my body relaxes a bit and I take a few steps forward until I'm standing in the overgrown grass.

"Might as well," I whisper beneath my breath. "I'm here already."

I glance over my shoulder before I head deeper into the property. I head toward a patch of grass behind one of the houses. It's always brightly lit on days like today.

A gust of wind blows over me, pulling my hair along with it and sending a chill running down my spine. It's not cold out, but the air is cool against my face as I walk. I want to feel it all over my body. I want to feel it on my arms, on my legs, on the back of my neck. I want it to envelope me in its embrace and have it never let me go.

I breathe in deeply, closing my eyes and letting the feeling wash over me. It's the feeling only being here can give me. It's the feeling of freedom, and it's something I can never feel anywhere but here.

But it's missing something now. I feel free and welcome, just like I always have, but I feel alone now, too. I feel lost now, unlike before when I felt like this place was the only home I've ever had.

Footsteps rustle behind me, and my body tenses.

Damn it…

I should've left when I had the chance.

"Thana?" Chase's voice is hardly above a whisper, but I can hear him as clearly as my heart beating in my chest.

I turn around slowly, like I'll scare him off, but I can't tell if I'm actually afraid to scare him, or if I'm afraid to scare myself.

Before I get a chance to realize what I'm doing, I'm sprinting across the yard toward the nearest house. He could easily block my way back home, but he can't completely stop me from getting away from him. I can hide in here until he decides to leave, whether that be in the next few minutes, or tonight.

He calls after me, but I hardly register the sound of my own name as my feet beat against the ground and adrenaline rushes through my body.

I shouldn't have stayed. I should've left and gone

straight home. I shouldn't have even come here in the first place.

I pull open the door to the house and slam it behind myself. I lock it shut and lean back against it, my breaths coming in sharp gasps.

Chase tries to turn the knob on the other side, but he's not forceful about it. He seems to already know that it's locked before he even tries it. He gives up after a second and I can hear him sigh. "Can you please let me in?" he whispers. His voice sounds as broken as I feel.

Before I can catch it, a sob forms in the back of my throat and I'm crying again. I slide down the door until I'm sitting on the floor with my knees to my chest. "Please, go away," I beg, my voice hitching at the end of the sentence.

"I'm so sorry, Thana…" he whispers, but I can hear every word. "I like you. I like you a lot, and I thought that… I thought maybe you liked me too, and I know that's not something I should ever assume, but… I'm sorry. I thought-"

"Stop," I say. My voice is weak and it's hardly above a whisper.

"No. What I did wasn't right. I shouldn't have just… assumed that was okay. I had no right to-"

"*Stop*," I plead. The tears burn my cheeks and something inside of me is breaking more and more with every word he says. "I like you, too," I tell him, but I'm not even sure if he can hear me. "But I can't. I *can't* like you… I can't… I can't hurt you…"

He's quiet for a second, and I wish I was stupid enough to think he left while I was talking. "I… I don't understand. How would you hurt me?"

I close my eyes. I shouldn't do this. I shouldn't tell him, or show him, or even mention it. He shouldn't know. He *can't* know. But that doesn't stop me.

"Take a step away from the door," I tell him, "and watch."

Slowly, I pull my glove off of my hand. I pull at each of the fingers until they're loose, and watch as it slowly slips off of my hand. When the glove falls away, the sickly pale skin of my fingers is visible.

I look like a ghost. A grey, solid ghost.

I press my hand against the door and watch as the grey spreads like a disease on the wood. It flows like a puddle of water on the ground, pushing out in every direction until there's nothing left that isn't covered.

"What… what am I seeing?" Chase asks.

I climb to my feet and open the door, standing before him as the monster I truly am. "I did it," I tell him, holding up my hand. "That's what I do to things. I kill them." I gesture at the door half-heartedly. "Everything I touch dies." My eyes are downcast when I continue. "Mark wasn't at school today. And he's not coming back…" I swallow hard, but the tears start pouring from my eyes again. "I caught him harassing my sister. She got away, but I was mad and I pinned him against the wall. I pissed him off, and he touched me and… and he died…"

Chase stares at me, his expression unreadable.

I shouldn't have told him that, but I need him to understand. I need him to not want to be around me. I need him to know what I'm capable of.

"I *killed* him," I say through gritted teeth, as though it'll keep the words from having an effect on me. It doesn't help anything, though. The tears still continue to pour down my face and cheeks until they drip from my chin. "Everything I touch dies. It's why I wear the gloves. It's why I dress like this. It's why I look like *this*." I grab a lock of my hair with my ungloved hand, as if that will explain it all.

He's still watching me, waiting for me to say something more. I don't know what he wants to hear, but I know I won't be able to give it to him.

"I wanted to kiss you that day, Chase," I admit, unable to look at him. "I really did…" My voice breaks into a sob at the end of it. "But I can't… I can't hurt you, too…"

"But you didn't," Chase says, his voice soft, like he's talking to a wounded child.

It's the one way I've never wanted him to see me, and now he does.

"Thana, that's why I thought you hated me. I did kiss you." He says it carefully, each word cautious and slow.

"No." I shake my head, taking a step away from him. "You couldn't have. You'd be dead right now."

"An, your lip was bleeding that day," he says, but

I'm not sure where he's going with it. "You were chewing it and I hadn't realized you'd gotten that deep, but I know I kissed you because when you ran off, I could taste it."

"You could-?" I shake my head. "No. No, you couldn't have. It was the wind. That's all I felt. You'd be dead because that's not possible. The only person who can touch me is Daemon, and he's my brother so it makes sense. It's just… no."

The thought that maybe he can touch me too is terrifying, but I don't understand why. I wanted to kiss him, didn't I? I wanted to touch him and to feel his hand in mine and to not be afraid of hurting him.

"No," I say again, this time firmer. "It was a fluke if anything. Daemon touched me, and there was no doubt that he did. I'm not… I'm not risking that." I say it more to myself than to him.

"Thana, you don't scare me," Chase says. He's still looking at me like he's afraid to hurt me, but he's not looking at me like my siblings and parents always have. He's not looking at me like he's afraid.

"That's what scares me," I whisper, realizing it's the truth. "I can't hurt you, Chase."

"You won't hurt me," he tells me, his voice firm. He takes a step closer to me, resting his hands on my shoulders and looking into my eyes.

I want to push him away. I want to scream at him and run, but I want to stay here more. I want to stay here and never have him let go. I want him to hold me like he did at the beach. I want him to kiss me like he thinks he already did.

But I know I can have none of that, no matter how much I want it.

So, I steal myself from the feeling, and I pull away from him.

"I'm sorry," I whisper, backing away from him.

I turn to leave, but my arm scraps against something sharp on the door. I can feel it pierce my jacket and bite into my skin, but I bite my tongue to keep myself from crying out.

I don't give Chase enough time to say anything before I run off.

I don't stop running until I'm back home.

Chapter Twenty-Three

Fayre's pacing back and forth in the entryway when I push open the door and walk inside. She looks worried, but when she looks up and her eyes meet mine, it melts away into something I can't place.

"There you are!" she says, sounding relieved and also mildly exasperated. "Daemon was getting worried. And he's even distracted by Lauren." She smirks in the direction of the living room, where I'm willing to bet they are.

I roll my eyes. "I'm fine. I told him I'd be back before five, and it's before five."

My eyes still feel raw and wet, but if she can see it, she doesn't say anything.

"What happened to your arm?" She's eyeing my jacket where the door ripped it and punctured my skin. I still haven't looked at it, but it's throbbing still and my jacket is covered in blood. Her eyes trail down to my hand next. "And where's your glove?"

I pull my glove from my pocket and show it to her. I stuff it back in my pocket before I walk off toward my room. I can hear her trailing behind me, but I ignore her as I make my way down the hallway.

Daemon and Lauren are sitting on the couch in the living room, watching a movie. My brother glances up and meets my gaze, offers me a smile, then turns his attention back to the movie.

Lauren sits curled up on the couch with her head on my brother's chest and her arms wrapped around herself. Daemon has his arm around her shoulders, holding her close, as he grazes her upper arm tenderly with his fingers.

The same something I've been feeling for the past few days wants to break a little bit more at the sight and I turn away before it gets the chance to.

Fayre sits down on my bed when we get to my room. I keep a good distance away from her as I peal my jacket off, the blood making it stick painfully to my skin.

"Geez, Ana," she says. She comes over to where I am and examines my wounded arm. "Does it hurt?" she asks, lifting her fingers up as though she's going to touch it. She pulls away before she actually does, though.

I shrug, wincing when I do. "It's not that bad," I lie. The wound is deep and still gushing blood, but with a little pressure on it and time, it'll be fine. "I just really like hurting this poor left arm of mine, is all." I give her a teasing smile.

We both know that the joke is a poor attempt to hide something, and I have no doubt that she'll be asking about it here in a minute.

I go into the bathroom and find a cloth. I run it under the water for a second before I start dabbing at the wound slowly. It stings every time I touch it, the pain radiating all throughout my arm.

"What happened?" she asks. She's sitting on my bed again, her legs crossed at the ankles.

"I was at the abandoned property, and I kinda scraped it on a door," I explain. I dab at the scrape again, wincing as another stab of pain shoots through my arm.

Fayre purses her lips. "That's not what I was talking about. You were crying."

I rinse the cloth out, letting the rust-colored water run smoothly over my hands before flowing down the drain. The only time water runs smoothly over my skin is when my blood has tinted it, and the fact makes me remember what Daemon said in the car last week. I push the thought away before I have too much time to think about it, though.

I set the cloth down on the counter before I leave the bathroom and sit down on the bed next to my sister, glancing in her direction.

She seems older somehow since everything

happened. She's been acting differently all around, but most of it seems like stuff that will subside a bit once she's moved on from what happened. But I doubt the sudden air of maturity is something that will go away with time.

I sigh. "Chase tried to kiss me a few days ago," I explain, my voice hitching at the end of it. Tears don't start falling again this time, though, and I'm thankful for that.

"Oh." She doesn't look like she knows what else to say, and I can't blame her. I doubt she ever really thought about what me and Chase liking each other might actually mean. "What happened?"

"At first, I didn't move." I swallow hard, refusing to meet her gaze. "I wanted to kiss him. I really wanted to. But… that's not something I can have. I felt the wind or something, and I moved before he could. Chase thinks he really did kiss me, but he'd… he'd be dead if he did."

Fayre is quiet for a minute, and I think for a second that maybe she won't respond, but then she takes in a breath. "But what about Daemon?" she asks. "I heard the two of you a couple days ago. I know Dae can touch you. So… what if Chase is like him?"

I want to tell her that I planned to tell her about Daemon being able to touch me, but doing so would be an absolute lie. I hadn't known that she'd been able to hear us, but if I had, I wouldn't have tried to hide the fact so much over the past couple of days.

"Daemon thinks it might be because we have the

same blood," I tell her. "So that would mean I could maybe touch you and mom and dad too, but that's not something I'm going to risk. And, even if Daemon is right, Chase isn't related to me in any way, so…"

She nods, but she has a determined look on her face and I know she won't let it go. "So… have you talked to him?" she asks.

"Yeah…" It's not the answer I want to give her, but it's the truth. "I let everything slip. He knows about all of it." I sound defeated when I say it.

Saying the words out loud makes something in me feel tight. It's a similar feeling to the one I would get around Chase, but this is slightly different in some way. It feels less sporadic and crazy somehow.

"What did he say?"

I want to tell her that he didn't even hear me. Or that he didn't believe me and left thinking I was totally insane. But I had shown him what I can do. He'd seen it and I'd told him everything, and he *had* believed me.

"He said he isn't afraid of me," I answer, my voice hardly above a whisper.

Fayre's smiling when I look back up at her. It's enough to make a tiny bit of hope form in my chest, even though I know it shouldn't be there at all.

"Talk to him, Ana," she tells me. It's not a suggestion, but it's not a command either. "Maybe things will work out."

I shove the feeling down. I can't be hopeful for anything when it could mean someone else's life.

"No," I say. "I can't hurt him, Fayre. Hurting him is the last thing I will ever risk doing."

"You don't have to hurt him."

Her eyes are so kind and loving. It breaks my heart that she thinks this could ever work. That there's some way I could still at least be friends with Chase.

"He knows now," she says, like it's just another fact. "He's safe if he knows. And maybe you won't be able to be together, but maybe you can at least still be friends. Just think about it, okay?"

I sigh. "Okay. I'll think about it," I agree, because I know that's what she wants to hear.

Fayre leaves my room a little while later, telling me she has a call to make. She doesn't tell me who she's calling, but she calls so many different people all the time that even if she did, I doubt I'd know who she's talking about.

She closes the door softly behind herself, leaving me alone in my room with the blackness from my touch as company.

I pull my phone from my pocket and turn it on. The apple icon glows bright white on the screen before it fades away, replaced by the lock screen. I enter the code that I'm still not used to and go to my texts.

I have 27 unread texts from Chase, most of them from earlier today after I ran away from him at the abandoned property. I click his contact and scroll through the texts, my eyes only catching a few words. Multiple of the first ones are long paragraphs of text, but the more recent ones are just single sentences with no more than a few words. I delete all of them before I turn my phone back off and shove it deep into my pocket.

My room is dark, and the moonlight shining in is the only thing that provides me with any light. It glistens off of the slick, grey floor of my room, sparkling like the stars in the night sky. It reminds me of the beach and the way the water sparkled when the lights of the shopping center reflected off of it.

I climb off of my bed and walk over to the window. It's barely past dark outside, but the streetlights are already on. An occasional car passes, but after standing there for twenty or so minutes, I only see two.

Lauren's car is still in the driveway, but I can't hear their movie playing in the living room anymore, so I don't know where she and my brother are. My parents left a while ago. They'd planned to go out tonight, but I had completely forgotten until I heard them leave while Fayre and I had been talking. Well, while Fayre had been talking.

As quietly as I can manage, I push open my window. The glass panel slides up to the top, leaving an open space of about nine square feet.

A breeze blows through, pushing my hood off of my head and my bangs out of my face. It sends a shiver down my spine as it wraps around me.

Before I get the chance to convince myself that it's a bad idea, I climb through the window and fall gently into the grass alongside the house. I slide my window closed again, the locking mechanism clicking automatically back into place.

My bike is parked alongside the house, only a few feet away from my bedroom window. I pull the tarp off of it and leave it in a crumpled mess on the ground. I grab a large rock and put it on top of the tarp to keep it from blowing away. I'll put it back nicely on my bike when I get back, but I'm not worried about the state it will be in while I'm gone.

I pull it around the house until I'm in the driveway. I take my jacket off and tie it around my waist before I hop on, doing my best to steady my bike with my good arm. I'm not at all worried about riding one-handed, but I'm still not sure how my shoulder will take to it. I have no doubt that it won't be pleasant — at least at first — but the beach is too far to walk to, and I haven't ridden in forever and I miss it.

I kick off, steadying myself so sloppily that for the first few seconds, I think I'm going to fall and break another bone, but I manage to get it under control.

The streets pass in a blur of orange lights and shadows that dance messily in front of me. I'm riding too fast to pay much attention to my surroundings, which is really stupid, but I also don't care at the moment.

By the time I get to the beach, it's 9:00. The sun has

been down for the past hour and I've been riding for most of it. My legs are sore and my heart is racing in my chest. It's been a long time since I've ridden so far without a break.

There's no bike rack or anything at the makeshift beach, so I bring it with me and stand it up on its kickstand before I sit down in the sand.

It looks the same here as it did when Chase brought me. The lights still reflect off of the water's surface and the laughter is still coming from the open area between the buildings where a bunch of kids are playing. But there's a feeling missing. It feels like the same bland place it always did when I would see it. It doesn't feel as special as it did when Chase was here with me.

I hug my knees to my chest and close my eyes, willing the feeling to come back. I want to feel that fulfillment again. The happiness. I want to look over and see him sitting beside me. I want to see the sparkle in his eyes that I could never place, but I could always feel mirrored in my own.

I miss him, even though I know I shouldn't. I shouldn't care enough about him to miss him. He should just be another person on this planet to me. But he isn't. I shouldn't care about him, but I do.

And that's why I have to stay away from him.

Nothing bad can happen to him because of me. If I was any other girl, the worst I could do to him would be to break his heart. But I'm not any other girl, and even if I did already do that, I can still do much worse.

I lie back in the sand, my arms resting across my stomach so that I don't touch any of it. The stars above aren't bright. They're like tiny specks of light that are barely visible. I never thought about how few of them I can see until now. The numbers of stars are endless, but if I spent the night counting the stars I can see right now, I wouldn't have a problem doing so.

"Thana?"

I don't know when the tears started falling, but when I sit back up, I notice for the first time that my cheeks are wet.

"Honey, what are you doing here?"

One.

Her voice makes the tears worse, and before I know it, I'm sobbing again like a pathetic child.

"I killed Mark," I gasp, still not looking at her. I can feel her standing behind me. Her breathing is soft and even, but her breath catches when she realizes what I just told her.

More footsteps stop behind me, and I know my dad has followed her out of the car. I hadn't heard him until now, but there's no doubt in my mind that he heard my confession, too.

"I saw him harassing Fayre, and I got mad. I yelled at him, and I pinned him against the wall, but I wasn't going to hurt him." I don't tell them how badly I wanted to. "He touched my face. And... it killed him."

Both of them are silent for a second, but it doesn't take my dad long to break it. "What were you thinking?" he hisses. He'd be yelling at me right now if we were home, but we aren't, and anyone around could hear the conversation.

"I was thinking that he wasn't going to stop unless someone made him," I snap, turning around to face him. "If she got away from him, he would've followed her. She's my sister. To hell if I was going to let that happen!"

Hot, angry tears are rolling down my face in a steady stream. I know what I did was stupid. I know what I did can't be taken back. But I didn't have horrible intentions when I did it. My intentions were to keep my sister safe and to stop him from hurting anyone else. As foolish as it had been, I hadn't meant for it to go the way it had.

My dad runs his hands through his hair. If looks could kill, I'd be dead right now. "There's a principal," he snaps at me, his tone matching the one I just used. "There're police. There are people who deal with these things in ways that aren't *lethal*."

My mom goes over to him and rests a hand on his shoulder, but it's a poor attempt to calm him down.

"I know you care about your sister, but that doesn't make his death any less your fault," he tells me, his voice hard and firm.

The words are like a knife to the gut.

"You think I don't know that?!" I shout, climbing to my feet. My voice is shaky and my hands are clenched into fists. "I *killed him*," I say through gritted teeth. I blink repeatedly, trying to get the tears to clear, but it's a worthless attempt. "I watched him *die* because of *me*."

My mom looks clueless as to what to do to stop the argument between the two of us, but I don't think I'd be doing any better in her position. What can she do? My dad isn't wrong and I'm not either because we're arguing next to the same thing. I know it's my fault just as well as he does, and I'm just as mad at myself as he is.

"Can we just… can we just go home?" I ask, my voice hitching at the end of it.

My dad doesn't say anything in response, just grabs my bike and takes it over to the car. He unlocks the car and throws it in the trunk before climbing into the driver's seat.

I put my jacket on as I walk and my mom puts her arm around my shoulders once I have it on. She kisses the top of my head and holds me close. When we get to the car, she sits in the backseat with me and holds me.

She doesn't say anything, but I'm glad she doesn't. I don't know what I'd do with her as worked up as dad is.

Chapter Twenty-Four

A week and a half passes. They start construction on the abandoned property, which means that Chase's dad got the plans back sooner than he thought.

I can't go back now. I can *never* go back to the place that has always been my only home, but I don't even care half as much as I should. I was upset yesterday when I made my first attempt to go back since Chase found me there and I saw the large yellow machine parked in the yard, but it's passed more than I thought it would've already.

I haven't been able to think about the property. All I've been able to think about is Chase. He hasn't left my thoughts except for a few times, and when it does happen, it doesn't last long.

He stopped texting me a couple days after he found me at the property and I haven't heard anything from him since. He stopped looking for me at school too, and now I'm able to sit in my usual spot and not have to worry about him coming over. Instead, I see him talking with my brother and his crowd of people.

I wish it didn't still upset me as much as it does because I know this is how it should be. Chase and I never should've been friends. He should've met Daemon or Fayre and become friends with them long before he ever met me. He should've seen this weird, gothic freak when he saw me the first time, instead of a girl who fell off of her bike to avoid hitting him.

The thing that irritates me the most is that I shouldn't even be giving him a second thought. I should be furious that his uncle's company is taking away my sanctuary, but I don't even know if it was that anymore. Getting to know Chase changed it somehow, and it hadn't felt the same when I went back.

A gentle knock comes on my bedroom door, and I barely have enough time to look up before Fayre pushes it open and comes in. "You're going to the dance, right?" she asks, her eyes bright and hopeful.

The dance…

I forgot that was tonight, and, in all honesty, I hadn't cared that it's happening at all. I've gone to one school dance and spent every moment of it bored out of my mind.

"That's today?" I ask, making a face at the thought of attending.

A bit of Fayre's normal self has come back in the

past week, and I'm glad it has. She's still not the same as she used to be, but I think this is as close as she's getting. She's my sister, though, and I'll always love her no matter what changes about her.

She nods. "And I may have gotten asked to go," she says, smiling wider than the Pacific Ocean times ten. "Drake and his girlfriend kinda broke up and he kinda called yesterday and asked if I wanted to go with him." Her voice is high and squeaky and I almost want to laugh. "So, will you come, too? *Please?*"

I crinkle my nose. "What's the purpose of me being there? I'll probably embarrass you more than anything if he meets me."

"I want you there," she answers, matter-of-factly. "This is my first high school dance and there are only going to be a couple chances for me to go to with both you and Daemon there."

I sigh. I know exactly what she means and how much it means to her because she's talked about it a thousand times before, but that doesn't make me want to go any more than I already did. I can't dance because I can't risk touching anyone, I can't eat anything because it's mostly finger-foods, and, according to my last experience, I'm not a huge fan of the music they play at them either.

I want to tell her no, but then I look up and see the hopefulness in her eyes, and any willpower I had to turn her down vanishes into thin air. "Alright," I groan.

"Yay!" she squeaks, jumping up and down. "Thank

you!" She runs over to me and wraps her arms around me, squeezing the air out of my lungs.

"Ow, ow, *ow*," I gasp. "Still broken, Fayre."

She pulls away like I shocked her with a bolt of electricity. Her cheeks are the tiniest bit pink and she gives me a sheepish smile. "Sorry."

I shrug, but wince when I do because that was stupid. "Moron," I mutter to myself, and Fayre laughs at me.

She drops down on my bed beside me and lies down, her body sprawled out and taking up more than half of the bed.

"What am I supposed to wear?" I ask, genuine curiosity making its way into my tone. "It's semi-formal, isn't it? And, I'm no genius, but I'm pretty sure that means that something called 'dresses' are required, and we're talking about me." I gesture down at myself as if my usual outfit style has anything to do with why I can't wear a dress.

Fayre smirks up at the ceiling as if me not being able to wear a dress is a puzzle she's already beaten a thousand times. "Not a problem," she tells me, waving a dismissive hand in my direction. "You're my size, and I can totally make that work."

My eyes widen and I sit up straight. "Oh no. No, no, no. You're not planning to dress me up like a Barbie doll, are you?"

She snorts a laugh. "Obviously." She climbs to her feet and goes over to the door, glancing over her shoulder quickly before she leaves. "Let me go get the stuff and we can get started." She wiggles her eyebrows at me teasingly before she turns and heads out of my room.

She leaves so fast that I don't have enough time to remind her that the dance won't be for another few hours.

I pull my phone from my pocket and text her that I'm going to the kitchen to get a glass of water and that she can take her time. There's a smile on my face when I shove it back into my pocket.

Daemon is sitting at the dining room table when I get to the kitchen. He looks up at me when I pass but doesn't say anything before he goes back to the papers in front of him.

I grab a glass of water, down half the cup, and come back out. He doesn't pay me any attention when I sit down across from him. I eye the math homework in front of him, making a face at the confusing problems. "So," I say, "you going to the dance with Lauren?" I wiggle my eyebrows teasingly at him when he looks up.

He rolls his eyes at me and gets back to his work. "Yeah, but we're meeting up with our friends so it's not exactly a date."

"Ah, yes. You're band of weird, popular kids." I smirk at him. His friends aren't the mean popular kids, which is why I've always referred to them as "weird" instead.

"Says the gothic freak," he says, his expression matching mine.

I roll my eyes. "Touché," I grumble, sinking deeper into my chair as I cross my arms over my chest. Daemon gets back to his homework again, and I stay silent for all of two seconds before I clear my throat and make him look up at me again. "Is Chase going to be there?" My voice is hardly above a whisper.

There's a nervousness to my brother before he responds. He looks like he's trying to decide whether or not he wants to tell me the truth. It takes him a minute before he seems to decide and answers. "Yeah, he's coming." He eyes me with a look I can't place. "You're actually coming? Or are you just asking to be nosy?"

"I just need to account for the lack of available air capacity I'll have in my lungs if I see him there, is all."

Daemon snorts a laugh and shakes his head. "I'll take that to mean you're coming."

I purse my lips. "Yup. And Fayre is dressing me up, which is going to be… fun."

He laughs. "Have fun with that. See, I never had that problem because she can't force me into a dress even if she tried because I'm not her size." He smirks at me before he goes back to his homework again.

"Lucky," I mumble beneath my breath, but I find myself not meaning it as much as I thought I would. I may not like the idea of being dressed up very much, but I do like the idea of spending time with my sister.

Daemon nods but he doesn't offer any more of a response than that.

"So… when did he become a part of your little group?" I ask. I've been wondering a bit, but right now I'm just using it as an excuse to start up another conversation. I know I should probably leave him alone to do his homework, but I somehow already managed to finish mine and I'd rather not wait alone in my room for Fayre to get back.

"The day after he tried to kiss you," he answers, not using the alternate version of specifying that same day. "He was sitting alone and Lauren thought it might be nice to invite him to hang out with us until you showed up, but then you never did. And you didn't come back to lunch for multiple days, so…"

"Ah," I say, because I don't know what else I could say in response to that. "I'm glad he's got a group of friends."

Daemon offers me a half-hearted smile, but there's a sadness in his eyes that I don't think he could hide even if he tried.

"ANA!" Fayre sings, her voice loud enough to make me deaf if she were standing next to me.

I don't say anything else to Daemon as I stand up and head back to my room. He glances up at me but doesn't say anything either. I get the feeling he doesn't have a clue what he's supposed to say, just like I have no idea what I want him to say.

When I get back, Fayre is standing beside my bed, a

bunch of dresses I didn't even know she had laid out in front of her. She picks up two, making sure I see them, then starts talking. "So, this one would work with your skin," she holds up the left one, "but this one would look nice with your eyes." She shows me the right one.

"Um, Fayre?" I say, an amused smile pulling at the corners of my lips. "They're both black."

"Exactly!" she announces, setting them both down and picking up yet another black one. "I think this one would complement your hair and the sling."

I snort a laugh and sit down on the bed. "Throw me in a cloak that covers me from head to toe, and you'd claim it shows off my legs," I tease.

Fayre nods. "Mhm, precisely." She sets the dress down and picks up another one. "But, in all seriousness, I think this one would look really nice on you." She holds up a flowy black dress with a V neck in the front and a low back. It has a shiny black waistband that looks like it should tie in the back, but doesn't, and it looks like it would come down to my knees.

"It's pretty," I tell her, meaning it, "but I can't wear that. Fayre, my back would be exposed and I do not have the boobs to fill that out." I point in the general direction of where the neck dips down to and make a face.

Fayre laughs. "You'll look amazing in it," she promises. "And I have a plan for the back." She picks up yet another article of clothing, this time what looks like the jacket piece of a pantsuit. It's the same shade of black as everything else, which means I won't absolutely destroy it.

"And my legs?" I ask, gesturing down at myself. "I don't need that much of a draft down there."

She rolls her eyes at me. "Go find a pair of leggings. I know you aren't that stupid."

"Never know," I say, smirking at her teasingly.

I grab a pair of leggings from my dresser before she hands me the clothing and sends me into the bathroom to change. I strip from the clothes I'm wearing, hanging my jacket on the towel rack and piling the rest of it on the toilet seat. I pull on the leggings before I slip the dress on over my head and zip it up in the back. The fabric is silky and smooth against my skin, and I curse myself for liking the feel of a dress.

Once I've got the leggings and the dress on, I slip the pantsuit-jacket-thing on to cover up my arms and my back. It leaves my chest bare still, but only a creep would touch me there on purpose, and I don't think I have to worry all that much about people knocking into me if I stay sitting at a table.

When I'm fully dressed, I leave the bathroom again. Fayre is sitting on my bed, as usual, with her legs crossed at the ankles.

Her eyes light up when she sees me and a grin that could challenge the length from the earth to the moon forms on her face. "Oh my god. Ana, you look so pretty!" She comes over to where I am and looks me over, her smile growing wider, if that's even possible.

"Okay!" she announces. "Step two: we gotta fix that hair of yours."

"What about my feet?" I ask, looking down as I wiggle my toes in my socks.

"You're what? Half a size smaller than mom?"

I nod.

"We'll just grab you a pair of her black dress boots," she says, shrugging. She says it so calmly; like she's done it a thousand times in the past week.

"Alright," I say, not sure if taking my mom's shoes is a good idea or not. "And also, rule number one about you doing hair and makeup on me: you have to wear gloves."

Fayre makes a face, like wearing the gloves will somehow make her work a thousand times harder, but eventually, she nods and agrees to it.

She leaves and comes back a moment later with a bunch of stuff in her arms, which she dumps in my bathroom before she beckons me in. She nods toward the toilet seat, telling me to sit down. I do and she turns back and grabs a pair of gloves.

She puts them on, then starts working on my hair. She brushes it thoroughly, then starts braiding it into multiple thick strands. There are four in total when she's done, which she sprays with something, and then undoes. When they're all undone, she plays with my hair a bit more before she pronounces that she's done.

Despite the fact that she's finished with my hair, she doesn't let me get up. Instead, she makes me sit there for what feels like another three years while she does her best to poke my eyes out with black pencils.

"Done!" Fayre says, right when I start wondering how likely it would be for me to actually escape if I started running now. She pulls her evil pencil back and puts a cap on it. I don't stop watching it until she's put it back in her bag, though. "Look, look, look!"

I sigh and climb to my feet. My reflection stares back at me when I look in the mirror. I look pretty; she got that right. The dress fits me nicely, just like she said it would. My chest is bare, and the neckline is a little low for my liking, but I don't look like I'm trying to show off anything. Somehow, the jacket and the leggings don't make it look bad, and, if anything, make it look classier.

My hair is wavy now, which looks nice with my face somehow, and my eyes are rimmed with dark pencil. It doesn't look ridiculous, though. It highlights my grey eyes without making them look pale.

I lean in closer to the mirror, staring into my own eyes, and my breath catches in my throat when I do.

"There are flecks of blue in my eyes," I whisper, which shouldn't mean nearly as much to me as it does. The fact that something in me is normal is amazing, though.

Fayre laughs, but it comes out in an amused breath of air. "I told you that a long time ago," she says. "You said you couldn't see it, so I figured it was a trick of the light."

I know she did, and so did Chase, but she's right because I didn't believe them until now, when I'm seeing it myself.

I take a step away and look at my reflection again. I sigh when I do, realizing something about it I don't like. "I look even more like a gothic freak," I say. My tone isn't defeated or upset. I just sound like I'm stating another fact of life.

"You look like you," Fayre tells me, which makes something in me feel whole somehow.

A smile touches my lips.

"Oh!" she says. She reaches behind her neck and unclasps her necklace before holding it out to me. "This'll make it perfect."

I take a step away from her when she comes closer to put it on me. "I can't wear that," I remind her. "Fayre, that's the necklace you *always* wear. I'm not going to destroy it."

"You're right," she agrees, and I think for a second that she's genuinely agreeing with me. "You'll make it better."

Before I can step away again, she reaches around my neck and clasps the necklace behind me. The weight of the pendant falls against my chest and is followed by the chain around the back of my neck. The metal is warm against my skin from my sister wearing it all the time, but I hardly notice it before it starts to turn a dull grey color.

When my touch has had its full effect, the necklace

looks like tarnished silver. The only thing that still looks the same is the gem in the center of the pendant.

Fayre smiles widely at me when I look up at her, and I realize she truly meant what she said. She thinks me touching it somehow made her necklace better. Like it means something more now that I've had my effect on it.

I have tears in my eyes when I cup her face like I've always seen Daemon do to her and like he's now started doing to me. "I hate you," I tell her, but there's nothing but affection in my tone.

"I love you, too," she says.

I pull her into a hug, making sure that none of her bare skin touches mine, and I hold her there for as long as I can.

Chapter Twenty-Five

Daemon pulls the car up in front of the school five minutes before the dance actually starts. There are a few other people here who're all standing outside talking, but I don't recognize any of them. After a few minutes, a few more people show up and I recognize Lauren in the group.

Apparently, she's the only person he was waiting for because as soon as he sees her, all of us get out of the car.

As soon as I'm out, though, I want to go back inside. I don't want to be here anymore than I've ever wanted to be at a school dance. The only reason I'm here is because Fayre asked me to come, but even that isn't feeling like a good enough reason to stay right now.

Fayre grabs my gloved hand and pulls me toward

the mess of people who are starting to head inside. She has a wide smile on her face and she looks so happy. I wish I could feel whatever she's feeling right now, but I don't even know what could make me look like that.

She doesn't pull me into any of the groups when we're inside. Instead, we go over to one of the tables and sit down. I know she's waiting for her date to get here, and once he's here, she'll no doubt be spending the rest of the evening with him, but I like having her company for the little amount of time I've got her.

We don't really talk, which would be hard to do over the music anyway, but it's nice to at least have someone sitting by me who actually knows I exist.

Drake shows up a few minutes later and comes over to our table. He offers me a smile, but doesn't say anything to me before he turns to my sister and they exchange a few words that I can't hear over the sound of the loud pop song on the speakers.

Fayre comes over to where I am a second later and leans close so that I can hear her when she talks. "We're gonna go get snacks," she tells me, and nods over in the direction of the table lined with all kinds of junk food.

I nod instead of trying to respond. She smiles before she practically skips back over to where Drake is and they leave.

I can feel someone watching me after they leave. The feeling settles itself over me in the form of an unease that I can't shake until I figure out who the person is.

I should know better than to look, but I do it, anyway.

And meet Chase's eyes when I do.

He's watching me with something I can't place in his expression. When I catch him staring at me, though, he turns away and back to the group he's with.

Daemon and Lauren are part of the group, but they're talking to another couple who look like they're also seniors. My brother has his arm around Lauren's shoulders and they both laugh at whatever the other two are telling them.

Not for the first time, a bubble of longing rises up inside of me. The conversation looks so easy, and, if I were anyone else, I could go over there and join in. But I can't do that. I'm the gothic freak of the school who is somehow related to Daemon and Fayre. And, on top of that, I could kill them…

I sigh and rest my arm on the table before I lay my head down on my forearm. I don't know how long I'm sitting there before I feel someone lay a hand on my shoulder.

Damn it…

My eyes snap open and an explosion of adrenaline rushes through me.

Please don't be Chase…

When I turn around, it isn't Chase staring back at me. It's Fayre.

I let out a breath and I can feel my body physically relax at the realization that it's only her.

She's smiling wide at me, but she shakes her head a second later and puts on a smaller one. "C'mon," she says, holding her hands out to me.

I stare at her hands like their covered in scales. I look up at her. "Huh?" I ask, because I'm a genius.

Her smile widens again. "Let's go dance," she says, grabbing my hand and pulling me up out of my seat before I have a chance to protest. "I already made Daemon dance with me. Now it's your turn."

I want to groan in protest, but I catch myself and let her drag me out to the dancefloor. There are about fifty other kids slow dancing, including my brother and his girlfriend. The sheer number of people makes me nervous, but Fayre pulls me to the edge of the crowd so that we're still on the dancefloor, but a decent amount of space away from everyone else.

"I don't know how to dance," I remind her as she lets go of my hand and spins around to face me.

She rolls her eyes at me, then takes my only free hand and holds it up in hers. "You've got a sling on. That makes it easier," she teases. She moves to put her other hand on my shoulder, then freezes, seeming to remember that it's broken, and puts it on my waist instead.

"Now what am I supposed to do?" I ask, glancing down at my feet like they're foreign objects.

"Well, to start, you move," she tells me, amusement in her tone. She takes a step and I follow her movements until we're taking a bunch of small steps and slowly turning in circles.

"People actually enjoy this?" I ask, crinkling my nose.

She rolls her eyes at me again, but she doesn't look all that annoyed. She must have expected that I'd be like this about slow dancing, considering how I seem to stick my nose up at a lot of things she likes to do.

The song takes about three hundred years to finish, and by the time it's done, I feel like I should've been dead a long time ago.

"Okay," I say, taking a step away from her once the song is over, "I'm never doing that again."

Fayre laughs, which isn't what I expected her to do at all.

After a moment, she stops and grabs my hand again. "C'mon," she says, pulling me away again. "I've got one more thing I need to make you do before my first dance is over."

This time I actually do groan. "So long as I don't have to slow dance for another thousand years, I suppose I can live with that."

"Oh, don't worry," she assures me. "I'm not signing you up for anymore dancing." She turns around and gives me a mischievous grin.

I don't have time to ask her why she was looking at me like that before she stops walking, taps a guy on the shoulder, takes a step away, and shoves me in front of Chase.

"Enjoy," Fayre says, then let's go of me and leaves.

I stare at Chase, my whole body stiff. I should run. I

should stop staring at him like I've never seen him before and leave.

But I can't do that for some reason. I can't make myself leave no matter how much I try.

I just stand there, staring up into his dark brown eyes, as something inside of me breaks even more.

Chase clears his throat awkwardly, which snaps me out of my trance. "What're you doing here?" he asks, looking more confused than I've ever seen him. There's hurt in his eyes too, but he does a decent job of hiding it.

"I… I don't know," I answer, and I find that it's the truth. I thought I came because my sister wanted me to, but I'm not sure if that's the whole reason anymore or not.

He stares at me, looking like he has no idea what to say, and I look away. My lip is raw from chewing already, and I've been standing here for less than a whole minute.

I want to tell him I'm sorry. I want to tell him that I want him back, even if I can only ever have him as a friend. But should I even do that? Can I risk something like that again?

Fayre was right. He knows now, so that makes him safer. But is anyone truly safe from me unless they're my brother?

"I miss you," I whisper, the words soft and broken sounding. It's more than I should ever tell him if I want him safe, but I can't seem to help but let the words come out.

Chase watches me for a moment, hurt in his eyes, but also something else I can't place. He opens his mouth to say something back, but if he did say anything, I can't hear him over the pain in my shoulder as someone bumps into me.

I bite my tongue to keep from flinching or even showing it as I look over at the girl beside me.

She's the same girl I overheard in the restrooms a couple of weeks ago. The one who thinks I'm a threat of some kind.

"Hey, Chase," she says, completely ignoring my existence. She laces her arm through his. "Dance with me?" she asks, but she doesn't wait for a reply before she pulls him away from me and toward the dancefloor.

I watch the two of them weave their way through the other dancing kids until they're near the center of the mess. The girl grabs Chase's hand, just like Fayre did with me earlier. She puts her other hand on his shoulder and he puts his other one on her waist.

They do the slow spin thing that Fayre and I did for a couple minutes, and something inside my chest feels tight. They're talking about something and Chase is smiling at her while he says something I can't hear. I can't see her face, but I'm willing to bet she looks just as happy as he does.

I let out a breath and turn my attention away from the two of them. I can't watch this, and I was stupid to think that I could ever even be friends with him still when I have so many feelings for him. That can never be me no matter how much I wish it could, and that hurts, but how much more will it hurt if the same thing that happened to Mark happens to him?

I can feel the tears starting in my eyes, and before they get a chance to fall and someone sees, I leave the gym. The dance is still another two hours long, and Daemon and Fayre most likely won't even notice I'm missing if I hide outside for the rest of it.

It's cool outside when I open the doors and walk out, and something about it is enough to break the dam I built up to keep my tears from falling while I was inside.

I'm not sure where I'm supposed to go, but if anyone comes outside like I did, I don't want them to see me like this. Daemon locked the car, so hiding in there isn't an option, but the football field will most likely be – and stay – vacant.

Before I give myself time to think through whether or not it's a good idea to hide there, I start walking. When I stop, I'm up at the top of the bleachers, the metal creaking uncomfortably beneath me.

I sit down in a corner, pressing myself deep into it as I pull my knees to my chest. I rest my arm on top of my knees and bury my face in it.

My sobs aren't loud, but they rock my whole body and burn the back of my throat. My tears are hot as they seep through the pantsuit jacket my sister lent me.

"An…"

My breath hitches and my sobbing stops. I don't

look up, though. "Go away, please," I beg, my voice barely above a whisper. I sound broken and I wish it wasn't so apparent.

"I…No," Chase says, and I can hear him step closer to me.

He sits down beside me, and a moment later, I feel him grab my hand and lace his fingers through mine.

My head snaps up and I pull my hand away from him, pressing myself deeper into the corner. "Don't touch me," I say, but it doesn't sound like a command, like I want it to. It sounds like I'm pleading with him.

"I'm not afraid of you, An," he tells me. He doesn't look away from me when he says it; like he wants me to see how much he means it.

I swallow hard and look away. "I'm afraid. I can't… I can't do that to you. I can't *kill* you. I couldn't live with myself if I did that to you…"

"You're not going to hurt me," Chase insists.

I want to believe him. I want those words to be true more than I've ever wanted anything, but I can't risk that they are. I can *never* risk something like that.

"And what if I do?" I ask. There's a challenge in my tone, but it's a weak one.

Chase sighs. "I kissed you that day," he says, and I so badly want to interrupt and tell him there's no way he could've, but he keeps going. "And I know you don't think it's possible, but I know I'm not crazy. I touched you, An. And I'm fine."

I remember him telling me he could taste blood

after I ran off, and how I chewed my lip until I was bleeding. I remember Daemon saying that maybe I can touch him because he and I share some of the same blood. I remember the blood in the sink after I cleaned my arm off and was rinsing out the cloth. I touched the water that was tinted red, and it ran smoothly over my hands.

And, at that moment, I realize what he's saying is true.

I won't kill him…

"I know…" I whisper, my voice barely audible.

Chase stays quiet after I say it, and I don't know what to follow it up with. Instead of talking, we lapse into silence. It's not uncomfortable, though. After everything that just happened, my mind is still spinning. I know I won't kill him. I have no proof and I'm still terrified that I could be wrong, but something in me knows I'm not.

"An?" Chase's voice is so quiet that I can barely hear him.

I look up.

"Can I kiss you?" he asks.

My heart skips a beat in my chest and my face feels hot. The nervous feeling I always get around him is back, but twenty thousand times stronger than it was last time.

"I'd rather you didn't," I answer, because as sure as part of me is, there's still a part of me that doesn't want to believe it.

"But do you want me to?"

Do I? I wanted him to last time, and I've wanted him to multiple other times, but is that something I'm stupid enough to want even when I'm fully aware of the risk? Is that something he's willing to risk?

I swallow hard. "Yes," I admit.

The word is barely out of my mouth when he kisses me.

His lips are warm against mine and adrenaline rushes through me at the feeling.

I close my eyes, and tears roll down my cheeks when I do.

He's still. Stiller even than I am.

I move away and I don't open my eyes. I just start crying again, white-hot pain erupting in my chest.

I killed him…

I never should've thought I wouldn't…

"Wow, that bad, huh?" Chase asks, and I can hear nothing but amusement in his tone.

My eyes snap open.

My face is covered in tears and I can't seem to stop crying even after I'm long passed positive that he's alive and not dying.

"I thought you were dead," I say, my voice somehow even despite the tears.

Chase smiles. "I mean, I freaked out a bit because, you know, you could've killed me."

I glare at him and punch him in the shoulder. "You told me you thought it would be fine and that you weren't scared!" I argue, but there's a part of me that feels close to laughter.

"I may have stretched the truth a *tiny* bit," he admits, giving me a sheepish smile.

I want to be mad at him, but I can't seem to pull it off. I want to shout at him that what he did was stupid and smack him across the face until it gets through to him, but all I can do is laugh. And it's not wicked or cruel or deceiving. It's genuine.

"I hate you," I decide, but there's something loving about my tone.

Chase smiles, shaking his head slightly. "I can live with that."

I roll my eyes and move closer to him, laying my head on his shoulder. He puts his arm around me a second later and pulls me closer to him. I can feel his warmth through the pantsuit jacket, and it sends a shiver down my spine. "Chase?"

"Hmm?"

"Can I kiss you?" I ask him.

He snorts a laugh. "Is that going to be a joke?" he asks, but instead of answering, I sit up and press my lips against his.

He kisses me back, and my chest explodes with something that's a cross between absolute fear and pure happiness. Whatever broke when I thought I'd killed him isn't broken anymore. I feel whole inside and happy.

I can touch him.

I can kiss him.

I don't have to be afraid of hurting him anymore.

I pull away from the kiss and rest my forehead against his. "Did you ever think I wouldn't make it into a joke?" I tease.

Chase smiles, the same thing I've never been able to place sparkling in his eyes. I know what it is now, though, because I can feel it in my own smile. It's something loving. Something that shows anyone who's looking a small glimpse right into our hearts.

I curl up next to him again and he wraps his arms around me, holding me tight.

"Okay," he says after a minute. "There's one thing that's been driving me crazy since you told me about the whole, 'when I touch things they die' stuff."

"Uh-oh," I tease. "What didn't add up?"

"Nothing," he answers. "But I do have to know one thing: do you actually have a problem with eating M&Ms that are different colors, or was that just made up because you didn't want me to see them changing colors?"

I can feel my face heat up and I'm glad he can't see it. "I actually don't like them," I admit. "They're gross."

Chase laughs, and the sound of it is enough to make me smile. "Good to know."

Despite the fact that I know we should probably be getting inside, I don't make a move to get up until my phone goes off in my pocket and I read the text from Fayre, asking where I am.

"Should we head inside?" Chase asks as I work on a response back to her.

"Yeah," I respond, sheepishly.

He smiles and kisses me again before he climbs to his feet and offers me a hand to help me up. I take it.

He doesn't let go until long after we're back inside.

Epilogue

Two months later…

I twirl around in the new dress Fayre picked out for me a few days ago. It's simple like the one she lent me for the dance. This one is lace and sleeveless with a V neck and a bow in the back. It hangs down to my mid-thighs and spreads out all around me when I twirl in it.

Fayre picked out the entirety of my outfit, but I prefer this one to the one she picked last time. I don't have to wear the leggings beneath this dress, which makes this specific outfit look a lot nicer, and instead of a pantsuit jacket, I've got a stylish leather jacket. She let me wear sneakers this time too, which is much better than my mom's heels.

"He's gonna die," Fayre says, giggling wickedly.

"Chase or Daemon?" I ask, and she laughs.

I like doing this with her. I like it when she dresses me up, and how we talk and laugh when she does. I'm still scared to touch her, and I still make her wear the gloves, but she's not stupid and I'm careful, too. I wish it hadn't taken me so long to realize that I don't always have to avoid people, even if I can't touch them.

"Thana, your boyfriend's outside!" my mom calls from out in the living room.

Boyfriend.

My heart skips a beat and my face turns red. Yup, he's my boyfriend. We determined that more than a month ago, but I still get nervous at the sound of the word and the thought of seeing him. Except, I don't even know if it's really nervousness anymore. Sometimes, it feels a lot more like excitement.

Fayre squeaks with excitement and jumps up from the bed. She heads straight for the door without even a glance over her shoulder in my direction.

I shake my head, rolling my eyes, as I follow her out of the room.

Daemon and Lauren are sitting in the living room when we walk past. Daemon looks up for a second, then back at the show they're watching, then back up at me like he just now realized I'm going out.

He squints his eyes at me and looks over my appearance. "What? You have legs?" he asks, laughing. Then he seems to realize something again. "Oh, wait. You have legs." He looks up at me again. "Nope.

Absolutely not. You're not leaving the house looking like that. Go put some pants on or something right now."

I open my mouth to respond, but Lauren smacks his arm to shut him up before I get the chance to. "Leave her alone," she tells him, then turns to me. "And, Thana, you look great."

I definitely like my brother's girlfriend.

"Thanks," I say, truly meaning it.

A knock comes on the front door, and before I get a chance to tell them goodbye and leave, Daemon is up and coming over in our direction and Lauren is rolling her eyes like she can't believe he's such an idiot. "Come on," he says to me, then proceeds to walk right past me and into the entryway. "We shouldn't keep your boyfriend waiting."

Oh, my god…

I roll my eyes and give Fayre a look, which she returns, and we both laugh. Daemon already has the door open and is talking to Chase when we get to the entryway.

I step to the side of my brother so that both of us are standing in the doorway.

"Whoa," Chase says when he looks at me. "An, you look-" Whatever he was going to say dies on the tip of his tongue when my brother fixes him with a look that could kill. "Absolutely scandalous!" he finishes, and I have to bite my tongue to keep from laughing.

Fayre snickers behind me and, when I turn to face her, she mouths, *"dead."*

I shake my head, a smile hiding in the corners of my lips, as I watch her walk off. She told me earlier she's got yet another call with a friend tonight, but I have my suspicions that it's someone more than just a "friend." And by that, I mean Drake.

"You ready?" I ask, before Daemon can get a chance to say anything else.

Chase nods.

"I'll be back by midnight," I tell my brother, which he doesn't look happy about, but he agrees to, anyway. He doesn't really have much of a choice, though. Midnight is the curfew my parents gave me.

Daemon gives me a quick hug. "Have fun," he says, and I can tell that he actually means it.

"So," I say to Chase, once Daemon closes the door behind me. "Where're we going?"

He wouldn't tell me no matter how much I pestered him to yesterday. He just asked if I was free tonight and left it at that.

"Still a surprise," he answers, winking at me teasingly. He grabs my hand and laces his fingers through mine before he pulls me closer and plants a kiss on my lips. "Grab your bike."

I raise an eyebrow at him, confusion bubbling up inside me. I do as he says, though, and grab my bike from alongside the house. "Why do I need this?" I ask as soon as I get back.

He's standing next to his own bike which is parked in the driveway next to my dad's truck. "Because it's not far, and I know you like to ride more than you like to be in a car."

I squint at him suspiciously but hop on my bike before I try asking again where we're going. I tug my dress down over my legs again when I sit. If I'd known I'd be riding my bike, I would've asked Fayre to come up with something easier to ride in. It's not difficult to ride in a dress, but it's a lot easier to ride in pants.

Chase leads me through the streets in the direction of what used to be the abandoned property but is now a construction site. He pulls up in front of it and stops, which confuses the hell out of me, but I do the same.

"What are we doing here?" I ask, staring at the giant yellow bulldozer in front of me.

Chase pulls his bike over to the machine and leans it against it. I have no idea what he's doing, but I follow after him and do the same.

He grabs my hand and leads me to the back of the thing, and that's when I see why he brought me here.

There are multiple slabs of cement laid in what seem like random places, and there's one right in front of me, but it's not like the other ones. There's a blanket set beside it with a small picnic basket sitting on top of it.

That's not the only thing that catches my attention, though. The old oak tree is still here. The same one that I used to climb all the time. I thought for sure they would destroy it because of how big it is and how much space it takes up, but they hadn't.

"Well?" he asks, once I've been standing there for at

least a couple minutes, staring at the place like it's the most beautiful thing I've ever seen.

"I love it," I tell him, a smile coming to rest on my lips.

Chase smiles and leads me over to the blanket. I sit down, tucking my legs beneath myself as he sits down across from me. The blanket itself is grey already, and when my legs touch it, it becomes the tiniest bit darker in color, but otherwise doesn't change.

"Oh," he says, grabbing the basket and opening it up. "Surprise." He pulls out a dish filled to the brim with brown M&Ms.

I laugh, my cheeks turning the tiniest bit red when I do. "You've got to be kidding me."

He winks at me teasingly. "Nope."

"You suck," I tell him, but I'm still laughing.

"I know."

I grab a couple of the M&Ms from the dish, careful not to touch the other ones, and pop them into my mouth. I chew them thoughtfully as I look around at the destroyed place. It looks nothing like it used to, and I miss it. This place isn't the place I once thought of as my sanctuary, and it never will be again.

"Isn't this technically trespassing?" I ask, nodding to the yellow construction tape that's set up around most of the property.

"I mean, my uncle owns the place and my dad is here to oversee the work, so…" He grins at me, but there's a hint of something mischievous in his smile.

"You didn't ask him if you could come, though, did you?"

He shakes his head, giving me an innocent smile.

"Definitely trespassing then," I conclude, shaking my head at him in mock disappointment.

"I learned from the best," he says, and I laugh.

I lie back on the blanket, looking up at the sky above. There are more stars here than at the fake beach when all the lights are on in the shopping center, but fewer than there are when the lights are off.

"So," Chase says, lying down beside me. "If you were a superhero in a comic book or something, what would your power be called?"

I turn and give him a look. "Are you serious?" It's hard to keep the humor out of my voice. Of all the things he could say about my ability, this is probably the dumbest by far. But… he didn't even turn me into a villain in a comic book. He turned me into the hero.

"What about something like 'The Touch of Death'?" he asks, pretending like he didn't hear what I said, even though I can see a smile playing across his lips.

"That's awful," I tell him, snickering as I curl up next to him.

"Okay, fine," he says. "What about 'Death's Touch'? Better or worse?"

I make a face. "Better, but still terrible," I decide.

I doubt there's anything good anyone could come up with for my ability, but I can't lie and say that I don't like that he's trying, even if it is the dumbest possible thing. His attempt is amusing, if nothing else.

Chase kisses the top of my head. "I think you liked that one."

"Mm," I say, rolling my eyes at him. "Yeah, I liked it about as much as a fish likes being on land."

I look up at him as a smile forms on his face, lighting up his features. It's the same smile he's always had, but somehow, it feels like every time I see it, I like it more. It's contagious in a way that makes a smile form on my own face every time I see it.

"What ever happened to you never smiling?" Chase teases.

"You came along and ruined me," I answer, smirking at him.

I look around the property again. It's in ruins compared to the wondrous state it used to be, but the stories are still here, even now that the old place is gone. Now, once they're finished with it, new stories will start, and they'll never stop.

This isn't the place that makes me happy anymore. It's not my home, but I have a new one now. I have my family, and I have Chase. They're what make me happy, and being with them is what makes me feel free.

I take Chase's hand in mine, intertwining my fingers with his. His fingers are warm against mine, and the feeling of his touch sends a thousand different feelings through me all at once.

"Thank you," I tell him, squeezing his hand lightly.

He squeezes my hand back. "For what?

I smile. "For ruining me."

Acknowledgements

So, first of all, I want to say that this book could not have been possible without the help of my amazing siblings. Or, at least, it would've been complete shit haha.

Thank you to my sister, Em, for sitting up late at night and listening to me talk on for hours about new plot lines and ideas, and for going over this story with me repeatedly and helping me fix the flaws. And thanks to my brother, Nate, for willingly reading my first draft and giving me your honest opinions. Y'all are amazing and I love you!

And, of course, I have to follow them up with one of my best friends, Gatlin, who also suffered through one of my earliest drafts and gave me a list of about a thousand grammar mistakes to fix. I love and appreciate you so much!

I also want to say thanks to my mom, who has always encouraged me to write and who has always been there to help me when I can't remember whether or not it's supposed to be "then" or "than". Thank you for being the best mom ever!

And, last but not least, Miss Gracie, my family cat, who provided me with endless snuggles while I wrote.

You guys are the best support system ever and I love y'all so much! <3

About Mase Evans

Mase Evans is a young adult fiction author. She writes work in multiple different genres, with fantasy, romance, and dystopian being some of her favorites. She enjoys writing her stories with emphasis on personal growth and relationships, with occasional outliers.

She grew up in Houston, Texas with her five younger siblings in an automotive repair shop run out of the home by her two parents. She began writing at the age of 10 and finished writing her first full length novel at the age of 14.

Evans continues to live in Texas with her partner, and her dog and cat.